Any man that ... attract the ladi...

There was no denying he was a fine figu... man, Madelaine acknowledged. Suddenly aware of the direction of her thoughts, she began to blush furiously. *She must be mad.* The man was a *servant*, for heaven's sake! And she, the Dowager Countess of Trent. What in the world had come over her? Surely she had not been reduced to hungering after a strong, handsome man, who, by all rights, should not have garnered a moment's notice?

Originally hailing from Pembrokeshire, **Gail Whitiker** now lives on beautiful Vancouver Island on the west coast of Canada. When she isn't indulging her love of writing, you'll find her enjoying brisk walks along the Island's many fine beaches, or trying to catch up on her second love, reading. She wrote her first novel when she was in her teens, and still blesses her English teacher for not telling her how bad it really was.

Recent titles by the same author:

BLACKWOOD'S LADY
LETTERS TO A LADY

AN OFFER
TO LOVE

Gail Whitiker

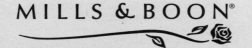

MILLS & BOON®

MILLS & BOON and MILLS & BOON with the Rose Device are registered trademarks of the publisher.

First published in Great Britain 1999
Harlequin Mills & Boon Limited,
Eton House, 18-24 Paradise Road, Richmond, Surrey TW9 1SR

© Gail Whitiker 1999

ISBN 0 263 81811 X

Set in Times Roman 10½ on 12 pt.
04-9910-82773 C1

Printed and bound in Great Britain
by Caledonian Book Manufacturing Ltd, Glasgow

Chapter One

'No, Lord Rakesley, I will not marry you,' Madelaine said. 'I have no wish to marry again and, as my circumstances here are quite comfortable, I really see no reason why I should.'

Percy Bedford, Viscount Rakesley, stared at the composed young woman in front of him as though she had uttered a string of obscenities rather than a politely worded refusal. Her clear grey eyes never wavered, and with growing alarm, Rakesley realised that his hopes of effecting an advantageous marriage to the lovely and extremely wealthy young widow in front of him were rapidly dwindling.

'But, my dear Lady Trent, I love you!' he professed, dropping to the floor at her feet. 'Have you no heart?'

'A heart? Indeed I have, Lord Rakesley, but love me?' Regretfully, Madelaine shook her head. 'No, I fear it is more what I have than who I am that you believe yourself to be in love with. But pray, do not think me unmoved by your proposal. Indeed, I am flattered that you would single me out for such an honour and I hope that I may continue to regard you as a friend.''

Her attractively low-pitched voice betrayed none of the amusement with which she viewed the anxious peer's proposal, and when no reply was immediately forthcoming, Madelaine folded her hands in her lap and fixed a patient smile upon her face. She had no doubt that poor Percy was trying to think of some excuse which would convince her of his eminent suitability and undying devotion—financial position notwithstanding. ''My lord?'' she prompted at length.

'Hmm? Oh, beg pardon, Lady Trent,' said Lord Rakesley, who had indeed been culling his brain in the hopes of finding some honeyed words of flattery with which to change her mind. But even he could not fail to recognise the note of finality in the young widow's voice. 'I take it you are…quite sure about this?' he ventured gamely.

Madelaine's smile was gentle, but firm. 'Quite sure. And I am confident that if you gave the matter adequate consideration, you would soon come to realise that we really should not suit. To be quite honest, I had believed you to be harbouring a *tendre* for Miss Elizabeth Horton.'

'Miss Horton!' A wave of colour suffused Lord Rakesley's cheeks. 'Lady Trent, I cannot imagine why you would say such a thing! Miss Horton and I are…barely acquainted.'

'Really? I had thought the two of you quite taken with each other at Lady Rutledge's ball.'

The colour deepened in the young man's cheeks. 'Well, perhaps we did…converse at some length, but I can assure you, that it was always you who were uppermost in my thoughts.'

Madelaine's smile remained gracious as she crossed to the bell pull and gave it a firm tug. 'It is most kind of you to say so, my lord, and for that reason, I say once again that I am flattered by your offer. But I fear you would do better were you to ask for Miss Horton's hand, than mine.'

'But, my dear Lady Trent, you have so much more—

that is—you *are* so much more, er…interesting than Miss Horton,' Lord Rakesley stammered desperately. 'She is but a…a Bath miss, while you are a sophisticated and elegant lady. And one who is lovelier by far.'

'Lovelier?' Madelaine's smooth brow furrowed. 'Surely you would not base so important a decision as marriage on something as ephemeral as the comeliness of a lady's face, my lord?'

'Of course not, Lady Trent—'

'But a good heart, now there is a more worthy prize for a man to aspire to, surely. Ah, Granger, good,' Madelaine said to the surprised servant, who had opened the door to find the chastised peer still down on both knees in front of his mistress. 'Lord Rakesley was…just leaving.'

Percy blinked his surprise. 'I was?'

Madelaine turned away to hide her smile as her visitor— aware that he had been caught in a most undignified position, and by a servant at that—hastily scrambled to his feet. 'Yes, well then, I suppose there is…nothing more to say on the matter,' Percy said, flustered at being observed in such a position. 'I bid you good afternoon, Lady Trent.'

'Good afternoon, Lord Rakesley. Oh, and Lord Rakesley?'

Ever hopeful, the young man turned. 'Yes?'

'Do give my regards to Miss Horton when next you see her.'

The faintly optimistic light which had appeared in the Viscount's eyes sputtered and died; muttering something quite unintelligible, Percy followed the implacable butler from the room, vowing never to listen to his mother's—or to his numerous sisters'—urgings again.

Not surprisingly, as soon as he had gone, Madelaine's smile faded too. 'Dear me, this is all becoming most tiresome. But then, I suppose it is only to be expected.'

Tucking the soft Kashmir shawl more closely about her shoulders, Madelaine turned and left the formality of the elegant Chinese drawing room for the one place in which she knew she would find solace—the small, but cosy rose parlour. Papered in a soft pink watered silk, it was a peaceful room; tranquil against the bustle of the London streets and shut off from the rest of the house. Madelaine had long since come to think of it as her own private sanctuary, and after closing the door behind her, she walked across the carpet to stand directly in front of the painting of her late husband who—though more like a father than a husband to her—had been a good and loving partner, and said, 'Oh, Edward, why did you have to die and leave me to the mercy of every fribble and roué in Town? Was I so very troublesome that you determined this to be my fair punishment?'

Some of the warmth which had always been present in the deep brown eyes seemed to shine down upon her now, and caused Madelaine to smile. 'Yes, I know. I am a wilful child, ever did you call me so. But, dear me, it is so difficult to know whom to believe. They all claim to love me, yet I fear it is not me they love at all, but that which you have left me. How am I to know who speaks the truth and who does not?'

Sadly, it seemed to be, of late, an all too valid question. As the widow of the late Earl of Trent, Madelaine was now a very wealthy and eligible young woman. She had been both married and widowed by the occasion of her twenty-fifth birthday, and was, if anything, even lovelier now than she had been six years ago when she had married the affluent and debonair earl.

Unfortunately, it was that very wealth which Madelaine was now finding to be such an onerous responsibility; serving, as it did, as an irresistible enticement to gentlemen in need of a prosperous wife. In fact, since putting off her blacks barely five months ago, Madelaine had been approached by no less than three gentlemen, all of whom had been anxious to proclaim their undying love and affection.

Still, at least forewarned was forearmed, Madelaine reflected philosophically. Had Edward not advised her that greed was one of the greatest impediments to true love?

'Madelaine? Where are you, my dear? Maddie?'

Madelaine spun around, her eyes widening in pleasure and surprise. 'Aunt Chloe?'

Unaware that her aunt was due back from Scotland today, Madelaine hurried towards the parlour door and threw it open—at precisely the same moment her butler went to open it from the other side. 'Oh, dear! I am sorry, Granger, I had no idea you were just there.'

'Quite all right, Lady Trent,' the elderly retainer assured her. Quickly righting himself, he smoothed down the front of his black coat, and announced in a formal voice, 'Mrs Merrill,' as though the presence of the lady behind him did not speak for itself.

Madelaine nodded, and carefully concealed her smile. 'Thank you, Granger. Perhaps you would be so good as to bring some refreshments for my aunt and myself.'

'Very good, my lady.'

After Granger made a much more dignified exit than he had entrance, Madelaine turned towards her aunt and fell, laughing, into her arms. 'Oh, Chloe, thank goodness, you are home! I have missed you dreadfully.'

Mrs Chloe Merrill, a handsome widow of seven-and-forty, was a lady of independent spirit and sound mental judgement. Though she laid no claims to beauty—her mouth being a touch too wide and her figure a shade too voluptuous—she was, nevertheless, a striking woman. She had the most warm and expressive eyes Madelaine had ever seen, and with her wonderfully thick, dark hair only lightly threaded with grey, she looked a good ten years younger than she was.

Madelaine had always felt closer to her mother's eldest sister than she had to any of her other aunts, no doubt due to the fact that Chloe was the only one who possessed both a sense of humour and a genuinely warm and caring nature. As a young woman, she had received a smattering of acceptable proposals, but having found none of them to her liking, had chosen to remain single, a decision which had brought about the condemnation of her entire family. Her mother had despaired of her, saying that as a single woman she would have no social standing whatsoever, and that once she reached the age of thirty, she would certainly not attract the attention of *any* reputable gentleman who might be in want of a wife.

Chloe had considered the arguments as a courtesy to her family, but she had not changed her mind. Nor had she come to regret her decision—especially after being left a considerable sum of money by a favoured and somewhat like-minded aunt. The unexpected inheritance had allowed her to move out of her parents' home and to set about leading the life of an independent and genteel spinster. Which she had—until the age of one-and-forty—when, to everyone's astonishment, she had met and married the illustrious Captain Arthur Oliver Merrill of the King's Own Horse Guards.

Madelaine smiled to herself as she thought back to that memorable time in Chloe's life. Certainly, she had never seen her aunt looking happier. It was clear from the start that it had been a love match, and for the first time in Chloe's life, she had truly blossomed. Sadly, however, it was not a union which was destined to last. After only three years of marriage—most of which were spent apart—the new Mrs Merrill had received word that her dashing husband had fallen at Talavera.

It was a crushing blow, and Chloe had felt it deeply. She had withdrawn from society, refusing to see anyone, and entertaining only a few members of her own family.

Madelaine had been one of those people. As the years had passed, and she had matured into a young woman herself, the relationship between the two women had become more of a friendship than a family obligation. Thus, when Madelaine had become a widow herself a year and a half ago, Chloe was the one who had been there to help her through the dark days, lending her support and comfort in a way that no one else had seemed able to.

'Well, my dear, I must say, it is marvellous to be back in London again,' Chloe announced brightly. 'And how much better *you* are looking than the last time I saw you. Your face is nowhere near as piqued as it was before I left.'

Madelaine smiled and waved aside her aunt's praise. 'Never mind me, come and sit down and tell me all about Scotland, because I am in a positive fidge to know. Is it as beautiful as Mr Scott writes of in his poetry?'

'It is every bit as splendid, though I must admit, I found some of the customs a trifle odd.' Chloe's lovely hazel eyes sparkled as she drew off her buttery-soft kid leather gloves. 'The Duke of Kenfield *would* have the bagpipes played every morning and night, and while I admit that I liked the sound of them well enough in the evening, I cannot say that I relished their being played in the hallway outside my door before the birds were even astir.'

'And what of the Duke himself?' Madelaine inquired, a smile tugging impishly at the corners of her mouth. 'Did you find his company enjoyable enough to offset the irritation of the pipes?'

'Impertinent creature,' Chloe replied fondly. 'I found

him to be a perfectly delightful gentleman who was as considerate of me as I could have wished. Just as he has always been. Though I feel it only fair to point out that he was equally charming to Lady Jane Tavistocke and Miss Harriet McClusky.'

'Tosh! I am sure it was only his inherent graciousness which made him appear so. Ah, thank you, Granger,' Madelaine said as the butler came in and set the tea tray next to her. 'Will you have tea, Aunt?'

'Thank you, my dear, I am positively expiring for a cup. And for one of Mrs Lutten's freshly baked scones,' Chloe said, eyeing the still-warm tea cakes with relish. 'Goodness, I did miss her cooking while I was away.'

'Fiddlesticks, I am sure the Duke's chef was more than competent,' Madelaine chided. 'So tell me, how many guests did his Grace invite to the house party?'

'Twenty in all, and a most congenial group they were,' Chloe said, reaching for a scone and biting into it with obvious enjoyment. 'I finally had opportunity to play a really good game of whist again.'

'Whist! Chloe, it is your fondness for the *Duke* that I am concerned with, not some silly game of cards,' Madelaine scolded her aunt affectionately. 'And if there were only two ladies out of twenty vying for Kenfield's attention, I cannot see that you had anything to concern yourself about. Everyone knows that you are far prettier than Lady Jane, and certainly a great deal more entertaining and sensible than Miss McClusky.'

'Perhaps, but who is to say that his Grace is looking for good sense in a lady?' Chloe said, delicately licking the crumbs from her fingers. 'Harriet McClusky is a pretty young thing with shining blonde hair and dimples a man could fall into. What does it matter if her conversation is found to be somewhat…short on substance? Have you ever known a gentleman to be put off by a woman's lack of intelligence before?'

Madelaine made a moue of disappointment. 'If the Duke is attracted to one such as that, he would certainly not be a worthy companion for you. I have seen the slightly glazed look which comes over your face when you are forced to endure the nonsensical chatter so often to be had in Society drawing rooms.'

'Never!'

'Oh yes, though you may rest assured, none but I know it,' Madelaine told her with a smile. 'No one suspects that, inwardly, you are miles away, dreaming of a handsome Duke who lives in the wilds of Scotland, and hoping that he shall come and lay his heart and his bagpipes at your door.'

'Madelaine!' Chloe burst out, trying to appear stern even as her mouth trembled with laughter. 'Truly, you are outside of enough, child! I do not long for the Duke of Kenfield to lay…anything at my door.'

'Fudge! Of course you do. And what is wrong with admitting it? The Duke of Kenfield is a most admirable gentleman, and since it is well known that he is looking for a wife, why should we not hope that it will be you?' Madelaine said in her usual forthright manner. 'Especially since I know that *you* are not indifferent to him. And given that he has not shown himself reluctant to share your company in the past, it seems to me that there is every reason to be optimistic.'

Chloe smiled, though the expression in her eyes grew suddenly wistful. 'I admit, I am not indifferent to the gentleman, nor can I deny that we have spent many a pleasurable afternoon together. But for all his attentiveness, do you hear him making an offer? He has never even hinted to me of such intentions. And surely he would have, if he held me in the kind of esteem you seem to think he does, Maddie. The Duke of Kenfield is not a man given to roundaboutation.'

Madelaine gave her aunt's hand an encouraging squeeze. 'I cannot imagine why the Duke has not spoken, Chloe, and indeed, I am rather surprised that he has not, given the way the two of you get on.'

Chloe shrugged her shoulders eloquently. 'It may simply be that he does not find in me that which he is looking for, my dear. But enough about that,' she said briskly. 'I have not asked how *you* go on. Was that Lord Rakesley I saw beating a hasty retreat as I entered?'

Madelaine nodded ruefully as she sat back in her chair. 'It was.'

'Well, I am glad to see that you have not been without the company of gentlemen during my absence. Has he called before?'

'Several times, though for the most part, I have managed to fob him off with an excuse.'

'Fob him off? Oh, dear, am I to assume that poor Percy came to offer his heart and home into your keeping?' Chloe said, the laughter bubbling up in her voice.

'You may, though Lord knows if you can call it much of a home. The last time I was at Rakesley Hall as a guest of Percy's sister, I spent a good deal of time walking around with my eyes turned upwards, lest I be felled by a suddenly loosed brick.'

'Mmm, probably the wisest thing you could have done, my dear,' Chloe murmured. 'I am sure it is only the wretched state of Percy's ancestral home which gave him the courage to speak to you today. He is not, by nature, a brave fellow.'

'Well, I certainly have no intention of seeing any part of Edward's fortune squandered on the restoration of Rakesley

Hall,' Madelaine told her aunt firmly. 'How that decrepit pile of bricks and mortar even remains standing is a mystery to me.'

'No doubt held together by the sheer willpower of the Rakesley Rabble,' Chloe said, smiling at her niece's averted face. 'I take it you declined the Viscount's offer?'

'I did, just as I declined Lord Murphy's and Mr Belton's before him.'

'Faith, Maddie! *Three* proposals in the sennight I have been gone? That is remarkable, even for you!'

'Actually, only…two in the past sennight,' Madelaine admitted in embarrassment. 'The other one I received… before you left.'

'Heartless girl, and you did not think to tell me?' Chloe scolded her. 'Fie, Madelaine, I am your aunt. I am supposed to know which gentlemen are making overtures towards you.'

'The truth is, which gentlemen are not?' came Madelaine's rueful reply. 'Since the day I came out of mourning, I have been the recipient of numerous such overtures. It appears that there are many gentlemen in need of a rich wife and, by virtue of Edward's benevolence, I am now the object of their affections.'

Chloe nodded sympathetically. 'Sadly, it is as it ever was. Last year, it was Lady Thornbury. She came out of mourning and was positively besieged, though I admit, by a considerably older crowd than you. And she not even as well situated.'

'To be honest, I do not know that age has any bearing upon the matter,' Madelaine replied. 'My suitors seem to vary greatly in age. The only thing they have in common is the stamp of desperation upon their faces and the smoothness of their lies. Indeed, I begin to wonder whether I shall *ever* be able to trust what a gentleman says to me again.'

Chloe studied her niece's face and was troubled by the doubt and uncertainty she saw lingering in the clear grey eyes. While she could not question the validity of what Madelaine was saying, she knew that it was wrong for someone so young and beautiful to harbour such bitterness. 'The fact that you have had the misfortune to solicit proposals from a few rakes does not mean that unacceptable proposals are all you can expect to receive, my dear. In case you need reminding, you were already quite nicely situated when Lord Trent offered for you, and you liked him well enough.'

'Yes, but you know as well as I do that I had little enough choice in that marriage, Aunt,' Madelaine reminded her. 'Papa arranged my engagement to Lord Trent. All that was left for me to do was agree. Fortunately, I was very fond of Edward, and happy enough to marry him, but had I not been, I doubt the outcome would have been much different.'

'Be that as it may, I was simply pointing out that there *are* gentlemen who will wish to court you for reasons other than your wealth. And I am sure that, amongst them, there will be at least *one* for whom you will be able to feel a genuine affection. It may just take a little time and patience to find him. Speaking of marriages, have you heard from the new Lord and Lady Trent yet?'

Madelaine shook her head as she reached for one of Mrs Lutten's scones. 'They are still away on their wedding trip. I did receive a brief note from Sarah telling me that they were safely arrived in Switzerland, but I have heard nothing from them since. No doubt they are too busy touring the countryside. I know that William was most anxious to show Sarah all of the wonderful places he used to visit as a boy.'

Madelaine's voice held a trace of wistfulness. It was strange to think of William—Edward's only son from his first marriage—as the new Earl of Trent. Or of his eighteen-year-old bride, Sarah, as the new countess. Madelaine hadn't been much older than that when she had married Edward and become Lady Trent herself.

'Well, I wish them both well,' Chloe said now as she set her cup and saucer back down upon the table. 'William is a fine young man. I thought it very good of him to be so concerned with your welfare, and to make sure that you were so comfortably situated after his father's death.'

Madelaine's eyebrows rose in surprise. 'It was Edward who ensured that my needs were taken care of, Chloe, not William.'

'Financially, yes, but it was William who allowed you to have the house in Cornwall,' Chloe pointed out. '*And* the use of this house for as long as you wished. As heir, he could have retained full possession of *all* his father's properties and left you to fare as best you could. Goodness knows, I have seen it happen often enough in the past—*especially* in the case of a second marriage, as yours was to Lord Trent.'

'Yes, but I think that I was luckier than most young women in my position,' Madelaine replied. 'William and I have always been on the best of terms. He never resented my marrying his father, because I think in his heart he knew how lonely Edward had been in the years following Penelope's death.'

'He may not have resented it, my dear, but I am sure he gave some thought to the possibility that you might have borne his father a son,' Chloe pointed out.

There was a brief silence before Madelaine sighed. 'There was very little chance of that taking place. You see, shortly after we married, Edward...informed me that he was in...declining health, and that it was...unlikely that we should have any children.'

'In declining health?' Chloe glanced at her niece, surprised and dismayed by the unexpected revelation. She knew how desperately Madelaine had longed for children, and had often wondered why, in the years following her niece's marriage to the much older Earl, that none had been forthcoming. Now she knew why. And to learn that the decision had not been one in which Madelaine had any choice caused her a deep and heartfelt despair.

'Oh, my dear, I am so very sorry,'' Chloe said softly. ''I had...no idea.'

'No one did.' Madelaine replied. 'It was not something I chose to discuss with my family, nor did Edward wish people to know that he was failing.'

'But...I am surprised that he would not tell *you* of his ill health before offering for you,' Chloe remarked tersely. 'You were only eighteen when you married him, Maddie. A young woman, with hopes and dreams of the future. Surely he must have realised that you would have wanted children of your own. And knowing that, was it not unfair of him to...trap you in a marriage where there was little chance of that ever happening?'

'Oh, but it wasn't like that at all. Edward did not trap me. He loved me,' Madelaine told her aunt earnestly. 'Indeed, if Edward had one fault, it was that he loved me too much. I think he suspected that we should not have many years together, and I believe that is why the settlement he made upon me at the time of our marriage was so very generous. Certainly it was far more than Papa was expecting.'

'Then you do not reproach him for his duplicity?'

'I have nothing to reproach him for. He was a good and loving husband to me all the years of our marriage, and he ensured that I was very well taken care of after his death.'

'But your desire for children—'

'Edward knew that I would be able to marry again and have the family I wanted, I am quite sure of that,' Madelaine replied softly. 'Which is why I cannot find it in my heart to reproach him, even for that.'

There was a brief silence as Chloe digested all she had heard. Then, with a sigh, she said, 'Well, I think you are being very noble about it all, my dear. I do not know of many young women who would look at it with such a kindly eye. But, all things considered, I suppose it has worked out for the best. You have two lovely homes, and enough money to keep you in comfort for the rest of your life. What does it matter if a few rakes try to turn your head with empty flattery? You are certainly intelligent enough to recognise the difference between a genuine expression of love and insincere commendation.'

A rueful smile touched Madelaine's lips. 'I should like to think I do. Certainly, I have been able to recognise the difference thus far. But I am sure you are right, Chloe. There must be at least *one* gentleman who will speak truly of his feelings for me. All I need do is find him—which I doubt I shall do in London, where everyone knows everyone's business and gossips about it interminably.'

'Never mind, Maddie. The Season is almost over and everyone is travelling down to the country. Come to think of it, did Lord and Lady Macmillan not extend an invitation for you to go and stay with them in Bath? They have a very fine house, and it is quite close to the Assembly Rooms, as I recall.'

'Yes, they did, but—' Madelaine ran her fingers over the delicate Ming vase on the table beside her, and suddenly began to smile. 'I think I have a better idea.'

'You do? Splendid. What is it, my dear?'

'I shall go to Pengarron.'

'Pengarron?' Chloe repeated blankly. Then, she remembered. 'Good Lord! You mean…all the way to Cornwall!'

'Yes, why not? It really isn't all that far. And what is a few days' journey compared to spending the rest of the summer on the coast?'

Chloe paused, her interest unwillingly caught. 'Pengarron is on the coast?'

'Indeed. Edward told me that on certain days you can hear the sound of the waves crashing along the shore. And apparently the house itself has quite a marvellous prospect.'

'Apparently?' Chloe repeated in surprise. 'Do you mean to tell me that you have not been to Pengarron?'

'No. Edward was always more partial to the house in the Cotswolds than he was to any of his other homes. He allowed that Pengarron had exceptionally fine shooting and fishing, but I do not think that he cared for the house overly much.'

'Then why did he buy it?'

'He didn't. His father did, years ago. Edward's mother, the Dowager Countess, lived there until her own death a few years ago. But now that the house is mine, I should very much like to see it.' Madelaine turned towards the older woman jubilantly. 'And *you* must come with me.'

'*Me?*'

'Yes. Oh, do say you will come, Chloe. We shall have the most marvellous time. And only think how very far away we shall be from London!'

Chloe regarded her niece with a dubious expression, her memories of Cornwall being vague—and none too favourable. 'I admit that a sojourn in Cornwall would certainly be getting away from London, my dear, but I fail to see how it would achieve the anonymity you crave. You cannot expect to go and live in one of your late husband's houses and not be recognised.'

'No, but I am scarcely likely to run into as many members of the *ton* in Cornwall as I would here or in Bath, where there are any number of large, neighbouring country houses, and all with owners who are very fond of visiting.'

'Yes, and why would they not be fond of it? After all, what else is there to do in the country?'

'Chloe, I am surprised at you. There are any number of delightful pastimes to be enjoyed in the country. Riding, for one. I have never been partial to the rather tame gallops one is forced to endure in Hyde Park.'

'Well, one could hardly do anything else without trampling someone,' Chloe responded wryly. 'And while I admit there are those whose feet I might like my mare to tread upon, it would certainly be *mauvais ton* to show it.'

'Indeed it would. And quite apart from riding, one can go for long walks in the fresh air, or visit a local fair. Read a book by the edge of a stream, or enjoy a picnic. And then, of course, there is always the seaside—'

'Stop, stop, this endless list of activities is simply too exhausting for me,' Chloe teased, holding up her hand to stem the flow of words. 'You need not work any harder to convince me, I shall be happy to accompany you to Cornwall. As long as you are sure that it will not be too much of a bother.'

'Dearest Chloe, it will be no bother at all,' Madelaine assured her, her eyes beginning to sparkle with anticipation. 'On the contrary, it will be splendid having you there.'

Chloe glanced quickly at her niece and was delighted to see how happy she was looking all of a sudden. Surely if the mere mention of a stay in Cornwall was enough to put the sparkle back in those luminous eyes, it was reason enough to go? Besides, what other plans did she have for the next few months?

'Do you know, it might just be fun at that,' Chloe relented good-naturedly. 'I have not been to the seaside in years. And who knows, by the end of the summer, you may even find yourself looking forward to the opportunity of returning to London.'

'Gracious, Chloe, why ever would you say that?'

'Because I cannot imagine that there will be much in the way of socialising going on down in Cornwall,' Chloe told her bluntly, 'and no doubt what little there is will be of an inferior nature to what you are used to. Indeed, it may be that even the attentions of the London gentlemen will not come so amiss after spending a few months mired in bucolic tranquillity.'

'Hmm, I cannot imagine that my feelings in *that* regard will have changed overmuch,' Madelaine replied drily. 'The *ton* will always be the same, whether it be in two months or two years from now. However, as you say, perhaps after having spent a few months away from them, I shall be able to be somewhat more...tolerant of their attentions.'

'Precisely. And, of course, there is always the possibility that you might meet someone in the country,' Chloe remarked innocently. 'There are, I believe, a few respectable titles in Cornwall.'

'Be that as it may, it will not be my reason for travelling down to Pengarron, nor my purpose for going about each day,' Madelaine assured her. 'I intend to devote myself to the pleasures of the coast, and to keeping *you* suitably entertained. That, I think, should be more than enough to occupy my time.'

Chapter Two

'Damn it, Thomas, I want Pengarron! It galls me to see it standing there empty!'

Gabriel Carew, Earl of Trevellyn, paced back and forth across the room, his hands clasped behind his back, his dark, flashing eyes focused on the carpet beneath his feet. Casually attired in buff-coloured breeches and a bottle-green kerseymere jacket that—had it been crafted by a tailor of any less distinction than Weston—would still have been unable to camouflage the width of his shoulders and the trimness of his waist, Gabriel had come in from his ride a few minutes earlier to find his good friend, Lord Keswick, awaiting him in the library.

'Trent never liked Pengarron,' Gabriel continued now as the older man looked on in amusement. 'He was always more concerned with his other estates than he was with this one. Witness the amount of time he spent here when he was alive. And now that his son has inherited the title and moved into the family seat in the Cotswolds, I fail to see any reason why Pengarron should not be offered up for sale.'

Lord Keswick, who was sitting very comfortably in an armchair and enjoying a particularly fine glass of his host's claret, crossed one booted ankle over the other and watched his long-time friend pace restlessly about the room. 'You may not see a reason for it, Gabriel, but there is one nevertheless. And a rather good one, I am afraid.'

Gabriel abruptly stopped pacing. 'And that is?'

'Trent's widow is in possession of the estate now. Her stepson gave it to her outright, along with his permission to use the town house in London for as long as she wished to do so.'

Gabriel's dark brows snapped together in surprise. 'He *gave* it to her?'

'Mmm. Caused quite a stir in London when word of it got out. Some gentlemen even began to wonder whether the new Lord Trent wasn't quite all about in the head.'

'Yes, I shouldn't wonder that they did. Most young men ascending to their titles are only too eager to increase the size and value of their holdings, not lessen them.'

'As you say. But it would seem that the new Earl is cut from a different cloth.'

'Perhaps.' Gabriel was silent for a few minutes, mulling over what his friend had told him. 'Still, I am surprised that I heard nothing about it.'

'I'm not. You were not long returned from France when it happened, and as you spent almost no time in London before coming down here, there was little chance that you would. But William was perfectly within his rights to give it to her. Pengarron wasn't the family seat, nor was it entailed to the title. His grandfather bought it when he was, himself, a young man, and any entail which might have existed ended when William reached the age of one-and-twenty.'

'But to *give* such a house away?'

Keswick shrugged. 'As you have already pointed out, Trent felt no affection for it. Obviously, neither did his son.

The only thing William *does* seem to hold in affection is his stepmother.'

'Humph. For all the good such a gift would do her.' Gabriel smiled mockingly. 'If the widowed Lady Trent has the use of an elegant town house in London, what could she possibly want with an estate all the way out here in Cornwall?'

'I have no idea, though far be it from me to know what motivates a woman to do anything. But tell me, Gabriel, why do *you* want Pengarron so much? After all, Carew is already the largest estate in the county, and the manor one of the finest in England. What could possibly be gained by the addition of a minor property like Pengarron to your existing holdings?'

'Who said anything about adding it to my holdings?' A slight smile broke through Gabriel's sternness and took the hard edge from his mouth. 'Has it not occurred to you that I might have another use for it altogether?'

'Actually…no.'

'What if I told you that I had it in mind as a gift.'

'A gift?' A gleam of interest appeared in Keswick's eyes. 'I would say that it would make a very nice gift indeed—depending on who you were intending to give it to. Pengarron would not suit everyone.'

'No, but I think it would suit John very well.'

'Your brother? Yes, dashed if it wouldn't,' Keswick agreed with alacrity. 'John has always admired the house—and there is no question that he loves the area. But tell me, does this sudden interest in buying Pengarron mean that he and Cassandra are coming home?'

'I expect them by the end of the month, all being well,' Gabriel said in satisfaction. 'With Cassandra breeding, John is anxious to get her back to England as soon as possible.'

'Yes, no doubt he is. But what of his own health? Has he recovered from his injuries well enough to travel?'

Gabriel sighed. 'His letters assure me that he has, but I still have my doubts. I know how serious his injuries were, and I am anxious to see for myself how far along his recovery really is.'

'Gabriel, forgive me for asking but, if your sister-in-law is breeding, and your brother still needs care, why are you so anxious to establish them elsewhere? Why not just let them live here at Carew until they are in a better position to look for a house themselves?'

'Because I think they deserve some privacy after everything they have been through, Thomas. And the simple fact of the matter is, John cannot afford a house right now. I can.'

'Well, yes, of course you can, there is no question about that,' Keswick allowed. 'But there is also no denying that it is an exceedingly generous gift.'

'No more generous than the new Earl of Trent giving his stepmother a house, I shouldn't think,' Gabriel drawled. 'However, it is no more than John deserves. I have missed my little brother, Thomas. I've never forgiven myself for…not being there the day he was shot.'

Keswick glanced at his friend sharply. 'Is that what this is all about? You are feeling…responsible for John's injuries?'

'I *was* his commanding officer.'

'Not that day. Argyle was. *You* were in a hospital recovering from injuries sustained two months earlier when you were blown off your horse—an accident that nearly cost you your *life*, my friend,' Keswick pointed out bluntly.

Gabriel heard the words, but now, as before, they made little difference. 'The fact remains that my younger brother was left to fight on while I languished in some…local hospital, nursing nothing more serious than a few cracked ribs and a broken leg.'

'It was a good deal more serious than that and you know it,' Keswick said in frustration. 'Damn it, Gabriel, why do you persist in playing down the seriousness of your injuries when you know how badly you still suffer with your leg? I have seen it give out on you any number of times.'

'Because I don't have a wife who is expecting a child in a few months' time,' Gabriel replied tersely. 'And now that John and Cassandra are finally coming home, I want them to have a home of their own. Somewhere to put down roots, and to raise a family. God knows they deserve it, especially Cassandra. That young woman has seen sights that would make a strong man blanch.'

At the thought of the gentle creature his younger brother had married, Gabriel's decision to buy Pengarron for them settled even more firmly in his mind. Cassandra deserved a lovely home after everything she had sacrificed to be with her husband. They were a marvellous pair and, not for the first time, Gabriel found himself wondering whether he would ever know a love like that; the kind of deep, selfless love that weathered all manner of storms, and cast aside doubts and misgivings. The kind of love that sent a gently reared young woman out on to the fields of war, offering help where she could, and all without complaint. Gabriel truly believed that buying Pengarron—the small but stately house set in a magnificent curve of land that adjoined his own—and giving it to them as a gift was little enough recompense.

If he could persuade the widowed Lady Trent to sell it to him.

'So, tell me, Gabriel, how do you go about buying Pengarron?' Keswick enquired, inadvertently tapping into Gabriel's thoughts. 'Do you approach the widow yourself and ask her to sell it to you outright, or do you go the circuitous route and involve lawyers?'

Gabriel's eyes hardened. 'I would have preferred to approach Lady Trent directly to find out whether or not she is interested in selling the property but, given the long-standing feud over the lake, and the bad blood between my father and old Lord Trent, I doubt that would be the wisest course of action. If Lady Trent knows about the feud, she is likely to refuse my offer on principle. For that reason, I think it would be best if I were to contact my lawyer and ask him to put forward an offer on my behalf.'

Lord Keswick's eyes narrowed thoughtfully. 'You mean…submit the offer anonymously?'

Before Gabriel had a chance to reply, the sounds of a commotion in the hallway beyond shattered the peaceful afternoon silence. Moments later, the doors to the library burst open, and two men spilled into the room. The taller of the two was Alfred Taylor, Gabriel's land agent at Carew. The man he was grappling with was the gamekeeper of Pengarron, a shady character by the name of Jake Diggs—a man whom Gabriel had never liked and certainly never trusted.

'Taylor! What is the meaning of this!' Gabriel demanded in a voice that cut through the air like the snap of a whip.

'Beg pardon, my lord, but I caught this one poaching down by the lake,' the steward said, holding the squirming man around the neck in a vice-like grip. 'He had a brace of pheasant, a freshly killed hare, and he was dangling a line in the lake.'

'Was he indeed? All right, you may put him down.'

'He'll bolt for sure, m'lord,' Taylor warned, not loosening his grip an inch.

'I don't think so.' Gabriel's mouth curved in a cold smile. 'Diggs and I already know each other, don't we,

Diggs? And he knows that he will have to take his chances with me if he does try to make a dash for it.'

Gabriel saw the colour drain from the man's face, and nodded his satisfaction. 'Let him loose, Taylor. He won't be running anywhere.'

The burly agent did as he was instructed, all but dropping the weaselly-faced man on the floor. Backing away, he moved no further than the library door, standing with his legs apart and his arms crossed, ready for trouble.

Meanwhile, Diggs rubbed a hand across his throat and looked daggers at the man. 'You bleeding great oaf! You nearly killed me! Just wait 'til I get my—'

'That will be enough, Diggs,' Gabriel interrupted in a soft voice that was edged with steel. 'You're not going anywhere until you tell me what you were doing.'

'I weren't doing nothing,' Diggs spat out, shiftily avoiding the Earl's regard.

'In a pig's eye. He was poaching, my lord,' Taylor spoke up. 'I caught him red-handed.'

Gabriel held up his hand, and silence descended once more. 'Now, Diggs, I shall ask you again. What were you doing down by the lake?'

'Nothing.'

'Nothing?' Gabriel replied quietly. 'You deny that you were poaching?'

'I shot the pheasant and the 'are on Pengarron,' Diggs replied with as much bravado as he could muster. 'There's no law that says I can't hunt on me own property.'

'No, there isn't. *If*, in fact, you were hunting on your own property,' Gabriel pointed out mildly. 'But how do you come to explain the fact that you were fishing in the lake—which just happens to be part of *my* property?'

Diggs's beady black eyes narrowed. 'I don't recall the ownership of the lake ever being properly settled, m'lord.

Besides, you can't nab me for poaching. I didn't have any fish. Your great lummoxing steward can attest to that.'

'Why, you little bas—!'

'Hold, Taylor,' Gabriel said quietly as Taylor took a threatening step forward. 'Nothing shall be gained by dealing Mr. Diggs a facer.'

'He'd be lucky that's all he got,' Taylor grumbled, but nevertheless resumed his position by the door.

'Well, Diggs, what have you to say in your defence?' Gabriel inquired.

Diggs laughed, a shaky, uncertain sound in the quiet room. 'What's this, then, a bleeding trial?'

'You could say that. Taylor is the prosecutor and I am the judge. Now, I repeat,' Gabriel said, walking up to the man and stopping only inches from his face, 'what have you to say in your defence?'

'I told you, I weren't doing nothing wrong,' Diggs replied, though with a good deal less confidence than before. 'Her ladyship is coming down and Cook asked me to bring in some game. And, as Pengarron's gamekeeper, I can hunt and fish as I like.'

Gabriel stopped short. Lady Trent was actually *coming* to Pengarron?

Carefully concealing his surprise at the unexpected news, he resumed his interrogation. 'You may indeed. But *not* on my property. And for that reason, I am giving you your marching orders. I expect you to be gone before sundown.'

Diggs blanched—before his face flushed an angry red colour. 'I don't take orders from you. Lady Trent is the only one as can fire me.'

'Is that so?' Gabriel's response was barely above a whisper. 'And if I told you that this was not the first time you have been suspected of poaching, what would you say?'

'I'd say you ain't got no proof.'

'All right. What about your weekly visits to the Three Feathers? Would Lady Trent be pleased to hear about those, I wonder?'

Diggs glanced up at the Earl in surprise. '''Tis nobody's business but me own what I do on me time off.'

'That is, of course, true,' Gabriel replied mildly. 'But I understood that drunk or disorderly behaviour on the part of *any* of Lord Trent's employees was grounds for immediate dismissal. And I should think that Lady Trent would be most upset were she to learn that you had been apprehended and charged on more than one occasion for just such…regrettable conduct.'

Diggs's voice was full of bluster. 'And I suppose you're going to tell her?'

'There will be no need to—because you will have gone long before she arrives.'

The smaller man's face took on a frightening appearance. 'I don't take kindly to threats, my lord,' he whispered. 'Not even from the likes of *you*!'

'You misunderstand me, Diggs. I am not threatening you at all,' Gabriel said, his eyes glittering ominously. 'I am *telling* you to get off Pengarron. If I ever see you around this part of the county again, you will have myself to answer to. And *that* you may take as a threat.'

Hatred flashed in the eyes that stared back at him. 'You've not heard the last of me, my lord.'

'For your sake, I hope I have.' Gabriel's voice was coldly devoid of emotion. He jerked his head at Taylor and said, 'Get him out of here, and make sure he's off Pengarron by sunset.'

'It will be a pleasure, my lord. Right then, let's be having you!' Taylor said with obvious satisfaction. He twisted the gamekeeper's arm around behind him and ushered him towards the door. 'And none of your tricks if you want to be using this arm again.'

When the agent and his captive had gone, Keswick turned to regard his host with a deliberate smile. 'Well, Gabriel, now you have set the cat amongst the pigeons. Firing Lady Trent's man without so much as a by-your-leave? Whatever will she say? Especially given that, if what Diggs says is true, the lady is due to arrive in the near future. She will be none too pleased to hear that her neighbour has fired one of her husband's retainers and that her first job will be to hire a new one.'

'She should be grateful to me for saving her the trouble of dealing with that scoundrel in the first place,' Gabriel muttered darkly. 'I never could understand why Trent took him on. As far as I'm concerned, Lady Trent is well rid of him. If need be, Taylor can keep an eye on Pengarron until the lady has an opportunity to secure a new gamekeeper.'

'Yes, no doubt she will be kept busy enough after her arrival meeting the denizens of local society,' Keswick speculated. 'Speaking of which, are you planning on attending Lady Westport's ball? I hear tell she has invited the cream of local society.'

'Yes, I suppose I shall have to. Far be it from me to pass up such a memorable opportunity,' came the uninterested reply.

'Was that a touch of sarcasm I heard?' Keswick sallied.

The corners of Gabriel's mouth lifted in a smile. 'You forget, Thomas, I have seen the cream this area has to offer, and I find it of very poor quality indeed.'

'Gabriel, you are a snob. If you were more apt to move in London circles, I would say that you were an insufferable snob, but in this instance, snob shall suffice. You should give some thought to marrying, old boy. It might sweeten your disposition.'

'Spare me. I do not need to hear it from you, as well as from my other all-too-vocal relatives, that it is time I beget the requisite heir. I shall marry when I am good and ready, and not a moment before.'

'That's all very well, Gabriel, but by the time you're ready, you may not be much good any more,' Keswick replied, chuckling. 'Still, Lady Constance seems happy enough to wait for you.'

Gabriel's face closed down. 'Lady Constance accepted Winchelsea's proposal three days ago.'

'Winchelsea!' Lord Keswick abruptly sat forward in his chair. 'But—good God, never say that she's actually *betrothed* herself to that coxcomb! Granted, he's well breeched, but—'

'Well breeched?' Gabriel cut in drily. 'Have you forgotten that he was the sole heir to the Gillis fortune?'

'Well, yes, I suppose he was, but…' Clearly at a loss, Keswick broke off, and then shook his head in bewilderment. '''Pon my word, Gabriel, I had believed the lady to be in love with *you.*'

'Obviously she found the idea of marrying a duke and becoming a duchess far more pleasing than aligning herself with a lowly earl,' Gabriel replied, his mouth twisting in a cynical smile. 'Do you know, I begin to believe that a poor man has an easier time of this love-and-marriage game. At least he knows when a lady is speaking truly of her feelings for him.'

'Yes, I suppose you are right. But, dash it all, Gabriel, I am sorry to hear the news. I know that you held the lady in some esteem. Still, there will be others, my friend.'

'Of course,' Gabriel said, striving for a supremely indifferent tone. 'Lady Constance was far from the only lovely young woman at court looking for a wealthy husband.'

'Do you know, it might not be such a bad idea to cultivate the affections of the little widow,' Keswick said thoughtfully.

'I *beg* your pardon?'

'Well, given the money Trent settled on her, at least you would not have to be suspect of *her* reasons for pursuing you.' Keswick glanced at his friend and smiled. 'Are you not in the least bit curious about her?'

Gabriel shrugged his shoulders in a very matter-of-fact manner. 'Why should I be? Even if I were looking for a wife, I would not choose to involve myself with a widow who was, by all accounts, quite happy with her first husband.'

'She was married to him but six years.'

'Long enough for comparisons to be made and, if I were the one found to be lacking, to have my failings pointed out with irritating regularity. I swore that I would not get caught in the parson's pound until some time past my thirty-fifth year, and as that is still nearly a twelvemonth distant, allow me to spend what little remains of my bachelorhood in relative peace. Granted, I have heard that she is attractive enough, but—'

'Attractive?' Keswick interrupted. 'Saying that Trent's widow is attractive is like calling the *Venus de Milo* an interesting sculpture. The woman is a veritable diamond, Gabriel! And from all I've heard, any number of gentlemen share that opinion and have been beating a fevered path to her door.'

'Yes, and no doubt in the hopes that the poor, bereaved widow will pour some bounty from her late husband's coffers into their pockets,' Gabriel commented drily. 'Hardly the makings of great romance.'

'When money is at the root of things, romance seldom is,' Keswick replied caustically. 'But what is that to you? Why not just introduce yourself to the lady and act the part of the accommodating neighbour? Seems to me that you owe her at least that much.'

'*Owe* her? Good God, Thomas, it is *she* who owes *me* for getting rid of that bad penny to begin with. Heaven only knows how long Diggs has been skimming a living from Trent's lands, let alone ours.'

'Be that as it may, I only thought—'

'Yes, I know what you thought,' Gabriel interrupted narrowly, 'and if it makes you feel any better, I do intend to ride over to Pengarron and do the pretty. *And* to explain the situation with regards to Diggs. But I will do so in my own good time.'

Keswick regarded his friend with a decidedly amused expression. 'I don't know why you are making this out to be such a hardship, Gabriel. You might be surprised to find that you actually come to *like* your new neighbour.'

'Whether I *like* her or not is not at issue here. What is, is Pengarron, and whether or not she is inclined to sell it. I would thank you to remember that and stop trying to meddle in my romantic affairs,' Gabriel said, though with a smile that robbed the words of any possible sting. 'But enough of this, you did not come here to involve yourself with my problems. Let us make haste and try out your new team.'

In the act of finishing his drink, Keswick glanced up at his host in surprise. 'How did you know I brought them?'

'Saw them on the drive. Thought they must be new, since all I've seen you drive to this point is greys. Look like prime cattle though, even from a distance.'

Keswick nodded his satisfaction. 'I was told they're the best, but I would value your opinion. I also figured a crack whip like you might like a chance to have a go with them.'

'Damn right I would,' Gabriel said, slapping Keswick on the shoulder. 'And I warn you, my friend, if I see that you

are still have trouble tooling the ribbons, even with such
prime cattle, I shall be forced to conclude that it is not the
horses who are lacking, but you!'

There was much to plan for the trip to Cornwall. Madelaine had never travelled so far from London before, and
given that she really wasn't sure how long she would be
staying at Pengarron, she decided that it would be better to
take more than she needed, rather than less. Chloe echoed
her niece's sentiments, so it was not surprising that when
the coaches set out early Wednesday morning, they were
laden with a daunting array of trunks, boxes, and portman-
teaus, all filled with a wide assortment of formal gowns,
day dresses, shawls, riding habits, and any other falderal
deemed a necessary part of any lady of quality's wardrobe.

Madelaine and her aunt rode in the first carriage, while
the two maids and the baggage followed in the second.
Thankfully, the weather was fine, and they made good
speed. Fresh horses were hired at each stage of the journey,
and at each of the overnight stops, Madelaine was greeted
with the courtesy and respect due her position and given
the best rooms available. They dined well, enjoying cold
ham or beef, pigeon or game pies, as well as an assortment
of breads and local cheeses. All in all, it made for a very
pleasant trip, as Chloe observed as they traversed the rugged Cornish countryside towards the coast.

'It is such a pleasure to travel in a well-sprung carriage,
my dear. I have certainly made worse trips, and to places
a good deal closer to London than this.'

Madelaine smiled her agreement. 'Edward was very particular about his conveyances. Indeed, I do not know that
I should have been so anxious to make the trip had I been
forced to endure the bumping and crowding of a public
coach. Or a hired one, for that matter.'

'I fear the amount of baggage we are transporting would have precluded either of those modes of travel, Maddie,' Chloe responded drily. 'We have baggage enough for ten, never mind two.'

'Ah, but we shall be well dressed, whatever the occasion,' Madelaine pointed out with a mischievous smile. '*If* we find that there are any occasions for which we will be required to dress!'

In truth, neither lady held out any great hopes for elaborate parties or balls being held in the wilds of Cornwall. The only titled families Madelaine had ever heard Edward refer to were Lord and Lady Westport, Sir Hugh and Lady Bourne, and of course, the Earl and Countess of Trevellyn, and even then, he had been reluctant to disclose much information about them. In the case of the Trevellyns, Madelaine had been left with the impression that relations between the two families had been strained at best. Something about a lake each family claimed as their own.

How silly, Madelaine reflected now as she glanced through the carriage window at the picturesque countryside beyond. With the hundreds of acres of land each family owned, why should it matter who controlled the largest portion of the lake? Surely there were fish enough in it for both?

When they finally arrived at the gates flanking the entrance to Pengarron, Madelaine breathed a heartfelt sigh of relief. Travelling in her late husband's carriage had afforded them a comfortable ride, but it had been a long and tiring journey, and she was glad to see it come to an end. She was also anxious for a first glimpse of her new home. Thus, when they rounded the last curve and the house came into view, Madelaine caught her breath in delight, totally unprepared for the stateliness of the building, and the perfection of its grounds.

It was not a large house, but it was possessed of an elegance and grace that Madelaine had not been expecting after the blunt uniformity of the other houses she had seen. Built out of warm, honey-coloured stone, Pengarron was set into a lush curve of land and backed by a towering stand of trees. A stream meandered off to one side, and just beyond, Madelaine thought she detected the shimmering surface of a rather large lake.

'Oh, how lovely,' Chloe said. 'And not at all what I had expected.'

'No, nor I, Aunt,' Madelaine admitted. 'I confess, I am very well pleased.'

The carriage drew round to the front entrance of the house, and even before the liveried footman had chance to let down the carriage steps, the front door of the house opened and an immaculately dressed butler stepped forward to greet them.

'Lady Trent?' he asked of the two ladies as they descended the carriage.

'I am Lady Trent,' Madelaine said. 'This is my aunt, Mrs Merrill. You must be Berkeley.'

The butler bowed from the waist. 'I am. And may I bid both of you welcome to Pengarron. I trust you had a good journey?'

Madelaine smiled as she started up the front steps. 'Thank you, Berkeley, it was most pleasant.'

As expected, the household servants were gathered in the hall to meet their mistress. They were arranged by rank, with the housekeeper, a soberly dressed woman by the name of Mrs Southerby, standing at the head of the line. Next to her was the cook, Mrs Banks, and then the rest of the footmen, housemaids, and the newly hired scullery maid. Once the introductions and inspection were completed, the servants scurried back to their respective places, with the exception of Mrs Southerby, who duly advised Madelaine and her aunt that their rooms had been made ready in the west wing.

'Perhaps you would like to speak with Mrs Banks regarding meals, Lady Trent?' Mrs Southerby said as they climbed the stairs.

'Thank you, Mrs. Southerby, but I think that can wait until the morning,' Madelaine assured her. 'My aunt and I will not be requiring much in the way of elaborate refreshments.'

'Very good, my lady.'

Madelaine's room turned out to be a large, elegant chamber which overlooked the formal gardens. It was richly appointed in cream and gold, with the furnishings being an interesting though eclectic mixture of Elizabethan solidness and Oriental fantasy. Chloe's bedchamber, which was almost as large, was located down the hall but one, and reflected its owner's passion for the more classic Grecian style.

'If there is anything else you need, Lady Trent, please do let me know,' the housekeeper said helpfully.

'Thank you, Mrs Southerby, I shall.' Madelaine untied her bonnet and set it on the bed. When she realised that the housekeeper was still lingering by the door, she turned back and said, 'Was there something else, Mrs Southerby?'

'Forgive me, my lady, I know it's a long time since, but…I just wanted to say how very sorry we were to hear about Lord Trent's passing. His lordship were a good man, and we were all sorry to lose him.'

Madelaine was touched by the unexpected declaration, and surprised that the woman would express sentiments over something that had happened some time ago. 'Thank you, Mrs Southerby, it is very kind of you to say so.'

The housekeeper curtsied respectfully. 'Goodnight, Lady Trent.'

When the door finally closed behind her, Madelaine sat down on the bed and took a long, deep breath. She was finally here. The long and tiring journey was over. She was home.

Home, Madelaine mused, glancing around the spacious chamber with an appreciative eye. How strange to think of Pengarron as home. And yet, that was precisely what it was—and a far more pleasant one than she had been anticipating. When she and Chloe had set out from London, Madelaine had had no idea what to expect. On the few occasions Edward had spoken to her about Pengarron, he had always referred to it as a somewhat dark house, with adequate gardens and a relatively pleasing prospect.

Upon her arrival at Pengarron, however, Madelaine had discovered that her late husband's description was not at all in keeping with the true manner of the estate. Pengarron was a house of some size, and it could not have been situated more perfectly on the grounds. Indeed, the view from this window was exceptional. And from what little Madelaine had seen of the rest of the house, she would not have said that it was dark at all. Certainly the wallpaper and the bed linens in this room were as elegant as she could have wished. The draperies looked as though they had been newly washed and hung—in fact, the entire house looked as though it had been scrubbed and polished for her arrival.

All in all, it made for a very pleasant introduction to her new home, and as Betty arrived to help her get ready for bed, Madelaine began to hope that everything else about her summer in Cornwall would turn out to be as gratifying.

Chapter Three

At ten o'clock the following morning, Madelaine met with Mrs Southerby in the hall, and began her tour of the house. It was a much larger house than it appeared from the outside and, more than once, the housekeeper had had to redirect Madelaine's steps as she went to turn into the wrong corridor. But then, after the relative simplicity of the town house in London, a house with three floors, numerous bedchambers, and a variety of saloons, parlours and drawing rooms was bound to be confusing.

The tour was followed by a review of the household accounts, which Madelaine found to be accurately documented and well laid out. Every last glass and thimble were accounted for, and she soon discovered that Mrs Southerby knew, to the last penny, where the household money was being spent. She doubted that any of the local merchants were able to get away with much with the housekeeper of Pengarron.

'Thank you, Mrs Southerby, I am well pleased with everything I have seen this morning,' Madelaine complimented her at the end of the hour, 'and I see no reason to disrupt what is obviously a well-run establishment. I shall inform you if there is to be any deviation from normal procedure, say, in the case of a special party, but other than that, the needs of my aunt and myself will be relatively simple. We plan to live very quietly throughout the summer.'

'Very good, my lady,' Mrs Southerby replied. 'Will there be anything else?'

'Yes, would you ask Berkeley to come and see me? There are a few matters I should like to review with him as soon as possible.'

'Yes, my lady,' the housekeeper said with a respectful curtsy.

Moments after she left, the door opened again and Chloe entered, attractively outfitted in a gown of dark grey cambric edged with ruffles of white lace at the wrists and throat. 'Good morning to you, my dear.'

Madelaine smiled, and stood up to kiss her aunt's cheek in greeting. 'Good morning, Chloe. How did you pass your first night at Pengarron?'

'Like a ship anchored in a snug harbour,' Chloe replied contentedly. 'I cannot recall when I slept more soundly. I almost fell asleep while my maid was brushing my hair.'

'I am delighted to hear it. Have you had breakfast?'

'Thank you, my dear, yes. Lucinda brought me up a tray. I must say, your cook does a lovely cup of chocolate. I found it quite to my liking.'

'I am pleasantly surprised to find nearly everything to my liking thus far,' Madelaine replied in some relief. 'The house is beautiful, the staff are efficient, and the feeling throughout is one of peace and tranquillity. I think it was a good idea to come here for the summer. Nor do I think that we shall suffer from the heat. The breeze blowing in off the sea is most refreshing.'

Chloe nodded, and gracefully sank into one of the damask wing chairs situated beside the fireplace. 'So, what have you planned for today?'

'Nothing of any import. I have already covered a good many things with Mrs Southerby, and shall have a word with Cook this afternoon. Currently, I am awaiting the arrival of Berkeley so that I can go over a few matters concerning the estate. After that, I thought perhaps we might take a turn outside. It is far too lovely a day to remain indoors, and after being cooped up in the carriage for so long, I thought you might enjoy a stroll through the gardens.'

'Hmm, I think I am rather more inclined to pass my time with a novel today, my dear,' Chloe remarked with a lazy smile. 'I am not as young as you any more.'

'Tosh! You have more energy than any woman I know. And I promise that we shall not go far. Unless you are interested in paying a call upon one of our new neighbours, that is.'

'I think I can forgo that dubious pleasure for a day or two,' Chloe remarked drily.

Madelaine chuckled. 'Now, Chloe, you needn't try to pretend that you are not curious about our neighbours. I know you better than that. Ah, Berkeley, come in.'

'You wished to see me, my lady?'

'Yes. I was wondering if there is a land steward or bailiff here at Pengarron?'

'No, my lady. Lord Trent only kept a small staff on, and matters pertaining to the grounds were handled by the gamekeeper.'

'I see. And what is his name?'

'That would be…Diggs, Lady Trent.'

Madelaine noticed the slight hesitation in the man's voice, but did not trouble herself to ask after it. 'Very well, would you ask Diggs to come and see me? I should like to know something about the size and extent of the—' Madelaine broke off when she realised that the butler was now looking somewhat uncomfortable. 'Is something wrong, Berkeley?'

'Well, not exactly wrong, my lady,' he said slowly. 'It is just that, well…Diggs is…no longer in your employ.'

'I beg your pardon? Do you mean to say that he quit?'

'No, my lady. It is my understanding that he was… dismissed.'

Madelaine blinked. 'Dismissed? By whom?'

'By…Lord Trevellyn, my lady.'

Lord Trevellyn? Madelaine was so taken aback by the unexpected disclosure that for a moment, she was rendered quite incapable of speech. *Lord Trevellyn had dismissed one of her servants?* But…that was preposterous! A gentleman would never do such a thing.

'Did you hear this from Lord Trevellyn himself, Berkeley?' Chloe enquired, when she saw that her niece was too surprised to.

'No, madam. It came to me via Everett, one of the young footmen. He said that he had heard it from Lord Trevellyn's own steward, Taylor.'

'Dear me, a convoluted trail at best,' Madelaine murmured when she finally found her voice, 'but one in which there would be much room for misunderstanding.'

'My lady?'

'Well, obviously Everett has misunderstood what the other gentleman said,' Madelaine replied. 'I cannot conceive that one of Lord Trevellyn's staff would know what a member of my own household was doing, nor can I believe that Lord Trevellyn would take it upon himself to involve himself in the running of Pengarron. As such, I am more inclined to believe that a misunderstanding has taken place somewhere along the way. And to that end, I should like to have a word with Lord Trevellyn's man myself. I do not like hearing that falsehoods are being spread by the servants.'

'With respect, my lady, Taylor is not the sort of man to spread falsehoods. He has been with the Trevellyn family for years.'

'Are you saying that you believe him?'

'I have no reason *not* to believe him,' Berkeley said tactfully. 'It is possible that, as you say, the information was not relayed correctly. Everett can become rather…excitable at times.'

'Exactly. Pray have one of the other footmen relay a message to Lord Trevellyn's man that I would speak with him.'

'You wish to speak with Taylor *yourself*, Lady Trent?'

'Indeed I do, Berkeley. I have no wish to jeopardise the man's position by going to Lord Trevellyn directly, but I will have the truth of the matter. I arrive at Pengarron to find myself without a gamekeeper and with no logical explanation as to why, when I know that Lord Trent was a good and generous employer—'

'He was indeed, my lady,' the butler was quick to agree.

'For that reason, I find it difficult to believe that a man would willingly give up a good position in his household. On the other hand, I find it equally hard to believe that a man such as Lord Trevellyn would stoop to meddling in someone else's domestic affairs. Granted, I have not yet made the acquaintance of the gentleman, but I would prefer to have this matter cleared up before I do. I cannot think that it would look well on my part to have an interrogation as my first meeting with Lord Trevellyn, rather than the polite social call it should be.'

Seeing that his mistress's mind was firmly made up, Berkeley inclined his head. 'As you wish, my lady. I shall have one of the footmen relay the message to Taylor at once, asking him to wait upon you. At what time would you like him to call?'

'The sooner the better,' Madelaine said, suddenly wishing that Edward was still alive. He would know how to deal with this so much better than herself. 'You may tell Lord Trevellyn's man that he may call upon me directly after lunch.'

'Very good, my lady. I shall see that the message is delivered immediately.'

After he had gone, Madelaine cast a curious glance at her aunt. 'How very strange. What do you make of all this, Chloe?'

'I am sure I do not know, my dear,' Chloe replied in all honesty. 'The idea of Lord Trevellyn high-handidly dismissing one of your own people does seem very strange, to say the least. But one thing I do know is that you cannot be without a steward or a gamekeeper. A property this size must be properly maintained.'

Madelaine nodded, then thoughtfully nibbled at her bottom lip. 'If Lord Trevellyn did not dismiss Diggs, why do you think he left? Surely he was not alarmed at the thought of working for me, rather than for my husband?'

Chloe let out a hoot. 'My dear girl, that is by far the most ludicrous notion I have ever heard. No one could possibly resent working for you. Still, it *is* rather strange the way he seems to have just disappeared. And so soon before your arrival. I wonder if perhaps your neighbour did turn him off?'

'No. I cannot believe that the Earl of Trevellyn would do such a thing,' Madelaine replied emphatically. 'It is clearly overstepping the bounds of propriety.'

'Perhaps it would be worth a call on him to find out.'

'As I told Berkeley, I should rather have this other matter

cleared up first. If not, it will linger in the back of my mind throughout the entire meeting with Lord Trevellyn, and possibly come out at a most inauspicious moment.' Madelaine paused for a moment, before adding, 'I wonder what Lord Trevellyn is like. I cannot remember having met him in London. Have you?'

'Yes, but it was some years ago,' said Chloe, 'and I am not at all sure whether I would know him now. He was away on the Continent for some time. Exceedingly good-looking though, as I recall.'

'Well, no doubt we shall stumble across one another in due course,' Madelaine said. 'But for now, I am far more interested in talking to the steward of Carew than I am to the master of it!'

As it turned out, however, neither the steward nor the lord of Carew Manor were in residence when Madelaine's note was delivered.

Gabriel had been intending to drive over to Pengarron in his sporty high-perch phaeton while his agent paid a visit to one of his oldest tenants, a woman by the name of Mrs Abbey. But when Taylor was unexpectedly called away to attend to an accident at another cottage, Gabriel had been obliged to pay the call on Mrs Abbey himself.

The elderly woman's cottage was located at the end of a very long road, with a driveway that was virtually impassable by carriage. For that reason, Gabriel had decided to make his way there on horseback. He knew that it would be easier to deliver the basket of foodstuffs that way than any other. He also knew, since he seldom managed to get away from her house without inflicting some small mark upon his attire, that it would be wiser for him to wear less formal clothing for the visit than he might otherwise wear.

He had no wish to be taken to task by his haughty valet for soiling his good clothes yet again.

As a result, when Gabriel's visit to Mrs Abbey was completed, he returned to Carew by way of the back fields, rather than by the main road. The trail was well known to him; winding like a ribbon through the lush fields and meadows he had grown up in, and it brought him, at one point, quite close to Pengarron. Close enough, that when Gabriel glanced towards the back of the house, he could see a young woman sitting in a shady bower in the garden. Her bonnet was lying on the bench beside her and all of her attention seemed to be focused on the book in her hand.

Even so, there was no denying that she was an exceedingly lovely young woman. Her profile was perfection; a pert little nose set above a soft rosebud mouth, cheeks high-boned and brushed with the delicate pink of a newly bloomed rose. Her hair appeared to him the colour of spun gold, with a few wispy tendrils escaping from the cluster of curls secured atop her head to dance naughtily around her brow, steadfastly ignoring the repeated attempts of her fingers to smooth them back into place.

Gabriel smiled as he drew the prancing stallion to a halt. Could this entrancing creature be the lady Trent had chosen for his second wife? For if it was, it came as no surprise to Gabriel that the older man had been so willing to disregard the considerable age difference between them and marry her.

As if suddenly growing aware that she was being watched, Madelaine stopped reading and lifted her eyes from the page. With unerring judgement, she turned her head and looked directly at the man seated upon the magnificent horse at the edge of the trees, and then blushed as she realised that he was staring at her rather boldly. *But who…?*

And then, Madelaine remembered. Of course, this must be Trevellyn's man come to see her. Granted, he had the hour a little early, but perhaps they took luncheon at Carew earlier than they did at Pengarron. Feeling considerably relieved, Madelaine set the book down and, raising her arm, beckoned for him to approach.

Across the width of the field, Gabriel gazed at the young lady who had calmly risen from her seat and now stood waving at him, with a marked degree of surprise. Surely it was not the custom of the Dowager Countess of Trent to wave at unknown gentlemen riding past her property? But then, perhaps this was not the mistress of the house at all, he thought, but a youthful companion, or a friend.

Curious, Gabriel turned the stallion's head in the direction of the house and rode towards her. 'Good morrow to you,' he said when he was close enough to be heard without shouting.

'Good morning,' Madelaine replied, lacing her fingers together in front of her. 'Pray forgive my casual attitude, but I had not expected you so early in the day.'

Gabriel's eyebrows rose a fraction. She had been *expecting* him? How strange, considering that he had not yet sent his card requesting permission to call.

'Have I the honour of addressing the Dowager Countess of Trent?' he enquired, not wishing to commit a grave social error.

The slow, deep voice sent an unexpected quiver along Madelaine's spine, and she hesitated before answering. He seemed to tower above her, this big, broad-shouldered man who sat so easily astride the magnificent stallion. His dark, wavy hair styled after no fashion but its own, and he had a face that was rugged rather than handsome.

As he gazed down at her, Madelaine was sure that she saw amusement glinting in the depths of those dark eyes, and unconsciously, she raised her chin. 'You have, and may I say that I appreciate your coming so quickly. I am sure that your duties keep you singularly well occupied.'

His *duties*? Gabriel swung down from the saddle, and offered her a quick bow. 'They keep me well occupied indeed, but I came as quickly as I could. I would not wish you to think that I was being in any way remiss in fulfilling my…obligations.'

Madelaine missed the slight note of mockery in his reply, being far more intent upon the question she was about to ask. 'Thank you, and please understand that I have no wish to cause any problems for you with your employer, Taylor. I simply wished to clear up this…misunderstanding as soon as possible. That is why I wrote to you directly, rather than go to Lord Trevellyn with the problem. You have my assurance that no word of our discussion need reach his lordship's ear, if you desire that it should not.'

Gabriel stared at the young woman in front of him as though she had spouted a mouthful of gibberish. *She thought that he was Taylor—and she had asked to see him personally?* But…what kind of nonsense was this? Why would Lady Trent need or wish to see the steward of Carew? And what was the nature of this…problem that she was referring to? Had Taylor been up to some kind of mischief for which he was now being taken to task? Mischief about which his own employer knew nothing?

'I…appreciate your candour, my lady,' Gabriel said carefully, and for the moment, in a tone that gave nothing away. 'Pray, tell me how I may be of service?'

'Well, it is in regard to my late husband's gamekeeper,' Madelaine began. 'Or, more correctly, to his *missing* gamekeeper, and the rumour that is circulating about his absence. A rumour that *you* are reputed to have told one of my servants.'

Trying to adopt the attitude of a menial, Gabriel lowered his eyes. 'Forgive me, my lady, but unfortunately, there are so many rumours circulating that I am not sure…to which one you refer.'

'I refer, Taylor, to the rumour that Lord Trevellyn dismissed my gamekeeper out of hand. I have been informed that *you* were the one who passed this information along to one of my younger footmen, and I thought that before meeting Lord Trevellyn, I should like to ascertain whether or not it was true, or simply a misunderstanding.'

Gabriel studied the upturned face of the lovely young woman in front of him, and was conscious of a number of emotions warring for uppermost place. He could see that she was very earnest in her declarations, and at the same time, very concerned about what she was going to hear. And, in all fairness, Gabriel knew that he should tell her immediately that he was not Taylor as she so obviously believed, but rather, the Earl of Trevellyn himself. But something held him silent. Something bid him hold his tongue until he was able to learn more about the lady, and the situation in which she found herself.

'Would it disturb you so much to learn that…Lord Trevellyn had dismissed one of your late husband's servants, my lady?' Gabriel inquired softly.

'Indeed, it would distress me greatly,' Madelaine replied without hesitation. 'It is not Lord Trevellyn's place to involve himself in the affairs of a neighbour. Especially one with whom he has not even made an acquaintance.'

'Yes, I can understand your feeling that way. I suppose there are still bad feelings over the matter of the lake,' Gabriel said slowly, watching for her reaction.

'The lake?' Madelaine stared at him blankly. 'I know little enough of this grievance over the lake, Taylor, and I certainly harbour no grudge against Lord Trevellyn because of it. It seems to me a silly matter between my late father-in-law and the previous Lord Trevellyn. *My* concern is with the current Lord Trevellyn, and the fact that he has taken it upon himself to meddle.'

'*Meddle!*'

The tone conveyed far more displeasure than it should have and, catching sight of the resultant surprise in Lady Trent's eyes, Gabriel chided himself for his carelessness. He had to remember that he was playing a part here, and that if he held out any hopes of carrying it off, his behaviour would have to reflect the subservience of the role.

'I…beg your pardon, my lady, I should not have spoken out in such a manner,' Gabriel said as humbly as he was able, 'but I have been with the Trevellyns…all of my life and have never once heard them accused of…meddling.'

Aware now that the tone had been one of offence rather than anger, Madelaine inclined her head in an apology of her own. 'Pray, forgive my choice of words, Taylor. Perhaps meddle is a touch strong. Indeed, I have yet to determine whether Lord Trevellyn did med—that is, involve himself in the situation at all. Which is why I asked to see you. I would like to discover the truth of the matter before meeting Lord Trevellyn for the first time.' Madelaine took a deep breath, and smiled uncertainly. 'So, I shall ask you outright. Did Lord Trevellyn dismiss my man, Diggs, as I have been led to believe?'

Gabriel hesitated. He was not sure that he wanted to give Lady Trent an answer to that question just now. If he did, and if he replied honestly, the meeting would be swiftly concluded, at which time Lady Trent would go back to Pengarron with her opinion of her new neighbour—as yet unseen—having already been formed. And it went without saying that it would not be a favourable one.

But that was not the only reason Gabriel found himself

reluctant to bring the conversation to a close. He realised, much to his surprise, that he was actually enjoying the opportunity of being someone else. There was a remarkable sense of…freedom in pretending to be someone other than Gabriel Carew, Earl of Trevellyn. The beautiful Lady Trent was not looking at him as a social equal, or as a prospective husband. She was regarding him as a steward; a servant in a rich man's household. And as a steward, Gabriel realised that, for the first time in his life, he was free of the social restrictions which normally bound him. There was no need for him to act like the lord of the manor now. He had only to behave with respect and courtesy towards a lady, and in turn, to see how she responded to him.

It was an intriguing prospect, Gabriel realised. To see what difference it made to others, if he were only the steward of Carew, rather than the master of it. Certainly, it would tell him a great deal about the lady herself.

'My lady, I wonder if I might ask you a question?' Gabriel said, deciding for the moment to play out the subterfuge.

'Ask what you wish, Taylor.'

'Did you know this person Diggs?'

Madelaine glanced up at him in surprise. 'No. How could I? I have never been to Pengarron before.'

'I thought as much. For, if you had known him, you would not have liked him.'

Madelaine's left eyebrow arched expressively. 'Indeed?'

'The man was a thief, my lady. A rogue, a scallywag, a ne'er-do-well. And, quite frankly, he was robbing your late husband blind.'

Madelaine gasped in astonishment. Lord Trevellyn's servant knew such things as this? Truly, matters were very much different here in Cornwall than they were in London.

'Taylor, I cannot imagine why—'

'Lady Trent, I wonder, have you seen anything of Pengarron, apart from the grounds which immediately surround the house?' Gabriel interrupted.

Madelaine blinked, caught off guard both by the question and by the disarming smile which accompanied it. 'I have seen nothing of Pengarron, because I no longer have a steward to show it to me—the reason for which I am trying to ascertain.'

'Then, might I suggest that I be allowed to take you around?' Gabriel offered. 'Having lived all of my life next to Pengarron, I think I can safely say that I know your lands as well as Diggs. And I would be pleased to show them to you in his absence.'

Startled by his directness, Madelaine found herself hesitating again. How very forward was this servant of Lord Trevellyn's. There was not a trace of subservience in his manner. Quite the opposite, in fact. He radiated an air of self-confidence that was entirely out of keeping with his position. And, while it was immediately evident that he had been well educated, both from the manner in which he spoke and from his general air of refinement, there was still something about the man that bothered Madelaine. Something that wasn't quite…right.

'You have not yet answered my question, Taylor,' she said quietly, trying to think what it might be.

'No, my lady, I have not. Now, will you allow me to show you Pengarron?'

Madelaine gazed up into the shadowy eyes of the man who had somehow taken control of this meeting, and opened her mouth to speak, intending to put him in his place.

She was dismayed when nothing came out. In fact, she was alarmed to find that her heart was beating rather faster than it ought to under the circumstances, and certainly more than was seemly. What manner of servant was this that addressed a lady so boldly? Did Trevellyn not teach his servants respect? But then, Madelaine had never met a servant quite like this before either. One who dressed as well as his master—and who brought the colour to her cheeks merely by the intensity of his gaze.

'You are uncommon bold for a steward, Taylor,' Madelaine observed in an attempt to discomfort him.

Her words met with little success, for he slowly began to smile. 'Aye, my lady, so I've been told. But we Cornish men are not like the dandies and fops of London society. We are not puppets made to dance at the fingers of those born higher than ourselves. I hold myself accountable to no man.'

'Not even to your lord and master?' Madelaine challenged.

'I am my own lord and master, my lady. But I am also loyal to the family I serve, and for whose lands and possessions I guard.'

That, at least, was not a falsehood, Gabriel assured himself. He had no wish to lie outright to Lady Trent; she didn't deserve that. All he wanted to do was spend a little more time in her company and thereby learn more about her *and* her plans for Pengarron. And if he was able to accomplish that by dressing in the guise of a servant, so be it.

Madelaine, however, found herself in a considerable dilemma. She had been unable to gain either clarification or denial from this man regarding the rumour surrounding Diggs and, as such, knew that the interview should swiftly be brought to a close. Why, then, was she so strangely reluctant to end their encounter? That made no sense at all. After all, why would she wish to remain in the company of a man who was beneath her in every way—yet one whose very presence was causing her pulse to quicken?

'And how do you propose to show me Pengarron, Taylor?' Madelaine heard herself ask, surprised that she would even consider his suggestion.

Gabriel's handsome features warmed to a smile. 'The only way it should be seen, my lady. On horseback.'

Madelaine tried to quell the quiver of anticipation his words evoked, but failed hopelessly. How desperately she had been longing for a good gallop over the open fields and rolling hills. Was that not one of the pleasures of country life that she had enumerated to her aunt? And was this not now the perfect opportunity of doing that, and of seeing her new home at the same time?

'Very well, Taylor, I accept your offer. You may take me around Pengarron, *if* Lord Trevellyn gives you his permission to do so.'

Gabriel's eyes narrowed. So, the lady was possessed of integrity as well as beauty. It made for a refreshing change. 'And how would you have me convey his permission, my lady? In writing, perhaps?'

Madelaine considered his suggestion for a moment, and then nodded. 'Yes, I should like to see a letter in his hand— *and* with his seal—condoning the time you may take to show me Pengarron.'

'I see no problem in securing such a letter,' Gabriel said, bowing. 'Shall I wait upon you later today?'

'No. My aunt and I were thinking of paying a call on one of our neighbours—'

'Not Lord Trevellyn, I hope?'

The words were out before Gabriel could stop them, and as soon as he saw the look on Lady Trent's face, he knew that he had erred. 'Forgive me, my lady, I did not mean to sound impertinent. It is just that…I know his lordship will

be…away from home this afternoon, and I thought to spare
you the time and trouble of riding over to Carew for no
good purpose.'

Madelaine eyed him with a cool appraising stare. It
seemed that this servant of Trevellyn's took a good deal
upon himself when it came to the well-being of his master.
'Thank you, Taylor, but it was not Lord Trevellyn that I
was intending to visit. I thought to pay a call on Sir Hugh
and Lady Bourne. However, I should be pleased to ride out
with you on the morrow. Shall we say…half past eight?'

'Half past *eight*?' Gabriel tried unsuccessfully to hide his
look of surprise. He had never met a lady who would willingly set foot outside her door before ten o'clock in the
morning—and certainly not when she was residing in the
country. 'Are you sure you wish to rise so early, my lady?'

'I can rise earlier than that when I've a mind to, Taylor.'
Madelaine smiled, glad to have finally been able to catch
him off guard. 'I am not so soft as you might think.'

'The thought never crossed my mind,' Gabriel assured
her.

The warm caress in his eyes brought a heated flush to
Madelaine's cheeks, and she quickly turned away. 'Shall
I…meet you at the stables?'

Gabriel shook his head, unwilling to risk recognition by
her servants. 'Perhaps we could rendezvous at the lake,
since it is closer to my own land, and to where I would
take you first.'

Madelaine looked at him quizzically. 'Your *own* land,
Taylor?'

'Beg pardon, my lady. Lord *Trevellyn*'s land,' Gabriel
said, amusement flickering in the depths of his eyes. 'Having lived here all my life, I sometimes tend to…think of it
as my own.'

For some reason, Madelaine found herself smiling back

at him. She supposed it was an understandable mistake. No doubt if she had spent her entire life in one house—whether it be as servant or mistress—she would probably be inclined to look upon it that way too.

'Very well. I shall meet you at half past eight by the lake. No doubt my groom will be able to lead me that far.'

Her *groom*? Gabriel swore softly under his breath. He had forgotten about the presence of the required groom. No lady of gentle birth—not even a widow—would risk incurring the censure of her peers by riding out with a gentleman unaccompanied. Unfortunately, there was nothing he could do about that now. If he questioned her decision to ride with an escort, it might only serve to arouse her suspicions more. All he could do was deal with the situation when it arose.

The sound of footsteps approaching from the direction of the house alerted Gabriel to the arrival of another person, and he glanced up in dismay. It was time for him to leave. He had no way of knowing whether the footsteps belonged to one of the household servants—who would certainly recognise him—or to one of Lady Trent's family but, either way, Gabriel knew he could not risk being caught out now. He had initiated a charade, and the revealing of it—if and when the time came to do so—would have to be effected with the utmost care and diplomacy. Which meant that he would also have to intercept the missive Lady Trent had sent to Taylor at Carew, before the steward had a chance to reply and thereby completely expose Gabriel's charade.

'Forgive me, my lady, but I fear I must leave,' he said abruptly. 'I have tarried longer than I should.'

'Yes, of course,' Madelaine replied at once. 'I am sorry to have kept you away so long, but I would like to thank you for coming so promptly.'

Gabriel flashed her a devastating smile as he climbed

back into the saddle. 'Until tomorrow, Lady Trent.' With that, he pressed his heels into the stallion's sides and was gone, leaving Madelaine to watch after him, her mind and her heart filled with a confusing jumble of emotions.

'Ah, there you are, dear,' Chloe said from the doorway. 'I have been looking for you this past ten minutes. Luncheon is ready.'

'Thank you, Chloe,' Madelaine replied without turning.

'By the by, did I hear you speaking with someone just now?'

'Yes. Lord Trevellyn's steward came by.'

'Ah, yes, the infamous Taylor,' Chloe remarked with a smile. 'Were you able to resolve the mystery with regard to your missing Mr. Diggs?'

'Not really,' Madelaine admitted ruefully, finally turning back to smile at her aunt. 'Taylor was remarkably adept at deflecting my questions. But I did discover one thing.'

'And what was that, my dear?'

Madelaine sighed as she fell into step beside her aunt. 'That the servants here in Cornwall are not *at all* like the ones we have in London!'

Chapter Four

Madelaine and her aunt did pay a call that afternoon—to
Ashcroft, the home of Sir Hugh and Lady Bourne, Madelaine's closest neighbours to the east. Lord Bourne was not
at home, but Lady Bourne and her daughters, Prunella and
Phoebe, were. And anxious to ingratiate herself with the
newly arrived Lady Trent, *and* to find out firsthand anything and everything she could about the lady she had heard
so much about, Lady Bourne set out to be as charming as
possible.

'My dear Lady Trent, how very good of you to call. And
Mrs Merrill, such a pleasure,' Lady Bourne said after the
introductions had been made. 'You cannot know how I
have been longing to make your acquaintance.' She led the
way into a small but pleasant parlour, and signalled to the
waiting maid to bring tea. 'Phoebe, Prunella, come and
make your greetings to Lady Trent and her aunt, Mrs Merrill.'

The two girls came forward, surprisingly with the
younger daughter, Phoebe, leading the way. She was a remarkably pretty child with dark eyes and dark hair, while
Prunella, a year older, hung back slightly, a meek shadow
compared to her vivacious sister.

'Good afternoon, Lady Trent, Mrs Merrill,' Phoebe said in a sing-song voice.

'Good afternoon, Miss Phoebe,' Madelaine greeted the girl politely. 'And to you, Miss Bourne,' she said in the direction of the older daughter.

'Oh, do come along, Prunella,' Lady Bourne admonished. 'We haven't all day.'

Madelaine saw the painful blush which spread across the girl's cheeks as she stepped forward to make her curtsy, and felt her heart go out to her. The state of affairs in the Bourne household was very plain to see. Phoebe, the youngest, was clearly the apple of her mother's eye. This was the daughter who would make the brilliant marriage—the one who would be deemed an Incomparable, and have her choice of any number of anxious suitors. Such a fate would be spared her as would likely befall her older, plainer sister, Prunella.

Still, after all of the introductions had been made, Madelaine found herself smiling upon the elder sister with far more warmth than she did upon the younger one. Phoebe had no need of such encouragement. Prunella had all that need, and more.

'And what do you think of Cornwall, Lady Trent?' Lady Bourne enquired anxiously. 'I dare say you find it a far cry from the glitter and excitement of London.'

'It is indeed, Lady Bourne,' Madelaine concurred. 'But it was that very quality which drew me to it in the first place.'

'You actually *wished* to leave London, Lady Trent?' Phoebe said, looking at her in astonishment. 'But how can that be? London is such a wonderful place. I do not think I would ever leave there if I did not have to. Prunella says that she did not like it at all, but I cannot wait to go up to make my come out next year!'

Surprised by the girl's boldness, but not by her enthusiasm, Madelaine smiled back, and was conscious of suddenly feeling very old and wise at twenty-five. Had she not felt much the same as Phoebe when she had been her age; eager to see the great city and anxious to discover what wondrous sights and adventures it held in store for her?

'No doubt, you shall have a splendid time, Phoebe,' Madelaine replied, 'because London *is* a beautiful and exciting place. But there are times when it is a relief to be away from it too.'

'La, I can scarce credit such a thing. Only think of all the exciting things one can do in Town,' the girl replied, clasping her hands together in delight. 'The shops, and the galleries. Carriage rides in Hyde Park, walks along the Serpentine—'

'Thank you, Phoebe, but I do not think Lady Trent needs you to enumerate all of London's attractions for her,' Lady Bourne said indulgently. 'I am sure she is well aware of what it has to offer.'

Chastised, but not in the least contrite, Phoebe flounced back into her chair and pouted. Prunella merely sat quietly in her straight-backed chair and gazed at the two visitors with an expression of awe, as if astonished that such glamorous creatures should actually be here in her house.

'Prunella, do stop staring!' her mother admonished firmly. 'Lady Trent and Mrs Merrill did not come here to be gawked at by you! Mind your manners, girl.'

The rebuke seemed unnecessarily harsh to Madelaine, but Lady Bourne quickly leaned over to whisper, 'Pray, pay no mind to my manner of speaking, Lady Trent. I can assure you, Prunella does not. The girl is a hopeless dreamer, and that is all there is to it. I have tried until I am at my wit's end to cure her of it, but still she does it.'

Madelaine turned a gentle smile on the elder sister, seeing the rosy blush of embarrassment which her mother's scolding had brought to her cheeks, and felt sorrier for the poor girl than ever. 'I do not mind, Lady Bourne,' Madelaine said kindly. 'When I was Prunella's age, everything seemed rather overwhelming to me too. I am sure she will be fine, given a little more time.'

The look of gratitude Prunella sent Madelaine's way was so warm and sincere that Madelaine could not help but be touched by it. Obviously, praise was not something the elder Miss Bourne was accustomed to receiving.

'Now, Lady Trent, will you have milk or lemon in your tea?' Lady Bourne inquired as the maid brought in the tea tray and set it on the small table next to her.

'Lemon, if you please, Lady Bourne.'

'And you, Mrs Merrill?'

'Milk, thank you.'

Lady Bourne poured tea for each of the ladies, adding milk or lemon as required, and then handed the delicate rose-patterned cups and saucers to Phoebe to pass around.

'First, let me say how very sorry we were to hear of Lord Trent's passing,' Lady Bourne said, anxious to get the obligatory regrets out of the way as soon as possible. 'He was a fine gentleman.'

'You knew my husband, then?' Madelaine enquired.

'Actually, no. But my husband did. And he told me many a time that Lord Trent was as fine a gentleman as you could have wished to meet, bless his soul.'

Madelaine she sat back and took a sip of tea. She found it incongruous that someone who had not actually met her husband was so willing to vouchsafe what a splendid fellow he had been. 'Thank you, Lady Bourne.'

'And, Mrs Merrill,' their hostess said, turning now to Madelaine's aunt, who had been quite content to sit back and watch the proceedings going on around her, 'I understand that you are recently returned from Scotland. Did you find the Duke of Kenfield's hospitality to your liking?'

Chloe all but choked on her tea. 'I...beg your pardon, Lady Bourne. But...how did you know of my visit to Scotland?'

'Quite by chance, actually,' Lady Bourne replied, pleased that she had been able to catch the illustrious Mrs Merrill off guard. 'One of my nieces was fortunate enough to have received an invitation to the Duke of Kenfield's house party as well. You may remember her. A charming girl, very pretty, with blonde hair and blue eyes—'

Chloe frowned. 'You cannot mean...Miss McClusky?'

'Yes, that's right. Dear Harriet wrote and told us all about it.'

Madelaine hastily turned away to hide her smile—and caught Chloe's eye in doing so. 'Is that not a coincidence, Aunt? Harriet McClusky—Lady Bourne's niece.'

'Yes, isn't it,' Lady Bourne replied, eager to validate the importance of her own connections—and thereby missing her visitor's gentle sarcasm. 'His Grace is a fine gentleman, is he not, Mrs Merrill?'

Chloe, who had quickly regained control of her own expression, regally inclined her head. 'He is indeed, Lady Bourne.'

'Harriet says that she is going to marry the Duke and become the next Duchess of Kenfield,' Prunella volunteered innocently.

'Prunella!'

The word reverberated around the room like a clap of thunder, and caused everyone in it to jump. 'Mrs Merrill, I do beg your pardon, but I fear that dear Prunella has spoken out of turn,' Lady Bourne said, turning a censorious eye on her daughter. 'Your cousin said no such thing, my dear. Harriet merely said that she had a lovely time at the

Duke's home, and that he would be…a most agreeable match for *any* young lady who was fortunate enough to catch his eye.'

Chloe did not miss the subtle reference to age, but her smile never faltered as she said, 'Indeed, his Grace is a charming gentleman, and one possessed of a most gracious nature. I declare, *all* of the ladies present were made to feel most welcome.'

'*I* think Lord Trevellyn is by far the most handsome gentleman *I* have ever met,' Phoebe proclaimed fervently, obviously feeling that she had been left out of the conversation long enough. 'Have you met him, Lady Trent?'

Madelaine glanced quickly at Lady Bourne, expecting her to reprimand her younger daughter for the untimely interruption, but soon realised that, unlike her sister, Phoebe Bourne could not put a foot wrong.

'No, I have not,' Madelaine replied, pointedly addressing her response to Lady Bourne. 'My aunt and I have spent the better part of our time since we arrived getting settled in.'

'Ah, then you shall no doubt have a chance to meet him at Lady Westport's ball,' Lady Bourne advised her. 'I assume you are going to the ball, Lady Trent?'

'I…do not think we have received an invitation.' Madelaine glanced at her aunt uncertainly. 'Do you recall having seen one, Aunt?'

'No, I do not. Certainly there was no invitation awaiting us when we arrived. But then, I doubt Lady Westport is even aware that we are here.'

'Oh, but you may be sure that she is,' Lady Bourne was quick to assure them. 'In fact, I am certain that two invitations were sent out.'

'Perhaps they will be there when we return, my dear,' Chloe said, her eyes brimming with merriment.

Abruptly, Madelaine looked away, her own lips twitching. 'Yes, no doubt they will.'

'Lord Trevellyn does not attend all the functions though, Mama,' Phoebe pointed out regretfully. 'He did not go to Rachel Beckham's ball, nor to Lady Upperton's musicale. He may decide not to attend Lady Westport's ball either.'

'Tosh, Phoebe, of course he will attend,' Lady Bourne assured the younger girl. Then, for her guests' benefit, added, 'Lord Trevellyn is somewhat reluctant to attend the many functions to which he is invited, which is a great shame since he is such an eligible bachelor. But, then, perhaps it is just as well. My Phoebe does not make her come out until next year, and I feel quite sure that, when she does, Lord Trevellyn will be utterly captivated by her charm and beauty. Phoebe has a lovely singing voice—don't you, my dear? And her skills at drawing and needlework are exceptional.'

Madelaine and her aunt smiled kindly, as they were meant to. 'I am sure the Earl will be thoroughly captivated by *both* your daughters, Lady Bourne,' Madelaine said kindly, and once again received an adoring glance from Prunella. 'But for the moment, I wonder, might I have some more tea?'

At length, the requisite time passed, and Madelaine and Chloe were able to make good their escape. At the door, Lady Bourne thanked them again most profusely for calling, and assured them that she would be dropping by Pengarron at the very first opportunity.

'And I do hope we shall see you at Lady Westport's ball,' Lady Bourne said as the ladies climbed into their carriage. 'I know there will be many people anxious to meet you.'

Assuring Lady Bourne that they would look for the invitations as soon as they arrived home, Madelaine signalled to the driver, and the carriage set off. Both ladies breathed a sigh of relief as they rounded the corner and the house—and its occupants—disappeared.

'Gracious, I hope they shan't all be like that,' Chloe commented wryly. 'Cornwall may have its attractions, but Lord save us from the idiosyncrasies of its inhabitants.'

'Yes, if ever there was a coming woman, it is Lady Bourne,' Madelaine agreed. 'But then, I suppose there is little enough else to divert her. No doubt the arrival of *any* newcomers in town, let alone a rich man's widow and her aunt, would be sufficient to draw comment.' Her eyes sparkled. 'I all but burst out laughing when she quizzed you about your visit to Scotland.'

Chloe gave a hoot. 'Oh, yes, indeed. And then poor Prunella stepping into the fray by voicing that ill-timed comment about dear Harriet's intentions of becoming the next Duchess.'

'Poor Prunella indeed,' Madelaine commiserated. 'I do not envy that unfortunate girl's position in the household, Chloe. She is definitely the ugly duckling in Lady Bourne's eyes. Still, I believe there is some spirit there, and hopefully, one day Prunella will come into her own.'

'Hopefully. But in the meantime, I do not give her much for her chances,' Chloe observed sceptically. 'Not with Lady Bourne so anxious to make a successful match for the younger girl. I am sure she would like to see Phoebe as the next Lady Trevellyn.'

'It would appear so.' Madelaine's lips curved upwards in a smile. 'I wonder what his lordship would say if he knew that his future were being so carefully planned!'

'No doubt we shall find out soon enough,' Chloe suggested, twinkling at her niece. 'Because I feel quite sure that if an invitation to Lady Westport's ball is not on the table by the end of the day, it will most certainly be in our hands before this time tomorrow!'

Chloe's word turned out to be unknowingly portentous. That evening, two invitations were delivered to Pengarron by special messenger, requesting the presence of Lady Trent and Mrs Merrill at a ball to be given by Lord and Lady Westport at their home, four nights hence.

Madelaine smiled as she perused the invitation and then set it down on the sideboard. Obviously, word had spread very quickly of their arrival in the area, fuelled in no small part by Lady Bourne's widespread network of relations. Surprisingly, however, it was not the excitement of the up-coming ball which prevented Madelaine from slipping into a peaceful sleep later that night. It was the thought of the tall, handsome man with whom she was to ride in the morning. A dark, secretive man who held the answer to the di-lemma of the as-of-yet unknown Lord Trevellyn's actions.

A man who, by rights, should have occupied no place in her thoughts at all!

At exactly half past eight the following morning, Mad-elaine and her groom arrived at the edge of the lake which formed part of the boundary between the Trent lands to the east, and the Trevellyn lands to the west.

It was a breathtaking sight, with the hills rising up in the background, and the grass running down to the edge of the water before them. Wild flowers bloomed in colourful pro-fusion around the lush green banks, while the dark emerald hue of the trees was reflected in the mirror-like surface of the water.

The day was as fair and as clear as Madelaine could have wished, and as she drew a deep breath of the clean morning air into her lungs, she was filled with a sense of peace and contentment such as she hadn't known in well over a year. Interesting, that it had taken only a few days away from London to effect such a difference in her outlook.

Taylor was already there, of course. Madelaine had seen him immediately upon coming over the crest of the hill, sitting relaxed and at ease in the saddle and surveying the land around him as though he owned it. In fact, dressed as he was in a multi-caped jacket over smooth buckskin breeches and gleaming black boots, Taylor looked far more the country aristocrat than he did a mere steward. He seemed to exude power and authority; all the things a servant should not.

'Good morrow, Lady Trent. 'Tis a lovely morning we have for a ride.'

His eyes were warm with admiration as they rested on her face, and Madelaine was dismayed to feel a blush creep up into her cheeks. She was wearing one of her new outfits this morning, an elegant riding habit of very dark blue cloth, with a rakish hat adorned with a wispy veil and a long curling feather tucked into its band.

Madelaine steadfastly refused to consider that she had worn it for any other reason than that she liked it very well. 'Good morning, Taylor. Yes, it is indeed a beautiful morning.'

The groom's head shot up in horror at his mistress's term of address. He abruptly opened his mouth to speak, when Gabriel suddenly shook his head—and winked.

Startled, the bewildered young groom closed his mouth. He said nothing, but it was evident from the look on his face that he was more confused than ever. Gabriel, however, merely smiled and said, 'This way, my lady.'

During the brief exchange of glances, Madelaine's attention had been focused on her mare, who had suddenly started fidgeting as a result of the stallion's proximity. Consequently, she had missed the interchange between the two men completely, and now, after getting the little mare back under control and urging her to a walk, she fell in beside Gabriel and gazed at his mount with a look of evident surprise. 'You ride a fine horse, Taylor. Is his lordship so generous with all of his servants?'

'No, but he is well aware of the amount of time that I spend in the saddle, and is generous enough to provide me with a decent mount. He is in this, as in most other things, unfailingly considerate.'

Madelaine did not see the way Gabriel's firmly sculpted mouth suddenly twitched, and she lapsed into silence again, wondering all the more about this omnipotent Lord Trevellyn.

Taking the lead, Gabriel urged his mount to a canter. He was anxious to begin showing Lady Trent her property, and anxious to start asking her questions. He knew that he would see soon enough whether she had any interest in Pengarron because, if she was anything like him, her feelings would be reflected in her eyes. There was no mistaking the reaction of one who truly had a love of the land. Gabriel had been born with it, as had his father, and his father's father before him. It was simply there, part of a Cornishman's lifeblood.

To that end, he showed Lady Trent as much of Pengarron as he could in the brief time that he had with her. He led her through the towering forests and the sun-dappled glades; across the wide open fields of grass and over gently flowing rivers. He even rode with her along the treacherous cliffs, pointing out the razor-edged rocks where the ships had foundered, after being lured to their deaths by the smugglers who stood watch along the shore—and then to the caves where the smugglers had stashed their ill-gotten bounty.

'The coast is alive with stories of the brave men who made their living by the sea,' Gabriel informed her.

His boldly handsome face briefly reminded Madelaine of some of the swashbuckling pirates of old, and she smiled mockingly. 'I would hardly call smuggling making one's living from the sea, Taylor, nor the killing of innocent men an admirable occupation.'

'Ah, but I did not say that it was admirable, my lady. I merely said that it was brave. Certainly, it was well talked about.'

'Nevertheless, you seem to hold these smugglers in some admiration,' Madelaine observed narrowly. 'Can it be that someone from your own family was so involved?'

'Surely you would not expect me to answer that truthfully, Lady Trent.'

'Why not? Do you fear retribution from the ghosts of the past?'

'I fear no man, living or dead, but I have no wish to be tarred with the same brush as my ancestors.'

Madelaine was tempted to say that she found the idea highly unlikely, but at the last moment changed her mind. It would not do to let Taylor think that she thought anything about him at all, though there was no doubt in her mind that many others would. Any man that handsome would naturally attract the ladies.

Still, there was no denying that he was a fine figure of a man, Madelaine acknowledged reluctantly as he set off ahead of her. His well-muscled legs were displayed to perfection in the snug-fitting breeches, and his broad shoulders more than filled out the jacket that he wore. Certainly he would garner many a sigh from the ladies in London, she was forced to admit. And indeed, none of the gentlemen she had ever met at *any* of the fashionable assemblies in Town would have been able to hold a candle to—

Suddenly growing aware of the direction of her thoughts, Madelaine began to blush furiously. *She must be mad.* The man was a *servant*, for heaven's sake! And she, the Dowager Countess of Trent. Daughter of Lord Derringham of Stokely Farm. What in the world had come over her? Surely she had not been reduced to hungering after a strong, handsome man who, by all rights, should not have garnered more than a moment's notice?

'Taylor!' she called, abruptly pulling in the mare.

Gabriel quickly glanced around, surprised to see that Lady Trent had reined in, and likewise brought the stallion to a halt. He hadn't missed the imperious note in her voice, and was amused to see that she was actually waiting for him to ride back to her side. Which he did, reminding himself that, in order to be convincing, he had to curb his natural inclination to take charge. 'Yes, my lady? Is something wrong?'

'No, not…wrong, precisely,' Madelaine replied, not quite sure what she hoped to gain by calling him back. 'I simply wished to…walk for a while. And to remind you that you still have not answered my question with regard to Lord Trevellyn's alleged dismissal of my steward.'

Gabriel drew a deep breath. 'Very well, my lady. We shall walk for a while. And at length I shall answer your question.'

'At length? Why not now?'

'Because first,' Gabriel said, quickly dismounting and holding out his hands to her, 'I should like to hear what you think of Pengarron, now that you have had opportunity to see a little more of it.'

It was a highly unusual question for a steward to put to a lady and, mindful of the fact that her groom was still in close range, Madelaine decided not to answer. She did, however, allow Taylor to help her dismount, a decision she regretted the moment she felt his fingers close firmly around hers. His skin was uncommonly smooth for a worker of the land, yet the strength in his hands made her uncomfortably aware of her own femininity.

She unhooked her leg from around the horn and slid down. Unfortunately, she had not counted on the unevenness of the ground, nor on the unsteadiness of her legs. When she suddenly stumbled, two strong arms reached out to steady her. They locked around her waist and pulled her upright—and far too close to that handsome face for comfort.

'Are you all right, my lady?' Gabriel enquired huskily.

Madelaine gave him a forced smile and a tense nod of consent. 'Yes...fine, thank you. I merely...stumbled.' She took a deep breath of air, surprised that she suddenly seemed to be having trouble getting enough into her lungs, and hastily stepped back from him. 'Thank you, Taylor, I am...quite able to stand on my own now.'

Gabriel likewise stepped back and abruptly removed his hands. *Dear Lord, she was beautiful. Her skin was like velvet and the fragrance of sweet roses seemed to perfume the air all around her.*

He gruffly cleared his throat as he reached for the mare's reins. 'Pardon, my lady. Shall we...walk for a while?'

At Madelaine's hesitant nod, Gabriel stood back to let her precede him. Then, falling in behind and still leading the two horses, he tried to figure out what the hell had just happened.

He wasn't supposed to be attracted towards Lady Trent. At least, not in the manner that he most assuredly was. If he felt anything for her at all, it should be in the form of...admiration for her spirit, or respect for her position. But not this...burning awareness of her as a woman. A longing that made his stomach tighten and his arms ache to hold her again. Even now, Gabriel found himself remembering with pleasure how incredibly soft and feminine Lady Trent had felt in his embrace. Funny that he hadn't felt this way about a woman—not even the most skilled of his mistresses—for as long as he could remember. If ever, in fact.

Ahead of him, Madelaine was quickly working to regain her own shaken composure after their brief and rather... intimate encounter. She told herself, in the most prosaic of terms, that her reaction to Taylor was completely normal. After all, she *had* very nearly fallen, and it was only natural that she would be suffering a few...breathless flutters by the gallant manner of his rescue.

'Tell me, Taylor, have you always...lived on these lands?' Madelaine asked, endeavouring to keep her voice as cool and indifferent as possible.

Glad to be given something to think about other than his jumbled emotions, Gabriel inclined his head. 'From the day I was born. I drew my first breath on Cornish soil, and 'tis here I hope to draw my last. As a boy, I rode over every inch of this property, and now, as a man, it is my privilege to guard it. But what of you, Lady Trent? What are your impressions, now that you have seen your late husband's property? Is it too wild and untamed for a London-bred lady?'

The rich timbre of his voice sparked an unwilling response in Madelaine. 'You seem...uncommon interested in my feelings for the land, Taylor. Why should it matter to you how I feel?'

'Because how a person feels about their land tells me much about the person.'

Madelaine stopped short and turned around. 'And why would you care to know anything about me?'

Yes, why did he want to know anything about her? Gabriel asked himself as he gazed down at her. What was this…indefinable attraction that he felt towards Lady Trent? Curiosity? Desire? Lust?

No, not lust, Gabriel decided, instantly rejecting the thought. He might be physically attracted to the lady—indeed, what man would not be—but she did not inspire that kind of reaction. Hers was a loveliness to be admired; to be revered.

Then what was it about Trent's widow that was affecting him in a manner that no other woman ever had before?

'Forgive me, Lady Trent,' Gabriel said quietly. 'I had no right to ask such things, either about your feelings, or about your person. I suppose I was merely asking because…the land fires such a response in me that I cannot help but think that everyone shares that feeling.' He glanced out towards the fields beyond her, and smiled wistfully. 'I could hardly expect a London-bred lady to share the sentiments of someone born and bred to the land.'

Madelaine studied the man in front of her, conscious of the pride in his eyes, and the confident set of his shoulders—and was disturbed by the nameless emotions he was arousing in her. She must be mad for even entertaining such thoughts. He was a steward, for heaven's sake. A *steward*!

'You might be surprised at what this London-bred lady can feel, Taylor,' Madelaine replied softly. 'No, I was not brought up here like you and, yes, I have spent most of my life in London. But that does not mean that I cannot appreciate what the good Lord put upon this earth. Heaven knows, I am sure He did not think that the sun rose and set solely on London.' Madelaine glanced out towards the rugged cliffs and then past them to the endless blue ocean beyond, and found herself humbled by the magnificence of it all. 'In fact, after seeing a place such as this, I wonder that people could ever truly enjoy the congestion of Town again. Is that what you wanted to hear, Taylor?' Madelaine turned to gaze at him boldly. 'Are those the kinds of sentiments you expected to hear from a typical, London-bred lady?'

The wind had whipped the colour into her cheeks and, just for a moment, Gabriel saw past the façade of the well-bred young woman. He saw the fire in her eyes, and the passion in her soul. And for that one brief moment, Gabriel found himself envying a dead man. Trent had tasted life with this woman. And nothing—not even death—could take that away from him.

'Perhaps not,' Gabriel admitted, meeting her gaze. 'But then, you're not a typical London lady. Are you, Lady Trent?'

Madelaine slowly shook her head, mesmerised by his stare. 'No, I don't suppose…I am.'

She stood that way for a long time; gazing up into eyes that were more compelling than any she had ever seen. Certainly, she stared at him far longer than Society would have deemed proper. But, in truth, she had no idea what to make of him. She saw no submissiveness in his eyes; no apology for who or what he was. There was only a calm assurance that he was, indeed, master of himself and his lands. Lands which, by a slight alteration in birth, he might have been lord over, rather than steward of.

Pity, Madelaine found herself thinking. He would have made an excellent nobleman. Indeed, far better than many she had met.

The soft nicker of a horse brought Madelaine's attention back to the present, and reluctantly, she tore her gaze from Taylor's. She could not allow her thoughts to keep drifting off like this. She was the Dowager Countess Trent. She had…a duty to her name. To her position.

Perhaps that was why, when Madelaine finally did reach

for her mare's reins, she did not look to Taylor for help, but signalled instead for her groom to assist her. And Gabriel, recognising her confusion, wisely said nothing. He stepped aside as the groom moved forward to give Madelaine a leg up, and swung easily into his own saddle. Gathering the reins, he turned towards her and said, 'Have you seen enough for one morning, my lady?'

Madelaine glanced at him once, before pointedly averting her eyes. She bent her head and pretended attendance on the arranging of her skirts. 'Yes, quite enough, thank you, Taylor.'

Her posture communicated far more than did her tone; for the first time in his life, Gabriel knew what it was to be summarily dismissed.

He discovered that it was not a feeling he liked.

There was no further conversation between Gabriel and Madelaine as they rode back to Pengarron. Madelaine purposely rode ahead of him, keeping her head high and her eyes forward so as to discourage conversation. It was as though, in some very fundamental way, she needed to make her position known. She was a countess, he was a steward. There could be no common ground between them. They both knew that.

Unfortunately, by setting herself apart from him, Madelaine did little more than thwart her own plans. It was not until she was safely back at Pengarron, and Taylor had left to return to Carew, that she realised she was still no closer to knowing what had happened to Diggs.

Taylor had not answered her question regarding Lord Trevellyn's purported firing of her man, which meant that the *only* way she was likely to get an answer now, was by risking another encounter with Taylor—or by asking the mighty Earl of Trevellyn himself!

Chapter Five

'Ah good, there you are, Maddie,' Chloe said, breezing into the green drawing room a little while later. 'I have been giving some thought to this ball of Lady Westport's. I thought I might wear my new grey silk. Do you think it will be too *risqué*?'

Grateful for the opportunity of being given something to think about *other* than Taylor and her alarming reactions to him, Madelaine considered her aunt's question. 'It may very well be, Chloe. Is the *décolletage* not a trifle low for the country?'

'Yes, I thought perhaps it was,' Chloe admitted. She glanced at her niece, and then twinkled. 'Which is precisely why I wanted to wear it.'

In spite of herself, Madelaine had to laugh. 'Oh, Chloe, you have no idea how glad I am that you are here with me. You bring everything…back into perspective somehow.'

'Back into perspective? Gracious, what an intriguing thing to say, Maddie. What in your life is out of perspective at the moment?'

Madelaine sighed. 'Nothing, I suppose. It is just that, at times, matters seem to get so dreadfully…confusing. Do you not find that, Chloe?'

'Well, yes, I suppose I do, occasionally,' she admitted. 'But what has brought on this sudden fit of the blue devils, dearest? Here you are, hundreds of miles from London and the obnoxious gentlemen of the *ton*. You have the sea air to breathe and the serenity of the countryside to enjoy. On top of which, you have Lady Westport's ball to look forward to. What more could a young lady ask?'

'What more indeed?' Madelaine said, as she kissed her aunt's cheek. 'But you did forget one thing.'

'I did?'

'Yes. You forgot to mention that I brought with me to Cornwall the best possible tonic I could. *You.* Now, how would you feel about joining me for a short walk before tea?'

Finding it a pleasing suggestion, Chloe nodded her agreement, and shortly thereafter, the ladies set out to enjoy a stroll through the extensive gardens which surrounded Pengarron. They admired the well-kept avenues, and marvelled at the magnificent profusion of flowers which filled the air with their heady scents of rose, jasmine and freesia. From there, they slowly meandered down the length of the drive, following its curves through the trees until, at length, they found themselves quite close to the main road.

It was at that point, and still hidden by a large clump of trees, that they heard the sound of a carriage approaching, and glanced up to see an elegant silver and black phaeton. It was drawn by two perfectly matched high-stepping blacks and was clipping along the road at a very smart pace. Unfortunately, it was difficult to discern any features of the gentleman who was driving it, but Madelaine could see that he had dark brown hair under a glistening black beaver. She could also see that he was definitely having trouble controlling the ribbons, and that he snapped the whip with a somewhat less than experienced hand.

'La, what an elegant-looking equipage,' Madelaine observed. 'Do you suppose it could be Lord Trevellyn?'

'I cannot be sure, my dear,' Chloe said, straining her eyes as the conveyance rounded the corner and disappeared out of sight. 'It might have been. He was travelling in the right direction.'

'But I wonder why he did not stop and pay a call? He must have heard of our arrival. The local gossip is nothing if not reliable.'

'I am sure that he does intend to call, Maddie,' Chloe reassured her niece, 'but I do not believe that he saw us just now. He seemed to be more concerned with controlling his cattle than he was in glancing about the countryside. Funny, I had expected Trevellyn to be a better whip than that. Still, they were a fine pair of horses, and if anyone could run them, it is Lord Trevellyn.'

'Be that as it may, he might at least have glanced up towards the house,' Madelaine said, sounding a little disappointed. 'He would have seen us then.'

'Judging from the way the blacks were pulling, I do not know that it would have been a good idea for him to lose concentration for too long, my dear,' Chloe said with a hint of laughter in her voice. 'Besides, I am quite sure that Lord Trevellyn was not expecting to see two ladies strolling about the lawns in the middle of the afternoon. It is much more the practice to sit at home and wait for people to come calling.'

'Yes, perhaps you are right. But then, I wonder if he will call, given what Edward has told me of this silly feud.'

'And what precisely is this feud about, Maddie?'

'It has to do with the lake which falls on the boundary of the two properties,' Madelaine told her. 'The old Lord Trevellyn claimed that it was his, while Edward's father said that at least half of it was on Trent land, which meant that it was ours. The result is that they refused to come to terms over the matter and ignored each other for years. They also made a point of jealously guarding the lake, refusing to allow the other to take out any fish.'

'Gracious, how silly,' replied Chloe, shaking her head. 'Men are such foolish creatures when it comes to matters of honour. Even the settling of such inconsequential matters as this raises their masculine ire to an unprecedented level.'

'How very true. But perhaps if it is a feud which Lord Trevellyn intends to continue, I should not be the one to make the first move. I have no wish to be thrown bodily from his front step.'

Chloe chuckled deep in her throat. 'I should like to see him try, my dear. I remember how you used to wrestle with the other children when you were still in the nursery. No one got the better of you, even then.'

'Ah, but my fighting days are long since over,' Madelaine replied. 'I am a lady now, and above such things. However,' she confided with a smile as she tucked her arm into her aunt's, 'I could sneak around to Carew at night and cut off the heads of all of his roses. *That* should tell Lord Trevellyn what I think of his silly feud!'

'Thank you, Gabriel, that was an excellent meal, as always.' Lord Keswick sat back and patted his ample stomach with the air of a man well satisfied. 'One of these days I shall endeavour to repay you for your generous hospitality, though I fear it may not be with meals as lavish as yours. Your chef is surely the finest in the county.'

'Never let it be said that hospitality is measured by the quality of meal served, Thomas,' Gabriel replied good naturedly. 'I enjoy your company, and like you to think of my home as yours.'

'You may be sorry you said that, my friend,' Lord Keswick commented ruefully. 'Once my two maiden aunts are returned to London, I shall be more than willing to remain at home, but until they do, I am quite happy to take myself off at every opportunity. I find the encroachment of one's family so disruptive to the normal harmony of a bachelor's existence. Speaking of which, have you kept to your promise?'

'My promise?'

'Yes. The one you made yesterday with regards to paying a call on the little widow.'

'Oh, that. Yes, as a matter of fact, I have. I went riding with her this morning.'

Keswick did not even trouble to hide his surprise. 'Well, never let it be said that you let the grass grow under your feet, Gabriel. And how went the conversation?'

'Well enough, given that she believed me to be a servant.'

'A *what*?'

'She mistook me for Taylor.'

'For Taylor? But…you bear no more resemblance to your steward than I do to my tiger, although there is, perhaps, somewhat more similarity in your heights.'

'The fact of the matter,' Gabriel replied narrowly, 'is that Lady Trent was expecting to see Taylor when I arrived, and naturally assumed, upon the arrival of a gentleman on horseback, that I was he.'

'I will not ask you why she was expecting to see your steward, Gabriel, but I will ask you why you did not tell her who you were at the first opportunity. I imagine you must have realised early on in the conversation that there was definitely a case of mistaken identity.'

'Within the first two sentences, actually,' Gabriel replied, chuckling. 'Tested my acting abilities, I can tell you.'

'Yes, I should think it did. You are many things, Gabriel,

but servile is not one of them,' Keswick drawled. 'So, why did you continue with the charade, once you knew enough to end it?'

'Because I was curious,' Gabriel admitted. 'Lady Trent had been led to believe that Taylor was responsible for spreading the rumour that I had sent Diggs packing, and thought to verify it with him before coming to me about it. Decided to give him the benefit of the doubt, as it were.'

'Decent of her,' Keswick commented. 'And did you tell her what she wanted to know?'

'No. I did an admirable job of avoiding her questions for the entire period of time that we rode together.'

'Really? I would wager *that* was more difficult than acting the part of the steward. So Lady Trent still doesn't know that you were the one who dismissed her steward, or that you are, in fact, Lord Trevellyn.'

'Correct.'

Keswick steepled his fingers in front of his face. 'I hope you know that this could get exceedingly complicated.'

'It could, if not handled properly,' Gabriel agreed. 'But, do you know, Thomas, I discovered, much to my surprise, that there was something remarkably…liberating about pretending to be someone else.'

'Liberating? What on earth do you mean?'

'I mean that today, I was given a glimpse into another side of life. Lady Trent did not see me as the Earl of Trevellyn, she saw me as a man.'

'You mean as a servant.'

'All right, as a servant, then. All I am saying is that she did not try to flirt with me, or feel forced to say polite things because they were expected of her. She acted in a manner that was completely open and natural—the way she would probably have acted with a servant.'

Lord Keswick grinned. 'Are you saying that you *enjoyed* being treated as a menial?'

At that, Gabriel chuckled. 'No. I am merely saying that it was refreshing for once to be viewed as something other than an eligible *parti*.'

'Well, I cannot say that I understand your reasons, Gabriel, but then, I am neither as young nor as handsome as you. I haven't a string of anxious young ladies and their mamas all running after me with marriage in their eyes. I just hope this little deceit doesn't backfire on you, my friend. But all that aside, what of Lady Trent? Were you able to find out anything that could be of use to you as regards her interest in selling Pengarron?'

'Not a great deal. The lady was very circumspect about answering my questions. To be quite honest, I am not sure that she knew what to make of me,' Gabriel confessed, remembering the uncertainty he had glimpsed in the widow's lovely grey eyes.

'I have no doubt that she found you extremely forward… for a servant.'

'No doubt she did. And, you may be correct in saying that I have set myself up for more trouble than I anticipated.'

'Oh?'

'How do I now revert to the part of Lord Trevellyn and retain any semblance of honour?'

'Why not just continue to play the role of the steward?' Keswick suggested. 'After all, if you are successful in buying Pengarron, and the anonymity of the offer is preserved, the lady may never have need of making your true acquaintance.'

Gabriel shook his head. 'I shall have to tell her sometime, Thomas. I played the part of Taylor today for a reason and, apart from Lady Trent's groom, no one else was around to see me do it. But I have no wish to make a fool of her in front of others. And, given that it is highly unlikely that she and I will not meet at some time in the near future, I can hardly expect to carry out such a farce amongst people I do know.'

'In that case, you will just have to make a full confession of it, old boy,' Keswick told him. 'And I admit, I should like to be around for it when you do.'

'Mmm. I wonder whether I should confess my guilt in a room full of people where she is less likely to tear a strip off me, or whether I should brave her wrath alone here.'

'Gabriel, you surprise me,' Lord Keswick said, feigning disappointment. 'I never suspected you of being a coward.'

'Fear of the lovely widow has nothing to do with it,' Gabriel was quick to assure his friend. 'I merely wondered which would garner me a less hostile reception if and when I do finally make her aware of the identity of her anonymous buyer.'

'You haven't changed your mind about buying Pengarron, then?'

Gabriel glanced at him in surprise. 'No. Why should I?'

'No reason. I simply thought you might have had a change of heart now that you've had a chance to meet the lovely widow. Thought you might have...welcomed the opportunity of getting to know her better. And having her live right next door seems to me to be the best way of doing that.'

'You forget, Thomas. If I am successful, John and Cassandra will be living at Pengarron, not Lady Trent.'

'Yes, but if for some unforeseen reason you do not succeed in buying Pengarron, John and his wife will end up here, and Lady Trent will *still* be your neighbour.'

Gabriel had to concede that his friend was right, but the thought of buying Pengarron had been with him for so long now that it was hard to imagine letting it slip away—even if he was finding himself somewhat intrigued by its owner.

'Well, over the next few days, I shall give some thought as to how to go about admitting my deception to Lady Trent,' Gabriel conceded. 'I have instructed my lawyer to present the offer, and God knows, the longer the charade drags on, the harder it will be to gracefully acknowledge my guilt.'

'Indeed. But do keep me informed on this one, will you, Gabriel?' Keswick said with a grin. 'I am looking forward to hearing how Lady Trent reacts when she discovers that the humble steward who showed her around her property is actually her covetous neighbour trying to inveigle her out of her property.'

Gabriel slanted him a caustic look. 'You make me sound quite reprehensible, Thomas.'

'Do I? Forgive me. It was never my intention.'

'Besides,' Gabriel said, 'once Lady Trent begins to feel the loneliness of living this far from London, I venture to say that she will pack up her bags and head straight back to the excitement of Town, vowing never to return again.'

'And there you shall be, the helpful neighbour just waiting to take Pengarron off her hands. Would that we all had such accommodating friends. Well, I wish you luck of it, Gabriel,' Keswick said, savouring the glass of very fine brandy that was always to be had at Carew. 'As for myself, I look forward to meeting the lady and to hearing exactly what she thinks of her fine house—*and* of her new neighbour!'

Gabriel's decision to make known his true identity to Lady Trent was not realised as quickly as he might have liked. The following morning, a young lad arrived from Pengarron with a letter addressed to Taylor, requesting his presence at the north end of the lake as quickly as possible on a matter of extreme urgency.

Alarmed by the tone of the note, Gabriel informed the lad that Taylor would come at once and sent him back to his mistress to relay the message. He then went up to his room and instructed his valet to set out the same clothes that he had worn the previous day.

Stonebrook drew himself up rigidly. 'The same clothes, my lord?'

'Yes.' Ignoring the shocked expression on his valet's face, Gabriel quickly donned the pair of old breeches—old being of the previous year's ordering—and then, to the valet's horror, the shirt with an offending smudge of dirt on one cuff.

'My lord, if I may say so, you *cannot* wear that out.'

Gabriel sighed. 'I am afraid I must, Stoney. I suppose it would be too much to hope that you have not had opportunity to attend to my Hessians?'

Stonebrook's nose quivered. 'Indeed I have, my lord, and in a very bad state they were. It took me hours to restore the finish.'

'Hmm, well, I won't be able to use them. What about my tops?'

'My lord?'

'You haven't polished those, I hope.'

'Well, no, my lord. You hardly ever wear them any more,' Stonebrook replied with the familiarity of a long-standing servant. 'But if you will give me thirty minutes, I shall endeavour to—'

'That won't be necessary. Bring them to me as they are.'

The poor man's face crumpled. 'My lord. Think of our reputation!'

Gabriel laughed. The man was more of a snob than he was. 'Never mind, Stoney. I shall see to it that yours remains untarnished. I shall tell everyone that you were indisposed and did not see me leave the house.'

Stonebrook sighed. 'Thank you, my lord.'

Minutes later, rigged out in the offending boots, smudged shirt and previously worn breeches, Gabriel swung into the saddle and cantered off in the direction of Pengarron. He wondered what kind of urgent matter could have warranted Lady Trent summoning him with such haste. At the same time, he admitted that he was pleased to have received the summons; welcoming it as an opportunity to spend a little more time in her company.

He found Lady Trent waiting for him at the edge of the wood. She was looking every bit as lovely this morning as she had on the previous one, dressed in a dove grey riding habit trimmed with black velvet frogging, and an elegant feathered hat in the same soft shade of grey. Behind the delicate veil, however, Gabriel detected sadness in those beautiful eyes. And to his surprise, she was alone, her groom being nowhere in sight.

'What has happened, my lady?'

'I…apologise for bringing you out so abruptly, Taylor, but I really did not know who else to call.' Madelaine's gloved hands flexed on the reins. 'I could not just leave her there like that.'

Gabriel was astonished to see the brightness of tears in her eyes. *'Her?'*

Without another word, Madelaine flicked her crop against the mare's withers and led the way into the woods. Gabriel followed close behind. They hadn't ridden more than two hundred yards before they came to a dense thatch of trees, and the sight which had obviously caused Lady Trent so much distress.

There, her hind leg caught between the bars of a cruel

trap, lay a small, golden brown doe, her limpid brown eyes glazed with fear and pain as she watched their approach.

'I found her when I rode out this morning,' Madelaine said softly. 'I have no idea how long she has been here.'

Gabriel's eyes darkened at the disturbing sight. 'Not too long, I shouldn't imagine, and certainly not overnight.' He swung down from the saddle and walked slowly towards the deer, not wanting to frighten the poor creature any more than it already was. 'But she is badly injured.'

Madelaine bit her lip. 'How could this have happened, Taylor? Surely Edward would not have ordered traps to be set on the property?'

'He did not, Lady Trent. This is a leftover from your gamekeeper.'

Madelaine gasped. '*Diggs* is responsible for this?'

Gabriel nodded. 'The woods are probably littered with them.'

'Can you do anything for her?'

Gabriel sighed. 'Yes. The only merciful thing there is to do. I shall go back to the house and fetch my gun.'

'A *gun*!' Madelaine gasped. 'But…surely that is not necessary.'

'I fear that it is, my lady. The leg is most certainly broken.'

'But…there must be someone who can tend to her.'

'Lady Trent, this is a woodland creature. One does not call in the local vet and say, please come and see to my deer. He will suggest, as I did, that she be destroyed.'

'No, there must be some other way. You told me yourself that you have lived here all your life. You must know of someone with the necessary skills.'

Gabriel looked at her askance. 'You cannot be serious?'

'I most certainly am.'

'But this is ludicrous! You cannot rescue every injured animal you come upon.'

Madelaine tilted her chin defiantly. 'I can if it is my wish to do so. This is my land, and that is my deer.'

'Lady Trent, I must object—'

'Taylor, you *forget* yourself!'

Seeing the sudden anger which flashed in those marvellous eyes, Gabriel clamped his mouth shut and turned away in frustration. *Damn it!* Damn this whole stupid farce. He should have just told her who he was when he had the chance. Now he was digging himself into a hole that was getting deeper by the minute!

'Look, even if I did know someone who could help the animal, how do you propose to get it out of the trap?' Gabriel flung back at her. 'I guarantee she will injure either you or herself in the process.'

Madelaine refused to budge. 'I assumed that the person who would minister to her leg would be able to get her out of the trap without causing her any further injury.'

'Oh, did you?'

'Yes. Now, do you know of someone who can take care of her or not?'

There was only one person Gabriel knew who had the skills necessary to deal with a situation like this. 'As it happens, one of my...that is, one of Lord Trevellyn's tenants occasionally takes in injured creatures. An old woman by the name of Mrs Abbey.'

Madelaine nodded. 'Good. If you would be so kind as to go and fetch her, I shall remain here with the deer.'

'You intend to stay here until I get back?' Gabriel asked in surprise.

'Well, I certainly do not intend to leave her here alone. If what you said about Diggs is true, he may well come back to see to his traps. If he does, I shall be here to stop him.'

Gabriel suspected that the likelihood of Diggs returning to the area was virtually non-existent, but he did not bother to tell her that. 'I would prefer that you do not stay here alone, Lady Trent. If you will return to Pengarron, I shall ride back to Carew and send one of the grooms to fetch Mrs Abbey. With any luck, she will not be out tending to some other sick animal.'

Madelaine looked up at him in surprise. Again, he had used that unexpected tone of command, as though everyone who worked at Carew were there to serve him.

'Lord Trevellyn must have a great deal of confidence in you, Taylor,' she observed drily. 'Has he told all of the servants that they are to obey you in his absence?'

For the first time since they had arrived upon the injured doe, Gabriel's grin flashed. 'To the last man, my lady. To the last man.'

Gabriel rode back to Carew as quickly as the stallion's legs would carry him. Though the day was still early, he did not care for the idea of Lady Trent sitting alone in the middle of a heavily wooded area with a wounded deer. Nature might very well take care of the poor beast before he returned, and Gabriel had no wish to see the lady so saddened. She obviously had a very soft heart when it came to animals.

Arriving in the courtyard of Carew, he brought the stallion to a dancing halt. 'Where's Taylor?' he barked to the stable boy who came running out.

'Up in the top field with two of the lads, m'lord, checking the wall.'

Gabriel nodded, and spurred his horse to a canter again. So much the better. The top field was the closest one to the road leading down to Mrs Abbey's cottage. If the old woman was there, Taylor could bring her back within twenty minutes.

Gabriel spotted his steward's muscular form immediately. He was overseeing the repair of a section of stone wall which had crumbled away. And he had two of the fine, strapping young farm lads with him.

Taylor looked up at the Earl's approach, and respectfully doffed his cap. 'Morning, my lord.'

'Morning, Taylor, I need you to do something for me. Lady Trent has found a wounded deer in the forest, caught in one of Diggs's traps.'

Taylor's eyes darkened ominously. 'That bloody—' He caught himself quickly. 'Begging your pardon, my lord. Would you like me to see to the deer now?'

'Yes, but not in the usual manner. I want you to go and fetch Mrs Abbey.'

One of the young lads glanced up at the Earl in surprise. 'You mean the old witch, my lord?'

Taylor frowned. 'That will do, Collins. Mrs Abbey is no witch, for all they say about her.'

'No, indeed she is not,' Gabriel agreed. 'She is merely an old woman who possesses an uncanny way with animals, and a remarkable knowledge of the healing properties of herbs and flowers. Lady Trent is hoping that the deer can be saved, Taylor. If it can be, Mrs Abbey is the only one who will be capable of doing it. However, if Mrs Abbey herself says that there is no hope for the animal, you are to deal with it as you see fit.'

Taylor nodded briskly. 'Aye, my lord. Right, then,' he said to the boys, 'you lads keep your backs to this. When you finish here, you can carry on down to the next gap.'

'Taylor, a word before you go.' Gabriel dismounted and drew the man to one side. 'I know this is going to sound a little strange, but I have my reasons for asking. When you bring Mrs Abbey to the glade, don't be surprised if you hear me refer to you as...Collins.'

Taylor stared at the Earl with a complete lack of comprehension. 'Beg pardon, my lord?'

'I shall endeavour to explain this to you more fully tomorrow. For now, I need you to pretend that your name is Collins. You see, Lady Trent believes that I am...you.'

Taylor grinned. 'You, a steward, my lord?'

'You find that amusing, Taylor?'

The grin quickly disappeared. 'Not at all, my lord. In the linden glade, you said?'

Gabriel nodded and hoisted himself into the saddle again. 'Yes. I'm going to ride back there now and keep Lady Trent company. I do not like the idea of her being alone with a wounded animal.'

'No, 'tis not wise, my lord.'

'As soon as I see you and Mrs Abbey approaching, I shall escort Lady Trent back to Pengarron, and leave you to deal with the situation.'

Taylor nodded. 'Very good, my lord.'

As Taylor headed off in the direction of the old woman's cottage, Gabriel rode back towards the linden glade. In spite of his reluctance to get involved with Trent's widow, he found himself forced to admire the woman's unusual courage and determination. Certainly no lady of his acquaintance would ever have volunteered to stay behind in a heavily wooded area to guard a wounded animal when there was any likelihood of the man who had trapped it returning.

But then, he was already beginning to realise that Madelaine Trent was quite unlike any woman he had ever met before.

* * *

In the silence of the wooded glade, Madelaine stood watch over the wounded doe, and tried not to think about the other creatures that might be watching them. She had never been alone in the forest before and, as she listened to the myriad chirps and twitters of the birds in the branches high above her, she was very aware of just how vulnerable she was.

The little doe lay still now, exhausted by her struggles to escape the dreaded trap. Madelaine glanced into the limpid brown eyes and knew a moment of hatred for the man who had caused the animal's suffering. She was very glad that the reprehensible Diggs was no longer in her employ—even if it was as a result of Lord Trevellyn's intervention. She only hoped that the Mrs Abbey whom Taylor had spoken of would be able to help the poor creature.

Thankfully, it was not long before she heard the sound of a horse's hooves. Madelaine held her breath for a moment, fearful that it might be Diggs, and then let it go in relief when she saw that it was Taylor. She was unable to conceal her disappointment, however, when she saw that he was alone. 'Oh, dear, was Mrs Abbey not there?'

'I cannot say, Lady Trent. I sent one of the lads to find her and bring her back here.'

'But…I thought that you would go yourself.'

Gabriel shook his head. 'Not at the risk of leaving you out here alone any longer than was necessary. Are you all right?' he asked softly.

Madelaine felt the strangest constriction in her throat as he drew his horse level with hers. *I am now*, she felt like telling him. But, afraid that he might misinterpret her meaning, and mindful of what had happened between them yesterday, she said only, 'Yes, thank you, I am fine.'

Gabriel studied her face, seeing the lines of worry and confusion there, and suddenly experienced an overwhelming desire to pull her into his arms. He wanted to hold her close, and to tell her that everything was going to be all right. But he knew that he dare not. For he knew that, as much as her voice had trembled just now, she would only be repulsed by such inappropriate behaviour. She believed him to be a servant—and the only way he could ever hope for any kind of closeness between them was to tell her the truth of his identity.

But he was reluctant to do that now while she was still so worried about the deer. No, better to wait until they were safely back at Pengarron. That would surely be soon enough, Gabriel told himself.

Chapter Six

Just over thirty minutes later, Madelaine found herself heading back to Pengarron for the second time that day, but in a much better frame of mind than she had been earlier. Mrs Abbey had come with one of Trevellyn's men by the name of Collins, and Taylor had left the wounded deer in their care.

Madelaine had not wanted to leave them. Curious, she had wanted to stay behind to see what the woman could do for the poor creature. But when Taylor had assured her that it was better that they not linger, Madelaine had reluctantly acquiesced and ridden back to Pengarron with him—*after* eliciting his promise that he would return to the glade and report back to her as soon as he could on the animal's condition.

As such, Gabriel escorted Madelaine back to the edge of the garden where he had first seen her. 'I shall take your horse back to the stables, Lady Trent,' he offered. 'You look like you could use some rest.'

About to object, Madelaine abruptly changed her mind when she realised that she was, in fact, rather weary. 'I think you are right, Taylor, thank you. And thank you for…everything you did this morning. I have no idea what I would have done without your help.'

Gabriel quickly dismounted and came around to assist her. Wordlessly, he put up his hand to help her, and this time, there was no hesitation on Madelaine's part. She felt neither surprise nor alarm at his touch, but instead, drew a measure of comfort from the strength of his hands, and from the authority he radiated. She slid down gracefully from her saddle and felt her legs tremble slightly as her booted feet touched the ground.

As she gazed up into Taylor's face, Madelaine saw again, not the face of a steward, but of a man; one who had had more effect on her emotions than any man she had ever met—and certainly far more than he should have. He was disturbing to her in every way. When he smiled, her heart danced with excitement. When his gaze travelled over her face and searched her eyes, Madelaine had to look away— afraid that he might see what was all too clearly written there.

But Gabriel already knew what was there. Because he had seen the confusion in her eyes, and he understood why it was there. The lady was attracted to him. Against her will—and certainly against her better judgement, she was drawn to a man that she could not have; a man who could play no part in her life. And that was her dilemma. Even now, her lips were slightly parted, her breath coming quickly as she stared up into his face, her mouth hovering so close to his that Gabriel needed only to bend his head to touch it…

'*Madelaine.*'

The name issued unbidden from his lips—and the moment it did, Gabriel knew that he had committed an unpardonable error. He had overstepped the bounds of propriety—and he had no need to hear from her just how serious his transgression had been. He saw the flicker of uncertainty disappear from Lady Trent's eyes, to be replaced by a look of shock, and then one of cool distance.

Gabriel bowed, but he did not apologise. He would not be that much of a hypocrite. 'I shall send word to you of the doe's condition. Good morning, Lady Trent.'

Madelaine watched him go, too shocked even to utter the briefest of goodbyes. She knew she should have chastised him for his inexcusable breach of etiquette. Her voice should have been filled with righteous indignation as she informed him that he had no right to address a titled lady by her given name, adding that even a *gentleman* would not be permitted to speak to a lady in such a familiar manner.

And yet, to her dismay, Madelaine realised that she could not bring herself to chastise him. She could not...humble him before her, and thereby widen the gulf which already separated them. Sadly, she could bring herself to do nothing more than watch him ride away, his back straight, his head held high—and wonder why he had not bent his head to kiss her when he'd had the chance.

The note arrived later that same evening. It was delivered by Berkeley, who brought it into the drawing room where Madelaine and her aunt were enjoying a hand of cards after supper.

'What's this, Maddie?' Chloe's eyes sparkled. 'Receiving letters from gentlemen already?'

As casually as she could manage, Madelaine took the letter and carefully broke the seal. 'I hardly think so, Chloe. Who would be writing to me?'

Lady Trent:
    You will be pleased to know that the doe is now in

the competent hands of Mrs Abbey, who expressed concern for the nature of its injuries, but did not feel them to be life threatening. You may visit the animal, at your leisure, at the cottage in the woods. I would be pleased to give you the address, or to escort you, as you prefer.

Your obedient servant, T.

'T.?' Chloe said, catching sight of the signature.

'Yes. It is from…Taylor,' Madelaine said, feigning indifference, 'regarding the deer I found in the woods today.'

'Rather an unusual way for a steward to sign himself?'

Madelaine shrugged and handed her aunt the note so that she might read it. 'He is a rather unusual man, Chloe, and quite unlike any servant I have ever met before.'

Chloe quickly perused the contents of the page. 'Certainly, he writes very well.' She handed the note back and returned her attention to her cards. 'Do you intend to go and see this Mrs Abbey?'

'I should very much like to. You cannot imagine how sweet was the little doe. Taylor was most gentle with her.'

Chloe risked a quick glance at her niece. 'And do you look to Taylor only for the address, or for his offer of an escort as well?'

'I have not yet decided,' Madelaine demurred. 'It would, I suppose, be easier to go with Taylor, since he already knows where the woman lives, than it would be to try to find it on my own. However, I am…reluctant to impose upon his time again when I have not even made the acquaintance of his master.'

'And so you find yourself in something of a dilemma.' Chloe smiled, and laid her cards down with a flourish. 'My hand again, I'm afraid.'

Madelaine sighed. 'Really, Chloe, I do not know why I bother to play cards with you, I have yet to win a hand.'

'You don't do badly when you concentrate, my dear, but I think your mind is elsewhere this evening. I think,' Chloe said intuitively, 'that it is more upon what happened in the woods today.'

To her dismay, Madelaine felt her cheeks begin to glow. 'Yes, I admit I was…most disturbed by the incident with the doe.'

Chloe saw the telltale colour in Maddie's face and felt a stirring of unease. 'Well, I am very glad that the little doe is going to be all right, of course, but perhaps it would be best if you did not go riding into the woods any more, child, and certainly not with Taylor. If what he says about these traps is true, you may find a good many more things in the woods that disturb you. Besides, it really is not the thing to keep bothering Lord Trevellyn's man, my dear. The Earl will not be pleased when he learns that you have been monopolising his steward.'

'Then he should not have turned mine away,' Madelaine replied mumpishly.

'We have yet to determine whether or not he did,' Chloe said diplomatically. 'But be that as it may, it would not do to offend your neighbour, Madelaine. You have your reputation to think of, and while we may be out in the depths of Cornwall, you know how quickly gossip can make its way back to London. And a reputation once lost is not so easily reclaimed,' Chloe said softly. 'You do understand what I am saying, don't you, my dear?'

Madelaine nodded. Yes, she understood. She understood that Chloe was warning her—in as tactful a manner as she could—that she must not allow her thoughts to dwell on the memory of Taylor's dark eyes and handsome face. She could not let herself be seduced, even in spirit, by a man who was her social inferior, no matter how well-educated or well-mannered he appeared to be.

For such conduct—indeed, such thoughts—would not be tolerated by Society, no matter what Madelaine's position in it!

Lady Westport's ball was, without question, the highlight of the local social scene, and Madelaine and Chloe set out for it in a spirit of considerable excitement and anticipation. Madelaine was wearing a lovely gown of shimmering grey satin, the overskirt caught up with clusters of pale pink roses and trimmed with an even softer pink lace. The *décolletage* was not as low as her aunt's but, as a recent widow, Madelaine knew it behoved her to show a greater sense of decorum. Her jewellery was expensive but not flashy, while the fan held between her gloved fingers was of a delicate rose and grey silk. The deep grey satin toque perched atop her golden tresses was the only other concession to her widowhood.

Chloe, as always, was striking in a gown of midnight blue silk, her bejewelled turban dazzling to the eye. She moved into Lady Westport's ballroom beside her niece, smiling and nodding at the locals, and was clearly amused by the openly curious glances they were drawing.

'Faith, Maddie, I do believe we are causing a stir,' Chloe whispered in her niece's ear. 'That woman over there looks near ready to faint.'

Madelaine tried not to laugh as she hastily averted her gaze from the woman who did, indeed, look in imminent fear of collapse, and asked, 'Are we that much out of step with the rest?'

'More like we are that many steps *ahead* of them,' Chloe commented drily. She viewed the outfits in the room with a disparaging eye. 'Gracious, only look at the styling of that woman's sleeves. That gown has been in the wardrobe for three years if it has been there a day.'

Knowing her aunt to be something of an expert on fashion, Madelaine did not trouble herself to argue. She had never really paid undue attention to her clothes, knowing that she had the time and the money to invest in keeping them *au courant*.

'Ah, now there is someone who could benefit by your guidance, Chloe,' Madelaine said, nodding in the direction of the windows, and the place at which Prunella Bourne stood, looking dreadfully uncomfortable and very nervous at her mother's side.

'Good God, why on earth would her mother dress her in such a hideous shade of yellow?' Chloe whispered. 'Surely she can see that it does nothing for the girl's complexion.'

'I have a feeling Lady Bourne is using Prunella's dowdiness to play up Phoebe's beauty,' Madelaine remarked sadly. 'She obviously knew how to make the most of her younger daughter's colouring and features.'

'Humph. It may help Phoebe, but it certainly will not help the older girl's chances of securing a worthy match,' Chloe remarked tartly. 'What can the woman be thinking of, parading her younger daughter about so openly? Surely she must realise that it casts her elder daughter into the shade.'

Yes, she probably did, Madelaine thought, her heart going out as it always did to Prunella Bourne. Unfortunately, it seemed to trouble her mother little more than that, and certainly not enough to make her behave in a more kindly manner towards her eldest girl.

As Chloe moved away to have a few words with their hostess, Madelaine walked further into the elegant ballroom. She smiled warmly at a few of the ladies who nodded respectfully in her direction, but sensed that they were nervous about coming forward to make her acquaintance.

What a wall of reserve a title created, Madelaine reflected dimly. It prevented people from behaving in a natural manner, and yet it did not necessarily make for a better person. Witness Taylor, for example.

Madelaine coloured, dismayed to find herself thinking about the man yet again. It seemed to be all she was capable of doing lately. She had had no contact with him since that morning in the woods, yet he had crept into her thoughts with startling regularity. He had even appeared in her dreams one night, causing Madelaine to blush deeply at the memory of exactly...how he had appeared.

But she was very careful not to allow any mention of Taylor creep into her conversations with her aunt any more. Madelaine had not missed Chloe's subtle warning the other evening at cards. Taylor was a steward; a cultured and refined one, perhaps, but a steward nevertheless, and Madelaine had no business thinking about him in any way other than that. Or remembering the strength in his hands when they had rested lightly on her waist, or the way his eyes had glowed when they had smiled down into hers. His deep, melodious voice should not have caused a frisson of awareness to spread throughout her body, warming her like the heat from a fire. She had absolutely no business thinking about a man who was, in every way, her inferior.

And yet, Lord help her, that's all she seemed able to do! 'I must truly have windmills in my head,' Madelaine admonished herself softly. Only think what Taylor would say if he knew what she was thinking. Imagine how he would laugh. The Dowager Countess Trent—and a steward. She could almost hear the richness of his laughter; a rolling, throaty chuckle that was so incredibly sensuous the very thought of it set her pulses to racing.

Madelaine closed her eyes and sighed. Funny how even the memory of it was enough to fill the space all around her; the sound so close that Madelaine felt he could almost have been in the room...

'Good evening, Lady Trent.'

Madelaine's eyes flew open. *Taylor?*

Incredulous, she spun around—and gasped in disbelief. It *was* Taylor. *Her* Taylor—but looking for all the world like a confidant of Brummell himself. In an exquisitely tailored black cutaway coat, satin breeches, and silk stockings, he was dressed every bit as well as the most prominent gentlemen in the room.

Madelaine struggled with the impossibility of such a thing happening. *'Taylor?'* she whispered in disbelief.

'Forgive me, Lady Trent, it was not my intention to startle you.'

'Startle?' Madelaine echoed. 'Startled does not even *begin* to describe how I am feeling at this moment,' she told him in a hushed voice, her luminous eyes wide with astonishment. 'Are things so very much different here in Cornwall that a steward is invited to attend gatherings such as this?'

'On the contrary, things are not that...different at all. Which is why I wanted to speak with you,' Gabriel told her earnestly. 'I fear there is...something that I must tell you, Lady Trent. Something which I should have told you much earlier in our acquaintance, but for which the opportunity never seemed to arise.'

Wondering what the nature of this alarming disclosure could be, Madelaine frowned. 'What is it you wish to tell me, Taylor? Surely it cannot be that bad?' Suddenly, Madelaine blanched. 'Pray do not tell me that Lord Trevellyn has dismissed you for spending too much time with me.'

At that, Gabriel managed a small smile. 'No, my lady. Would that it were something so…uncomplicated.'

Madelaine's feathery eyebrows knit together in an expression of surprise. 'You do not consider being turned off a complication?'

'Not in this instance, no. You see, what I have been wanting to tell you—or rather, what I *must* tell you, is that I am not really Tay—'

'Ah, there you are, Gabriel,' Lady Westport interrupted, her polished voice effectively cutting across his words. 'Thank heavens, I have found you. Pray, forgive the interruption, Lady Trent, but Lady Bourne has been quite relentless in her search for this gentleman and has sent me to track him down. I fear I must commandeer him for a moment.'

Madelaine glanced at her hostess in bewilderment. 'Lady Bourne has been looking for *Taylor*?'

Gabriel flinched. 'Lady Trent, I—'

'Taylor?' Lady Westport repeated, puzzled. 'My dear Lady Trent, I fear I do not know who you are talking about.'

Madelaine glanced at Taylor quizzically. 'But I thought—'

'Dear me,' Lady Westport interrupted again, 'can it be that the two of you have not been properly introduced?'

'I fear we have not, Lady Westport,' Gabriel answered before Madelaine had opportunity to, 'though I was just about to remedy that situation.'

Lady Westport laughed, her ample bosom bouncing. 'Well, I would not have credited it, given that the two of you are neighbours. I thought surely you would have made each other's acquaintance by now.'

Madelaine slid disbelieving eyes towards the man she

had believed to be a steward, and tried to ignore the sudden rushing sound in her ears. *'Neighbours?'*

'But of course. Lady Trent, allow me to present Lord Trevellyn. Your new neighbour at Carew.'

Madelaine could not have looked any more surprised had someone told her that Lord Rakesley had suddenly become a millionaire. She stared up at Trevellyn as though horns had sprouted from his head. *'Lord* Trevellyn?' she repeated blankly. 'Earl of Trevellyn?'

Gabriel nodded slowly, keeping his eyes fixed firmly on her face. 'One and the same, I am afraid.'

Lady Westport watched the two people in front of her with unconcealed amusement. 'Well, Gabriel, I can see that the two of you have much to talk about, so I shall simply tell Lady Bourne that you are otherwise engaged. No doubt her impatience can hold a little while longer.'

'Thank you, Sophia.' As the grand lady moved away, Gabriel turned back to Madelaine with an expression of guilt upon his face. 'Lady Trent, believe me, I wanted to tell you before but—'

'But you were enjoying your game a little too much, is that it, *Lord* Trevellyn?' Madelaine asked coldly.

'That was not the way of it at all. It was never my intention to deceive you,' Gabriel told her quietly.

'Wasn't it? Pity, because you gave a very good imitation of doing just that!'

Madelaine felt the blood begin to pound in her temples as she realised the full extent of the humiliating trick he had played on her. The man had lied to her. Worse, he had made a *joke* of lying to her. He had pretended to be someone that he was not—and a *servant* into the bargain—and had never once evidenced a shred of guilt at doing so. Oh, that she should have been so gullible.

'It is a shame you chose to come tonight, Lord Trevellyn,' Madelaine said scathingly. 'You might have been able to carry on fooling me for some time yet, since I am not that quick to catch on to deception. Especially where I do not expect any. You must think me extremely naive.'

'Lady Trent, I can assure you—'

'Taking me around my own property,' Madelaine continued with a bitter laugh. 'Asking me what I thought of it. Pretending to love the land—'

'No. That was not a lie,' Gabriel interrupted. 'I do love the land. Nor was I trying to make a fool of you as you seem to think, or to take advantage of the fact that you were new to the area.'

'Then I should like to know what you *were* doing, my lord, since I confess to having no idea whatsoever!' Madelaine struggled to find a handhold on what was left of her dignity. 'Why did you not tell me who you were the first time I called you Taylor?'

'Because I was…curious.'

Madelaine stopped short. 'Curious? About what?'

'About why you were expecting my steward, rather than myself, to come calling on you. I would have thought that the only gentlemen from whom you would have been expecting visits were myself, and possibly the vicar.'

Madelaine sent him a withering glance. 'At least the vicar's appearance would have given him away. How was I to know that you were the Earl? You certainly did not look like one.'

Recalling that he had been dressed in a somewhat less than formal fashion that day, Gabriel smiled sheepishly. 'As it happens, I was dressed that way for a call I was paying on Mrs Abbey.'

Madelaine blinked. 'You mean, the lady who saw to the deer?'

'Yes. She lives at the end of a very long drive which is

more of a quagmire than it is a road, and as such, I felt it prudent to wear clothing of a more…casual nature. And that being the case, I—' Gabriel abruptly broke off as he realised that their prolonged conversation was earning them a number of interested looks from passers-by. 'Lady Trent,' he said, lowering his voice, 'might I suggest that we remove ourselves to somewhere more private in order to continue our conversation?'

'I see no need to remove ourselves for anything, Lord Trevellyn,' Madelaine informed him haughtily. 'And certainly not for a more private conversation. I have nothing further to say to you, other than that I am appalled and hurt that you would treat a lady, and a newcomer to the area, in such a shabby and ungentlemanly manner. If this is your idea of civility, I understand why my late husband had so little good to say about the Trevellyns of Carew. Good evening, sir!'

With that, Madelaine picked up her skirts and walked away, aware that her heart was beating uncomfortably fast. Her face felt stiff and she knew that her colour was unbecomingly high, but she was so angry that she could not help it. Who did he think he was, playing merry with her like that? Did he think that she had no feelings? That…just because she was from London and not of *good Cornish stock*, that she could be lied to and made to look a fool?

Madelaine thought back over the times they had spent together—and groaned aloud as she recalled some of the more memorable things she had said to him. In particular, to the way she had…interrogated him; all but ordering him to answer her questions. No wonder her groom had looked at her askance. He had heard her talking to the distinguished Earl of Trevellyn as though he had been nothing more than a steward! No doubt *that* had made for some amusing gossip in the servants' hall that night.

But what was worse, Trevellyn had gone along with it all—and without hesitation.

Well, that was fine, Madelaine decided, opening her fan with a practised flick of her wrist and plying it to her burning cheeks. Not even the knowledge that the man for whom she had felt such an overwhelming attraction was actually an Earl offered her any kind of comfort now. Whoever or whatever he was, he had lied to her without compunction. He had taken advantage of her naiveté and made her look a fool. And for that she would not forgive him. The mighty Earl of Trevellyn had had his laugh; he had played out his little game at her expense. And as far as she was concerned, it was the last game he was ever going to play with her.

And then she remembered. *Diggs!*

Madelaine moaned softly. Botheration! Now she would *have* to talk to the Earl whether she wanted to or not. Because she had yet to learn whether or not Trevellyn was responsible for her steward's absence. Certainly, now that she realised who and what he was capable of, Madelaine had no doubts that he had, indeed, stepped in and dismissed the man. If he could treat the lady of the manor so shabbily, he would certainly have no hesitation about belittling the lady's servants.

'Ah, there you are, my dear,' her aunt said, arriving at her side in a rustle of silk and lace. 'I have been looking for you. Do you know that…Maddie, are you all right, dear?' Chloe asked, halting in mid-sentence. 'Your colour is dreadfully high. In fact, I do believe that your cheeks are brighter than the roses on your gown. I know it is dreadfully warm in here, but—'

'You will never guess who I just met, Aunt Chloe,' Madelaine interrupted in a voice that was high and overly bright. 'Our elusive neighbour, Lord Trevellyn.'

Chloe's eyes widened. *'You met him?* Good heavens, and

you did not think to call me over immediately. La, Maddie, I am in despair of you. If I have heard that man's name mentioned once this evening, I have heard it a dozen times. No, make that two dozen. Phoebe Bourne mentioned it a dozen times in my hearing alone.' Chloe began to scan the faces amongst the crowd eagerly. 'Well, which one is he? Point him out to me and then I insist that you introduce us.'

'I shall point him out to you, Aunt, but I shall not introduce you.' Madelaine's eyes hardened. 'I shall spare you that ignominious pleasure.'

Chloe turned to regard her niece with a look of utter bewilderment. 'Maddie, what in the world are you talking about? If I did not know better, I would swear that you were—' Chloe stopped, and gazed more intently into her niece's face. 'Oh, dear, you *are* angry, aren't you? But what has happened? Surely Lord Trevellyn has not offended you in some way?'

'I fear I have, Mrs Merrill,' a masculine voice cut in smoothly behind them. 'And rather grievously, I am afraid. But it was completely unintentional, as I have been trying, at some length, to assure Lady Trent.'

Chloe turned around, her eyes widening in pleasure and surprise at the sight of the very handsome gentleman who was waiting to address them. 'Madelaine?'

Madelaine kept her face pointedly averted. In a voice that was as cool as she could make it without sounding rude, she said, 'Aunt Chloe, permit me to introduce the Earl of Trevellyn. Lord Trevellyn, my aunt, Mrs Chloe Merrill.'

'Mrs Merrill,' Gabriel said, bowing over Chloe's gloved hand. 'I hope you will forgive my interrupting you just now, but Lady Westport told me who you were, and I was most anxious to make your acquaintance.'

'The honour is mine, Lord Trevellyn,' Chloe replied, mo-

mentarily dazed at finding their neighbour to be every bit
as handsome and charming as she had been led to believe.
She heard her niece's barely disguised snort and raised an
eyebrow. 'I understand that you and my niece have already…met?'

'We have.'

'And that you have…had words?'

'I fear I did not show myself to best advantage.' Gabriel's voice was apologetic. 'I have just been telling Lady
Trent that I would very much like an opportunity of explaining myself.'

Chloe looked at him in surprise. 'Why? What have you
done?'

About to explain, Gabriel suddenly spotted Lady Bourne
and her daughter, Phoebe, across the room from them and
realised that they were looking rather hopefully in his direction. 'I think that now is not the best time to discuss it,
Mrs Merrill. Perhaps I could call upon you tomorrow at
Pengarron, that I might explain my actions more fully.'

'I see no problem with such a visit,' Chloe replied without hesitation. 'Do you, Madelaine?'

Madelaine lifted her chin. 'If you would like to entertain
his lordship, Aunt, I see no reason why I should object.'

'Maddie, I hardly think the Earl is coming to see me—'

'I should be delighted to see *both* of you,' Gabriel said
quickly, aware that his apologies were not going to cut any
ice with the younger lady—and that the Bourne females
were bearing down upon them. 'I am well aware that I owe
Lady Trent a considerable explanation as well as an apology, but I hope that, once the details of my behaviour are
set forth, she will understand my motives a little better, and
be able to forgive my subterfuge.'

'Your…subterfuge?' By now Chloe was totally intrigued. 'Yes, Lord Trevellyn, you may indeed call upon

us tomorrow. I admit, I am curious beyond all to hear this…explanation of yours—as well as to find out what prompted the need for such a confession in the first place.'

Gabriel smiled, and bowed again. When he turned to face Madelaine, however, his smile faded. 'Until tomorrow, Lady Trent. And may I say again that I meant no harm. I hope you will give me the opportunity to convince you of that on the morrow.'

Madelaine finally turned around and returned his gaze with one that was just as direct, but a great deal more reserved. 'You are welcome to call, my lord. Whether I am in attendance is another matter entirely.'

Something flickered in the depths of Trevellyn's eyes, but he said nothing. He merely bowed and then quietly moved away. As soon as he was out of hearing distance, Chloe turned to regard her niece with an expression of astonishment. 'Madelaine, what in the world has come over you? You were positively rude to the gentleman. Indeed, for a moment there, I feared the two of you were going to come to blows.'

Madelaine followed the Earl's retreating back with her eyes, refusing to acknowledge how beautifully his jacket lay against the breadth of his shoulders. 'Tosh, you should know me better than that. I would not allow any man to disturb me to that degree.'

Chloe also turned to gaze rather thoughtfully after the Earl. 'I don't know about that, Maddie. It seems to me that the Earl of Trevellyn has already disturbed you a great deal more than any other man you have ever met. What on earth has he—'

'Lady Trent, Mrs Merrill, I thought I spied the two of you here,' Lady Bourne said, sweeping down on them like a bird of prey in search of its dinner. 'But what a pity we missed Lord Trevellyn. I thought he might like to speak to my Phoebe.' Lady Bourne breathed a regretful sigh. 'Such a charming man, is he not, Lady Trent?'

'I am afraid I cannot say, Lady Bourne,' Madelaine answered politely. 'We only met this evening, and I had very little opportunity to converse with him.'

'But do you not find him to be the most handsome of gentlemen, Lady Trent?' Phoebe sighed dreamily.

'To be honest, I have very little opinion of the man one way or the other.' Madelaine's reply was intentionally sharp. 'I have noted, however, that he seems to possess both a smooth tongue and a very high opinion of himself, two characteristics which I have never held to be particularly admirable in a gentleman. Still, I am sure there are ladies enough who would argue the point with me.'

'Madelaine, perhaps you would care for a glass of ratafia?' Chloe suggested hastily. 'Like you, I find it rather warm this evening.'

'I do not find it in the least—'

'If you will excuse us, Lady Bourne, Miss Phoebe.' Chloe smiled brightly and swiftly drew her niece away, well aware that the Bourne ladies were staring after Madelaine in open-mouthed astonishment.

'Chloe, why did you pull me away like that?' Madelaine asked in annoyance.

'Because I was afraid you were about to commit a social *faux pas* for which we might never have heard the end. What do you mean by calling Lord Trevellyn vain?'

'I did not call him vain.'

'Not in so many words, perhaps, but the intention was certainly there,' Chloe said in an urgent whisper. 'And for one who is anxious to keep a low profile in the county, you are definitely going about it the wrong way. No doubt it will be all around tomorrow that you find Lord Trevellyn an insufferable prig.'

'On the contrary, I do not find him a prig,' Madelaine replied.

'I am very glad to hear it.'

'I believe him to be a liar and a rogue, but hardly a prig.'

'Maddie!' Chloe gasped, glancing around nervously. 'The man is an Earl. You cannot go around calling him a liar.'

'I can and I will.'

'Gracious, what did he do?'

'The poor man, as you so kindly call him, pretended to be his steward, Taylor.'

Chloe stared at her in disbelief. 'I *beg* your pardon?'

'I thought I spoke clearly enough.'

'You spoke very clearly indeed. Are you saying that Lord Trevellyn was the gentleman who took you around Pengarron…in the guise of…a steward?'

'Yes.'

'Dear me, no wonder you were so impressed with him.'

Madelaine flushed deeply. 'I was not impressed with him at all.'

'That was not my recollection of the events.'

'Then I fear your recollection is in error. *I* found the man to be overbearing, forward, stubborn, and…rude!'

'There, you see? I said that he made quite an impression on you, and he has,' Chloe continued mildly. 'But what I cannot understand is why in the world he would pretend to be a servant.'

'That is precisely what I intend to find out. And in case you are wondering, I do intend to be there when Lord Trevellyn calls tomorrow,' Madelaine said fiercely, 'because I am very curious to hear what he has to say.' Her eyes glittered with barely suppressed anger. 'I want to know exactly what manner of man pretends to be a steward, when he is about as far removed from being a servant as I am from being a lamb!'

Chapter Seven

Gabriel was shown into the parlour at Pengarron at precisely half past two the following afternoon. He was impeccably turned out, his buff-coloured pantaloons fitting snugly to his well-muscled thighs while the dark maroon jacket accentuated the trimness of his waist in comparison to the width of his shoulders. His neckcloth was arranged in a perfect Mathematical and his highly polished Hessians reflected a sheen so deep that it was possible to see the pattern of the carpet in them.

'Lord Trevellyn, my lady.'

'Thank you, Berkeley.' Madelaine smiled politely at her guest as the butler withdrew. 'Good afternoon, Lord Trevellyn.'

'Lady Trent.' Gabriel sketched her a formal bow. 'Thank you for agreeing to see me. I trust you are in good health after the events of last evening.'

'I am very well, thank you.'

Gabriel carefully hid his amusement at the coolness in her voice. He was encouraged by the fact that she had been willing to see him, but he knew better than to read anything more into it than that. The lady was curious. At the mo-

ment, that was probably the only thing he had going for
him.

Gabriel turned to greet Lady Trent's aunt, who had been
watching, with interest, the interplay between the two of
them, and his voice warmed appreciably. 'Mrs Merrill, how
charming you look this afternoon. Indeed, the two of you
appear more like sisters than aunt and niece.'

To Madelaine's astonishment, her aunt actually started
to blush. 'My lord, you are too kind. A touch shortsighted,
perhaps, but definitely too kind.'

Gabriel smiled, bringing into a view a most attractive
dimple in his left cheek. 'I assure you, my eyes are quite
sharp, Mrs Merrill.'

Madelaine fiddled with her lace handkerchief, trying to
ignore the light-hearted banter that was taking place between her aunt and her new neighbour. 'I must say that
your own appearance is not to be found in any way lacking
this morning, my lord,' she commented stiffly. 'Indeed, it
would be impossible to mistake you for *anyone* but the lord
of the manor today.'

Gabriel's expression did not change as he turned to regard his hostess. 'I did not wish you to think that I
was…unaware as to the proper manner of dress when paying a formal house call, Lady Trent. However, I admit that
my appearance on the occasion of our last meeting was
affected for your benefit.'

'As, I expect, was your appearance on the occasion of
our first one.'

Gabriel smiled, and shook his head. 'On that, I beg leave
to differ. As I started to tell you at Lady Westport's last
evening, the first time I saw you, my manner of dress was
solely as a result of the call I was intending to pay on one
of my tenants; a visit necessitated by my steward being
unexpectedly called away.'

'Ah, yes, your steward.' Madelaine's eyes flashed a challenge. 'I assume that would be Taylor?'

'That would, indeed, be Taylor.' Gabriel glanced quickly at Madelaine's aunt. 'Am I to understand that you have now been made aware of the details of my…deception, Mrs Merrill?'

Knowing that Madelaine's eyes were upon her, Chloe was careful not to appear as entertained by the proceedings as she felt. 'Yes. My niece did inform me of it, er, briefly last evening.'

'In that case, I had best explain myself as quickly as possible.'

'Yes, Lord Trevellyn, do.' Madelaine looked up at him expectantly. 'I am anxious to hear how you intend to justify your conduct.'

Gabriel cleared his throat. 'Perhaps I should begin by answering the question you put to me on the occasion of our first meeting, Lady Trent.'

Madelaine frowned. 'I…do not recall the question, my lord.'

'Really? I am surprised that you do not, since it was of such importance to you at the time,' Gabriel remarked idly. 'You asked me if I had, in fact, dismissed your man, Diggs.'

Madelaine was so surprised that he would choose to start his explanation with the very question he had been so careful to avoid that she could do naught but nod.

'The answer is, yes, I did dismiss him,' Gabriel said. 'I did so because, as I told you the other morning, Diggs was a thoroughly reprehensible man. He was robbing your husband blind. And he would have continued to rob *you*, without thought or compunction.'

Chloe gasped her dismay. 'He would have stolen from a woman?'

'Indeed. Such was the kind of man he was.'

'Scoundrel! How was he accomplishing this thievery, Lord Trevellyn?'

'Through poaching, for the most part,' Gabriel informed her. 'Lady Trent was unfortunate enough to have found evidence of that in the linden glade. I had Taylor make some enquiries, and you would be amazed to learn of the extent to which Diggs took advantage of Lord Trent's absence. He was supplying the butcher, amongst others, with fresh rabbits, grouse, partridge, and even fish, which Lord Trent's absence made it very easy for him to procure.'

'Was he, indeed?' Chloe retorted, her brows drawing together in a frown. 'Then it is a good thing you turned him off, Lord Trevellyn. Madelaine would have had her hands full with one such as that.'

'On the contrary, Diggs had everything so nicely arranged that Lady Trent would have had no idea that she was being so ill used.'

Against her will, Madelaine felt her gaze caught and held by his. 'But why? My husband was a kind and generous employer, Tay— Lord Trevellyn. I know for a fact that he paid his servants far more than most.'

Gabriel heard the sorrow in her voice, and briefly wondered at its source. Was it simply regret that one of her husband's retainers had cheated him—and that he would have continued to cheat her? Or did her grief stem from the mere mention of Lord Trent's name? Because if that was the case, it meant that the lady was obviously still in love with her husband.

Gabriel was surprised to find that the knowledge disturbed him.

'Unfortunately, Diggs required more than just an average wage, Lady Trent. You see, on top of his propensity for poaching, he was also a compulsive gambler. I have been informed that he was a regular at the Three Feathers in town.'

Dismayed by the extent of the man's treachery, Madelaine stared down at the carpet in silence. It troubled her to know that someone whom her husband had hired and paid good money to had thought to take such blatant advantage of him. She also knew that Lord Trevellyn was right. Given her own inexperience in matters such as these, she would never have discovered Diggs's dishonesty. His little operation, as Trevellyn called it, would have continued unchecked, long after her husband's death.

Madelaine swallowed uncomfortably. 'It would appear that I...owe you an apology, Lord Trevellyn. At least as regards the matter of my steward. I now understand that you had my best interests at heart when you dismissed the man. And I confess, after seeing evidence of his work, I can only be relieved that you took it upon yourself to do so. It is better to be without a steward than to be deceived by a dishonest one.'

Gabriel was not sure that he liked seeing his feisty lady humbled in front of him, but he dutifully acknowledged her thanks. 'If I may, Lady Trent, I have spoken with Taylor, and he has agreed to oversee the running of both properties until such time as you are able to hire a new steward. And, since I did take it upon myself to dismiss Diggs, I would be happy to undertake the interviewing of potential candidates and then meet with you to discuss a suitable replacement, if that meets with your approval.'

Madelaine hesitated. It was a generous offer, indeed, but she wondered whether it was right to accept it. She had been painfully rude to Lord Trevellyn last night, which made his offer now seem even more altruistic.

Chloe, however, sensing her niece's reserve, and knowing the reason for it, spoke up for her. 'That would be most kind of you, Lord Trevellyn. Like myself, Madelaine is not used to dealing with matters such as these, and I know we should both be grateful for your advice.'

Gabriel watched Madelaine for a moment. 'Lady Trent, have I your agreement in this matter?'

Madelaine looked up at him, and allowed a hesitant smile to play around the corners of her mouth. 'Yes, I suppose you have. Thank you, Lord Trevellyn, it is a most generous offer, and I am grateful for your assistance. I hope you will also convey my thanks to Taylor for looking after Pengarron. I am sure he will have his hands full attending to both properties.'

Seeing her smile, Gabriel suddenly felt as though a weight had been lifted from his shoulders. 'I shall do better than that, Lady Trent. Since it is only right that you be able to recognise the man who will be looking after your property, I shall introduce you to Taylor at the first opportunity. I would not want another case of mistaken identity arising as a result of your seeing, what you might perceive to be, a stranger riding around the grounds.'

Abruptly, Madelaine began to laugh. 'No, indeed, my lord. Two Taylors visiting Pengarron was enough for anyone, I should think.'

'As for the second part of the explanation,' Gabriel continued, 'I wonder if I might not explain that over dinner tomorrow evening at Carew.' His smile was warm, his eyes lingering darkly on the soft curve of Madelaine's lips. 'I would very much like to show you and Mrs Merrill my home, and to enjoy the pleasure of your company at greater length.'

Madelaine hoped he would not see the way her hands suddenly began to tremble. 'My lord, it is really not necessary.'

'Perhaps not, but I would be honoured if you would

agree to be my guests regardless. After getting off to a rather shaky start, I certainly owe you that.'

Madelaine's indecision lasted only a moment before she said, 'We should be pleased to accept your invitation, my lord. Would we not, Chloe?'

Relieved to hear the lightness back in her niece's voice, Chloe inclined her head. 'Delighted, Lord Trevellyn. It is most kind of you.'

'Kindness has nothing to do with it, Mrs Merrill,' Gabriel said, smiling down at Madelaine. 'I am merely anxious to re-establish trust.'

'Well, Maddie, I think this calls for a celebration,' Chloe announced, rising and crossing to the bell pull. 'On the most satisfactory conclusion of this business, I think we should offer Lord Trevellyn a glass of champagne, both to thank him for his kindness, and to assure him that there are no hard feelings over this most unfortunate misunderstanding.'

'There are, I hope, no hard feelings, Lady Trent?' Gabriel said.

Madelaine knew that his eyes were on her, and felt the warmth rise to her cheeks as a result. 'None on my part, Lord Trevellyn, though perhaps I should withhold comment on that until *after* you have explained why you felt the need to pretend to be…someone you were not.'

'That is only fair,' Gabriel agreed. 'As such, I will not expect any comment from you until I have had the opportunity to do so.'

Madelaine graciously bowed her head, hoping he did not see the smile which hovered about her mouth.

Yes, it seemed that the summer in Cornwall was going to be a good deal more interesting than she had thought!

Madelaine spent extra time over her toilette for her dinner with Lord Trevellyn the following evening. Because, while she was reluctant to admit it, even to herself, Madelaine realised that she was very much looking forward to the evening. Her animosity towards the Earl had lessened considerably since their meeting the previous afternoon, due in no small part to the nature of the news he had given her.

Madelaine had been horrified to learn that one of her husband's own people would stoop to stealing. She had heard that such things went on, of course, but knowing of Edward's beneficence, she had not expected to find it happening within her own walls. The fact that she had saddened her; as did the knowledge that, without Lord Trevellyn's intervention, it would likely have continued unabated.

Quite apart from that, however, Madelaine found herself looking forward to spending an evening in the company of a man to whom, even in the guise of a steward, she had been unaccountably drawn.

She blushed now as she recalled her reaction to him that first morning when he had taken her around the property. She should have realised straight away that something wasn't right. Even then, the man had seemed too noble to be anything but the lord of the manor. The pride in his eyes as he had looked out over the lands, the calm assurance that he was, indeed, his own lord and master, had made for an ill fit with the role he was playing.

The question remained, why had he tried to play the part in the first place?

Madelaine admitted that she was very interested in hearing his explanation for that!

Gabriel was waiting at the door when Madelaine and her aunt arrived at Carew. He tried not to stare as his butler removed Madelaine's velvet cloak, revealing the whisper-soft gown of lavender silk beneath, but it was very hard not to. Caught high under the bust as fashion decreed, the bodice was cut low enough to display the fullness of a smooth white bosom, while evening gloves covered her arms to just below the delicate band of embroidery encircling the puff sleeves. The same shade of lavender was then repeated in the shimmering silk ribbon that wound attractively through her hair.

Madelaine had chosen to wear one of Edward's wedding gifts with the gown this evening, knowing that the breathtaking necklace of diamonds with a single amethyst drop was a perfect compliment to the simplicity of the gown. She blushed as she saw Trevellyn's eyes linger on the magnificent gem which nestled invitingly in the shadowy cleft between her breasts.

'You look lovely, Lady Trent,' Gabriel said sincerely.

His voice was soft and caressing, yet totally lacking in the cloying undertones that Madelaine had so often heard in the voices of other gentlemen who had paid her compliments. She blushed as she caught Chloe's knowing eye. 'Thank you, my lord. You are very kind.'

Tearing his eyes away from Madelaine, Gabriel then smiled upon her aunt, who was looking radiant in a gown and matching turban of very dark green silk. 'And once again, Mrs Merrill, I might think that you and Lady Trent were sisters. The gown becomes you exceedingly well.'

'Do you know, Maddie, I think I begin to like it more and more here in Cornwall,' Chloe observed with a laugh. 'Perhaps the sea air is more restorative to my system than I thought!'

Madelaine laughed. 'I have heard that the Regent positively swears by it. Look how long he spends at Brighton.'

'But I wonder…is it the sea air or the fact that Brighton

is so far removed from London which makes it such a favourite haunt of Prinny's?' Gabriel commented. 'Given his recent unpopularity, it hardly surprises me that he would feel the need to flee the excesses of Carlton House.'

'Mmm, so that he can flee to the excesses of the Pavilion.' Chloe sniffed disdainfully as they moved into a magnificent room, the walls of which were hung with pale blue silk. 'Did you hear about the dinner party he hosted, my lord? Over thirty entrées. I ask you, where is the need for such pretentiousness? Or such gluttony?'

Madelaine chuckled as she took a seat close to the window. 'I understand that most of the guests were too stupefied to do much beyond listen to the band when the meal was over.'

'No doubt that had something to do with the amount of port and Madeira served after the meal,' Gabriel supplied, 'on top of the wines we had with dinner.'

'We?' Chloe blinked. 'Oh, dear. Am I to understand that *you* were in attendance, my lord?'

Gabriel laughed. 'I am afraid so, Mrs Merrill. Though not a close confidante of the Regent, I *was* invited to that particular dinner. But I do share your opinion that such lavish displays are not only unnecessary, but highly imprudent at a time when the Corn Laws are still in effect, and taxes on basic goods are making it more and more difficult for the common man to put food on his table. The Regent does not endear himself to his people by indulging in such displays of excess, I can assure you.'

Madelaine watched as Lord Trevellyn calmly poured out two glasses of sherry, as well as a brandy for himself, and then carried them across the room. To say the least, she was surprised by his sentiments. Most gentlemen of her acquaintance were openly envious of the excesses of the court, and spent a good deal of their time wishing that they might be invited to enjoy them. Whereas Lord Trevellyn, it seemed, had not only *not* enjoyed his time at Brighton, but was unashamed to admit it.

Madelaine glanced towards the entrance to the room as a tall, well-built man suddenly appeared in the doorway. She saw him hesitate uncertainly, and then look towards Lord Trevellyn, whose back was turned towards him. By his dress, he was clearly not an invited guest, even though the buckskin breeches and tweed jacket were of good quality. But it was the familiarity of his face which caused Madelaine to frown. 'My lord, it would appear that you have another guest.'

Turning, Gabriel smiled, and motioned for the man to come in. 'Not exactly a guest, Lady Trent, though he is someone I should like you to meet. May I introduce the true land steward of Carew, and your temporary one, Mr Alfred Taylor. Taylor, Lady Trent, mistress of Pengarron.'

'Good evening, Lady Trent.'

Madelaine's eyes had widened at the mention of the man's name, and then suddenly, she remembered where she had seen him before. 'But...I thought you told me that his name was Collins?' Madelaine said, recalled to the incident with the deer in the linden glade.

Gabriel had the decency to blush. 'Yes, well, I couldn't very well introduce him as Taylor, when I had already told you that *I* was Taylor, could I?'

Madelaine's eyebrow rose slightly. 'Another deception, my lord?'

'I prefer to think of it as...a small but necessary extension of the first, Lady Trent,' Gabriel said humbly.

Deciding that she would let it go at that, Madelaine smiled up into the steward's face, liking the honesty and the openness she saw there. 'Lord Trevellyn has informed me that you have kindly offered to look after Pengarron until I am able to find another steward, Taylor. I am most grateful to you.'

She was surprised to see the man's ruddy cheeks darken. ''Tis no trouble, my lady. I know Pengarron almost as well as I know Carew. It won't be any trouble minding them both for a bit.'

'I am relieved to hear it. And please do come and see me about anything which you feel I should be apprised of.'

At the steward's nod, Gabriel said, 'I have told Lady Trent that since I was responsible for dismissing Diggs, I shall take full responsibility for hiring his replacement. Can you look after putting out the word for me, Taylor?'

'Aye, m'lord. It will be a pleasure. Begging your pardon, my lady,' Taylor said, 'but you're well rid of Diggs. He was a bad one, and no doubt about that.'

'Yes, so I learned the other morning,' Madelaine replied softly. 'I understand that you carried the little doe back to Mrs Abbey's cottage, Taylor.'

'Aye, m'lady, I did. But she were only a wee thing, so it wasn't a bother.'

'Nevertheless, I am grateful for your help with her.'

Gabriel was amused to see the man's cheeks darken even further and knew that he was uncomfortable at being the centre of attention. 'Thank you, Taylor, that will be all. I shall see you in my study tomorrow morning at ten. We can go over the details then.'

'Yes, my lord. Good evening, Lady Trent. Ma'am.' he said, bowing to Chloe and then taking his leave of the party.

When he had gone, Madelaine turned back towards Lord Trevellyn and smiled. 'That was very good of you, my lord, thank you.'

Gabriel picked up his glass. 'I thought it wise that you meet Taylor as soon as possible. It is my wish that he begin a thorough examination of the estate to see just how much neglect Diggs has been guilty of. I feel sure there will be a number of repairs required to fences and gates, and I have already told him to remove any traps he finds. I have no doubt that the grounds are littered with them.'

Madelaine's eyes darkened again at the thought of Diggs's cruelty. 'Thank you, Lord Trevellyn. I should be grateful for any reports that you are able to give me as to the condition of the property, and I shall see to it that monies are made available for any expenses which are incurred. I will not allow Pengarron to fall into a state of disrepair.'

Gabriel smiled his approval. 'Of course. And if you will permit me, I shall continue to send reports to you in London after you have returned there. That way you will be able to stay abreast of what is happening at Pengarron, until such time as you decide what you want to do with it.'

Madelaine glanced at Lord Trevellyn over the rim of her glass. 'What I want to *do* with it?'

'Yes. Well, it is, after all, the most distant of your late husband's properties,' Gabriel said, maintaining a carefully detached expression. 'And as I understand, you have been given the use of a town house in London for as long as you wish. I merely assumed that you would not wish to be burdened with the responsibility of an estate so far from London, when you were unlikely to live in it.'

Madelaine was prevented from having to reply by the arrival of yet another gentleman; this one, clearly an invited guest.

'Ah, Thomas,' Gabriel said, relieved by the interruption. 'I was beginning to wonder where you were. Come and meet my new neighbours, Lady Trent, and her aunt, Mrs Merrill. Ladies, my good friend, Lord Keswick.'

Keswick made his bows. 'Lady Trent, Mrs Merrill, a pleasure, most assuredly. And Gabriel. I do apologise for my somewhat late arrival, but I fear I had a bit of trouble negotiating the turn at Tynamere.' He glanced at his host sheepishly. 'Team rather got away on me, I'm afraid.'

'Ah, so it was *you* Madelaine and I saw driving that splendid pair the other day,' Chloe said. 'I thought at the time they looked a touch…high-spirited.'

Gabriel tactfully smothered a smile, while Lord Keswick cleared his throat. 'Yes, well, I admit I am still getting the feel for them, Mrs Merrill. Quite a bit different from my last team, you see. Not the same manner of cattle at all. Are they, Gabriel?'

The Earl quickly banished his smile. 'Not in the least. Sherry?'

Lord Keswick gratefully nodded and then took a seat beside Chloe. 'And how are you enjoying your stay in Cornwall, Mrs Merrill?'

'I am finding it entirely to my liking, Lord Keswick.' Chloe twinkled at her niece mischievously. 'I have been told that the sea air agrees with me.'

'I am sure that it does. Brings out the colour in the cheeks,' Lord Keswick concurred. 'Might be a bit harsh on a younger complexion like Lady Trent's, of course, but I should think it would do very well for yours.'

Chloe's smile abruptly faded. 'Really.'

'Indeed. And Lady Trent,' Keswick said to Madelaine, 'this is, I believe, your first visit to Pengarron?'

Madelaine fought to keep her lips from twitching. 'It is indeed, Lord Keswick. The first time I have been to Cornwall, actually.'

'And what do you think of our part of the world?'

'Like my aunt, I find it most agreeable. A refreshing change from the bustle and congestion of London.'

'Yes, I have always thought so,' Keswick said amiably, 'though I must confess, after rusticating down here for a few months I am happy enough to return to Town. Personally, I have always cared more for Shropshire or the Cotswolds than I have for Cornwall and Devon. Speaking of which, I understand the new Lord Trent and his young wife will be taking up residence at Trent Hall.'

'Yes. William has always loved the house there, and it will be a wonderful place for them to raise a family.'

'So you have no regrets about coming here?'

'None at all. I find there is something rather wild and exciting about this part of the country, do you not think so?'

'Well, yes, I suppose you could say that. What do you think, Gabriel?'

It seemed to Madelaine that Lord Keswick was having trouble keeping a straight face, though she was quite at a loss to understand why. She had not found anything particularly amusing in the conversation thus far, apart from Lord Keswick's inadvertent blunder with regard to Chloe's complexion, and she wondered that he was suddenly and pointedly avoiding her eyes.

Even more surprising to her than that, however, was the fact that Lord Trevellyn seemed almost relieved when dinner was announced a few moments later. He rose quickly and offered her his arm, leading her into the dining room, with Mrs Merrill and Lord Keswick following behind.

And to her surprise, he made no further reference to Cornwall at all.

As expected, the meal which was presented to them in the splendour of the formal dining room at Carew was, quite simply, superb. Each course was perfectly prepared and served, from the delicate consommé soup to the succulent baron of beef. And it went without saying that the wines Lord Trevellyn had chosen to accompany each course were a reflection of his connoisseur's taste and discernment.

Fortunately, the wine also helped to alleviate some of the constraint which the diners had felt upon their arrival at the table, and after a somewhat stilted start, conversation began to flow again. Madelaine was relieved to see that her aunt eventually warmed up to Lord Keswick—who managed not to commit another social blunder—and that the two were able to converse with some degree of affability. As for herself, she was anxious to bring the conversation back to a topic which Lord Trevellyn had briefly touched on earlier, and which, to Madelaine's way of thinking, had been passed over with remarkable expediency.

'Lord Trevellyn, I was surprised by the comment you made earlier with regards to my continued ownership of Pengarron. I take it by your comment that you are of the opinion I should sell the property?'

Her eyes on Lord Trevellyn's face, Madelaine failed to notice the sudden interest in Lord Keswick's.

'Sell Pengarron?' Keswick glanced towards his host with an ingenuous smile. 'Upon my word, whatever introduced such a topic into the conversation?'

'Lord Trevellyn kindly offered to keep me apprised of the situation here at Pengarron after I returned to London,' Madelaine explained, 'and until such time as I had decided what I wanted to do with the property.'

'Personally, I think it is a very good idea that the property be sold,' Chloe spoke up unexpectedly. 'As I have already told Madelaine, there is no reason for her to live so far away from London when she has the use of the town house in Mayfair. And given that she has the wherewithal to buy an establishment of her own, why would she not buy one closer to Town? Pengarron is a lovely property, but it is so very far away, and Madelaine is much too young and beautiful to bury herself away in the depths of the country. Do you not agree, Lord Trevellyn?'

'Chloe, *please*!' Madelaine said, blushing hotly, 'I am sure that Lord Trevellyn has no opinion on the matter.'

'Tosh, of course he has an opinion, my dear,' Chloe asserted calmly. 'Gentlemen always do. I venture to say even Lord Keswick has one.'

'Well, yes, as it happens, I do, Mrs Merrill,' Lord Keswick spoke up. 'And I tend to agree with you, that it would be advisable for Lady Trent to consider selling. Certainly, it would be difficult for any young woman to look after an estate of this size, especially if she is not planning on living in the place year round. I think this unfortunate episode with Diggs is ample evidence of that.'

Madelaine glanced at him in surprise. 'You knew about that?'

'Lord Keswick was here the afternoon Taylor caught Diggs poaching and brought him in to see me,' Gabriel explained quickly.

'And what was your opinion of the man, Lord Keswick?' Chloe enquired.

Keswick sucked in his breath sharply. 'Nasty bit of goods, Mrs Merrill, very nasty indeed. Totally lacking in conscience. Sort of chap who would steal from his own mother. Sad to say there are fellows like that around—and that the late Lord Trent was unfortunate enough to have employed one.'

'Well, thanks to Lord Trevellyn, we no longer do employ him,' Chloe observed tartly, 'but that is just my point. Why should Madelaine concern herself with the running of a house that she is unlikely to live in for more than a few months a year? Lord Trevellyn, surely you would not advise her, as a lovely and eligible young widow, to hold on to Pengarron when she could do so much better living in London?'

Gabriel rubbed his finger over the etching on his wine glass, surprised to find himself uncomfortable with the conversation. He assured himself that it was strictly as a result of the frank and open discussion they were having with regard to Pengarron's future—and *not* to the fact that Mrs Merrill seemed to consider him of no possible interest to her niece as a potential husband at all—that lay at the root of his displeasure.

'There is no doubt in my mind that *any* young lady with inclinations towards marriage would be better served by spending her time in London, Mrs Merrill,' Gabriel replied circumspectly, 'where the number of eligible gentlemen is tenfold over what it is in the country. However, given that I, myself, am loathe to spend any more time in London than is absolutely necessary, I am probably not the best person to ask. The decision whether or not to live in London is surely Lady Trent's to make.'

'But you have not said whether you think my niece would be well advised to sell Pengarron,' Chloe persisted.

Quite unintentionally, Madelaine came to his rescue. 'I think that Lord Trevellyn might have difficulty answering that question, Aunt, given his strong feelings about the land. I believe he would have trouble believing that anyone would wish to live anywhere other than Cornwall.'

'On the contrary, this is a harsh land, Lady Trent, and not for everyone,' Gabriel acknowledged. 'The moors are bleak, and the coastline rugged and unforgiving. But when one is born to the land, it becomes more difficult to see its flaws. You learn to appreciate the good with the bad. As to the wisdom of selling Pengarron, I think that is a decision which Lady Trent must make for herself.'

Lord Keswick glanced at Gabriel sharply, while Chloe,

seeing the lull in the conversation as an appropriate time for her and Madelaine to withdraw, graciously rose. 'Come, my dear, I think it is time that we retire to the drawing room for tea and leave the gentlemen to their port.'

Madelaine smiled hesitantly. 'Yes, of course.'

The gentlemen rose and bowed politely as the ladies withdrew. Not until the door closed behind them, however, did Lord Keswick turn a curious eye towards his host and say, 'Well, Gabriel, you astonish me. Lady Trent all but *handed* you the opportunity you were looking for. She asked you point blank for your opinion with regards to her selling Pengarron—and you let it pass. Why? I thought you would have welcomed the chance to convince her to sell.'

Gabriel poured out two glasses of port and handed one to his guest. 'I did not think it wise to make my opinions on the matter known at this time.'

'At *this* time? Pray, what was wrong with *this* time? Even Mrs Merrill expressed her sentiments on the subject.'

'Yes, and as Lady Trent's aunt, Mrs Merrill is free to make her point known whenever she feels inclined to do so. I am not in that happy position.'

Lord Keswick's eyes narrowed thoughtfully. 'Do you want to know what I think?'

'No, but I fear I am to hear it nevertheless.'

'I think you are starting to have second thoughts about the whole thing.'

'Nonsense!'

'In fact, I would even go so far to say that you are beginning to have feelings of affection for the lady—'

'*Rubbish!*'

'—and that you are reluctant to proceed with your plan and thereby force her back to London.'

'For your information, I am not forcing her anywhere— and it is certainly of no consequence to me where she lives,' Gabriel asserted bluntly. '*If* I were interested in Lady Trent, and *if* I were inclined to press my suit, I could certainly travel up to London and do it there.'

'But you do not like London, remember?' Lord Keswick said, grinning. 'You made it quite clear that you endeavour to spend as little time in Town as possible. So do you not think that following Lady Trent to London—when you have no other earthly reason for going there—would exhibit to others a certain partiality for the lady?'

Gabriel sighed. 'Why is it that, just because I do not choose to discuss the lady's possible inclination towards selling Pengarron, I have suddenly changed my mind about buying the house, and am now chasing up to London to romance her?'

Thomas raised the cut-crystal glass to his lips and took a mouthful of port. 'I do not know. That is what I am asking you, my friend.'

'And *you*, my friend, read a great deal more into a conversation than is really there,' Gabriel commented drily.

'Do I?' Lord Keswick smiled complacently and took another mouthful of port. 'I wonder.'

Chapter Eight

In the drawing room, Chloe saw to the pouring of the tea while Madelaine sat at the pianoforte and ran her fingers lightly over the keys. She played whatever tune came into her head, her thoughts not on the music but on the subjects upon which they had touched during dinner—and in particular, on her selling Pengarron.

It was not the first time she had considered the possibility. Her lawyer had already advised her that it would be a good financial decision, and she knew of Chloe's feelings on the matter, given the unrestricted use of the town house in London. But for all that, Madelaine was still reluctant to part with Pengarron. Perhaps because it had once belonged to Edward, and because his son had made it a gift to her in the hopes of seeing her established there. Also, now that she was actually living in the house, Madelaine found that she liked it very well indeed. So much so that the thought of selling it held little appeal for her.

She refused to consider that her reluctance had anything to do with the presence of the very handsome and charming gentleman living right next door. After all, why should that be of any importance to her? But surely a man as astute as

Lord Trevellyn would not have suggested that she consider selling it unless he believed it to be in her best interests?

'That was lovely, Maddie,' Chloe said as her niece finished up the sonata she was playing, and then rose to join her on the settee. 'You play the instrument beautifully.'

'It is an exceptionally fine instrument,' Madelaine told her with a smile. 'And one upon which it is easy to produce a lovely sound.'

'Not unless you know where to place your fingers, my dear. Sadly, I was never an accomplished player,' Chloe confessed. 'I could neither play nor sing, and my father used to say that it was kinder to the company if I merely offered to turn the pages for those who could. But never mind that, what do you think of Lord Trevellyn now that you have had an opportunity to spend some time with him? Is he not all that is polite and charming in a gentleman?'

Madelaine felt a blush steal into her cheeks. 'He is charming indeed, Chloe.'

'And handsome enough for any lady, I should think.'

'As you say.'

'I thought his conduct with regards to your steward perfectly justified after hearing the reasons for it. I hope you feel no malice towards him for his behaviour.'

'I feel no ill will towards Lord Trevellyn whatsoever. Indeed, I am indebted to him for his timely handling of the situation,' Madelaine agreed slowly. 'But I am still curious as to why he felt the need to pretend to be someone that he was not.'

'Then perhaps it is time I gave you an answer to that question, Lady Trent,' Gabriel said quietly from the direction of the door.

Madelaine started, embarrassed and dismayed that he had overheard her remark. 'Lord Trevellyn, pray forgive my thoughtlessness—'

'It was not thoughtless at all,' Gabriel assured her as he and Lord Keswick advanced into the room. 'I am well aware that I owe you an explanation regarding my charade as Taylor, and that it is long overdue.' He hesitated a moment, and then glanced towards the French doors. 'Perhaps I might do that while showing you the view of the lake from the balcony. There is a full moon tonight, and it is a particularly breathtaking sight.'

Madelaine glanced uncertainly at her aunt. 'I...do not think it would be polite to leave my aunt.'

Lord Keswick, catching the momentary look of disappointment in Gabriel's eyes, hastily cleared his throat. 'Mrs Merrill, I wonder if I could interest you in a game of cards until Trevellyn and your niece return?'

Cognisant of the fact that Lord Trevellyn wished to speak to Madelaine alone, and always agreeable to a hand of cards, Chloe nodded. 'Very well. But I give you fair warning, Lord Keswick, I am an accomplished player, and I cannot abide cheats.'

Lord Keswick flushed. 'Mrs Merrill! I cannot imagine why you would even feel the need to say such a thing. I am an honourable gentleman, above all.'

'Hmm, we shall see.'

Gabriel turned in time to see Lord Keswick wink at him, and Mrs Merrill smile her approval at her niece. Thus reassured, he bent to offer his arm to Lady Trent. 'Shall we go, my lady?' he enquired.

Madelaine glanced up into Trevellyn's handsome face and, aware that she no longer had any excuse not to go with him, she slowly rose and placed her gloved hand lightly upon his arm. In silence, she allowed him to lead her out onto the privacy of the balcony.

It was a perfect night. The full moon smiled down upon the lake like a ghostly face checking its reflection in a watery mirror. A light breeze blew across the fields, ruffling the leaves on the nearby trees, and in the distance, Madelaine could just hear the sound of the waves crashing upon the rocks. It was a mournful sound, and involuntarily, she shivered.

'Are you cold, Lady Trent?' Gabriel enquired solicitously.

'Not at all. It was merely the sound of the sea. It is a powerful sound, is it not, my lord?'

'It is, indeed. And a frightening one when one is out in a small boat being blown in towards the rocks.'

Madelaine glanced up at him, but could see only half of his face in the shadowy moonlight. 'Have you found yourself in such a situation, my lord?'

'Once, many years ago, when I was a boy. I had gone out with a friend of mine who, as it turned out, had even less experience of sailing than I. We had rowed out some distance when the weather turned nasty, and the waves began to swell. That was when we discovered, much to our dismay, that we were too close in to shore.'

'Goodness, what happened?'

Gabriel chuckled. 'We were extremely fortunate. I managed to steer the boat into a small channel that led into a cave I knew about. Once we were close enough, we jumped out and scrambled up over the rocks before the waves had opportunity to crush us up against them.'

Madelaine's eyes were wide. 'Were you frightened?'

'Terrified,' Gabriel confessed with a laugh, 'though, of course, we never admitted it to anyone. But to this day, I remember the sound of the waves. Indeed, I do not think I shall ever forget it. But that is not why I brought you out here, Lady Trent.' Gabriel paused, and turning to face her, drew a deep breath. 'I came out here to apologise. I should not have pretended to be Taylor that first day we met. It was wrong of me, and for that I am deeply sorry.'

Madelaine gazed up at him thoughtfully. 'Why did you do it?'

'For two reasons, actually. The first was simply because I wanted to know why the widowed Lady Trent was expecting to see one of my servants. I thought that perhaps Taylor had been up to some kind of mischief, and I was curious to discover what it was. Especially when I learned that it had something to do with someone I hadn't even met.'

'I thought you professed to having implicit trust in your servants,' Madelaine said impishly.

His smile matched hers in liveliness. 'I do. But that is not to say that I know what they are doing every minute of the day—or with whom.'

Madelaine inclined her head in silent acknowledgement of the point. 'And when you realised what it was I wanted to see Taylor about, and that we were, in fact, talking about something which concerned you personally, why did you not tell me who you were then?'

'Because I wanted to learn more about the widowed Lady Trent before I revealed my own identity,' Gabriel confessed.

Madelaine frowned. 'But why? And why did you feel you had to do it in the guise of a servant?'

'Lady Trent, I may live a long way from London, but I know something of what goes on there. I wanted to know why a beautiful young widow would come all the way to Cornwall, when she was reputed to lead such an...active social life in London.'

Madelaine frowned. 'An active social life?'

'Indeed. I know that since you have emerged from mourning, you have been approached by any number of gentlemen, all of whom claim to have lost their hearts to you, when in fact all they really want is a chance to get at your late husband's money.'

Madelaine was thankful for the darkness which hid her flaming cheeks. 'You certainly do not mince words, my lord.'

'No, because I see no merit in it. I know all too well how it feels to be courted solely for one's money, or social standing, Lady Trent. In that, our situations are not all that different.'

'Dear me. Am I to assume that you even know the identity of the gentlemen in question?'

'One of them I can claim an acquaintance with. The others I know by name or reputation.'

Upon hearing this, Madelaine felt thoroughly discomfited. 'I am almost afraid to ask what else you know of me, my lord,' she said. 'Given such an in-depth knowledge of my life, I fear you might be persuaded to tell me…what I ate for breakfast this morning.'

Gabriel threw back his head and laughed. 'Alas, I fear I am not that well informed about you, Lady Trent. I suspect I would have to place spies at Pengarron to discover such intimate details about your everyday life—'

Abruptly, Gabriel broke off. The statement had been intended innocently enough, and yet he was astonished by the realisation that he *wanted* to know the more intimate details of her life. He *wanted* to sit across from Madelaine Trent and see what she ate for breakfast. But that was ridiculous. It wasn't Madelaine Trent he wanted. It was her house.

Wasn't it?

'Lord Trevellyn?'

Gabriel turned to look at her—and was astonished to discover that he was no longer sure what he wanted any more. 'Forgive me, Lady Trent, my thoughts were else-where. You were saying?'

Madelaine heard the sudden reserve in his voice and wondered at its cause. A moment ago they had been en-joying a laugh together. Now, there was almost…a wari-ness in his tone.

'I said, that…I understand what it is to be aware of one's true source of attraction to another person. And, yes, I think I can understand why you might have wished to be some-one else. In truth, there have been many times since Ed-ward's death when I have felt the same way.' Madelaine's smile turned wistful. 'I constantly find myself questioning what people say to me, especially gentlemen who seek to know me better. I am well aware that there are many men in need of a rich wife and, after a while, it becomes difficult to know who is speaking the truth and who is lying.'

Gabriel could see that her confession was heartfelt, and knowing of his own duplicity with regard to Pengarron, he experienced a sharp stab of guilt. What would she say, he wondered, were she to learn that *he* was after something of hers as well, albeit something that he was more than willing to pay for, and handsomely?

'I should not have lied to you, Lady Trent, no matter what my perceived justification for doing so,' Gabriel said quietly, aware of the confusion in his own mind. 'And again, for that, I apologise. I had no wish to deceive you, nor to embarrass or to hurt you. I hope you can find it in your heart to accept my apology and to forgive me.'

Madelaine felt an impish desire to tease him further, but when she saw how serious was the expression in his eyes, she abruptly changed her mind. 'Yes, my lord, I will for-give you. I cannot abide lies, but in this instance, I believe I understand the motivation behind it. And perhaps it is just as well. I doubt I would have ordered the Earl of Trevellyn about in so high-handed a manner.'

Gabriel heard the laughter in her voice and smiled somewhat ruefully. 'Perhaps the Earl did deserve a bit of a set down. It certainly gave him an appreciation for the way Taylor must have felt upon occasion. Perhaps it will even serve to teach him to address his staff more temperately in the future.'

Madelaine laughed softly. 'I am relieved there was something to be gained by the experience, my lord.'

Gabriel gazed down into the sweetness of the face turned up to his, and suddenly felt a fierce desire to kiss her—an urge he knew he dare not give in to. Because he wasn't Taylor any more. He was the Earl of Trevellyn, and, as such, a gentleman bound by Society's rules. He would not trespass on her again. Instead, he reached for her hand, and raising it to his lips, pressed a long and lingering kiss against the back of it.

Madelaine drew in her breath, aware of a painful constriction in her throat as she watched him. She felt the warmth of his mouth through the silky fabric of her glove, and saw the look in his eyes when they finally rose to meet hers above it. 'My lord—' she whispered huskily. 'I think perhaps we should…return.'

Gabriel sighed, and reluctantly let go of her hand. 'Yes, your aunt will no doubt be wondering at our delay.'

Madelaine nodded, wishing that her heart was not beating quite so fast. It made it very difficult to speak to him in a normal tone of voice. 'Thank you, Lord Trevellyn.'

And as they had come on to the balcony, so did Madelaine place her hand once again upon Lord Trevellyn's arm and allow him to lead her back inside.

Madelaine lingered longer abed the next morning than was usual for her; not because she was tired, but because she kept going over in her mind the events of the previous evening. And, in particular, to what had happened between herself and Lord Trevellyn on the balcony.

Madelaine knew that there was no logical reason for his brief caress to have startled her so. After all, she was hardly a green girl, forced to profess ignorance about what went on between a man and a woman. She had been married for six years, and she knew what took place in the bedchamber. But she knew that she had never experienced with Edward the kind of fire Gabriel's brief touch had ignited in her last night.

She closed her eyes as the strange fluttery feelings began again. She recalled the manner in which Lord Trevellyn had raised her hand to his lips and kissed it, remembering the look in his eyes when he had straightened—and the quickening of her pulse when he had spoken to her in that low, husky voice. But…what did it all mean? She was willing to admit that she was…attracted to Lord Trevellyn, but did she dare entertain hopes that he might return those feelings? Certainly, the apologies he had offered her for his conduct had been both sincere and believable, and his actions in regards to Diggs positively admirable.

But did that mean that he held her in any special affection? Or were his actions towards her merely those of a gentleman towards a lady?

After finishing her chocolate, Madelaine slowly dressed and went down to the breakfast parlour. She found her aunt already seated at the table, and looking quite splendid in a flowing black silk robe that was embroidered with bright peacocks and other unusual birds.

'My word, Chloe, you do look exotic this morning. Wherever did you find such a marvellous creation?'

'At a mercer's in Cheapside,' Chloe admitted, spreading

a thick dollop of orange marmalade on her piece of toast. 'He gave it to me for next to nothing after I showed him the pattern I had in mind. It does elicit the strangest reactions from the staff, though.' She broke off, as Berkeley, at that moment coming into the room for the first time, stopped abruptly on the threshold and stared at her outright, lending immediate credence to her statement. 'There, you see?' Chloe whispered to her niece. Then, to the butler, said, 'Ah, good, fresh coffee. Would you be so good as to pour me a cup, Berkeley?'

The butler abruptly closed his mouth and nodded. 'Yes, Mrs Merrill.'

Madelaine's shoulders began to shake, and as soon as the butler departed, she burst into laughter. 'Chloe, you are incorrigible!'

'Yes, I know, my dear. Speaking of incorrigible, what is your opinion of your new neighbour now that all the... misconceptions have been cleared up?'

Madelaine concentrated on spooning sugar into her coffee. 'I find him to be a most...interesting gentleman.'

'Interesting!' Chloe wrinkled her nose. 'What an insipid way of describing him, Maddie—I was quite swept away by his charm. And those shoulders! Did you see how well his jacket became him? Cut by Weston himself, I'll vow.' She shrugged her own silk-clad shoulders eloquently. 'I cannot credit Lady Constance having preferred a purse-proud coxcomb like Winchelsea over such a man, whether he be a Duke or not. But there, I suppose there is no accounting for other people's taste.'

Madelaine's fingers stilled. *Lady Constance had been courted by Lord Trevellyn?* She had not considered that his affections might already be spoken for.

'Where did you hear that, Chloe?'

'From Lord Keswick. He informed me of it over cards.

PLAY "LUCKY 7" AND GET

FOUR FREE GIFTS

HOW TO PLAY:

1. With a coin, carefully scratch off the silver box at the right. Then check the claim char
   to see what we have for you – **FREE BOOKS** and **GIFTS** – **ALL YOURS! ALL FREE**

2. When you return this card, we'll send you specially selected Mills & Boon® romances
   from the Historical Romance™ series and the gifts you qualify for. These books have a
   cover price of £2.99 each, but they are yours to keep absolutely free.

3. We hope that after receiving
   your free books you'll want to
   remain a subscriber. But the
   choice is yours – to continue or

NO COST! NO OBLIGATION TO BUY!
NO PURCHASE NECESSARY!

The Mills & Boon Reader Service™ — Here's how it works

Accepting free books and gifts places you under no obligation to buy anything. You may keep the books and gifts and return the despatch marked "cancel." If we do not hear from you, about a month later we'll send you 4 brand new novels, and invoice you for just £2.99* each. That's the complete price —there is no extra charge for postage and packing. You may cancel at any time, otherwise every month we'll send you 4 more books, which you may either purchase or return to us, the choice is yours.

*Terms and prices subject to change without notice.

Mills & Boon Reader Service
FREEPOST CN81
CROYDON
CR9 3WZ

NO
STAMP
NEEDED

Apparently, he is a great friend and confidante of Lord Trevellyn's, and he told me that Lord Trevellyn held the lady in some affection. There was even talk of them marrying.'

'Did he say whether…an offer was ever made?'

'No, though Lord Keswick believes that one would have been, had the lady not chosen to accept Winchelsea's offer instead. By all accounts, Lady Constance treated Lord Trevellyn abominably,' Chloe whispered. 'She encouraged his suit, even professing to more than one person that she was in love with him, only to shift her affections to Winchelsea when he came into his title and inheritance.'

'A shallow game, indeed,' Madelaine observed. 'I am not well acquainted with the lady, but I would not have thought her so fickle.'

'No doubt she was impressed by the Gillis fortune. Winchelsea was the sole heir, you know,' Chloe advised her. 'And, of course, by marrying him she becomes a duchess, rather than a mere countess. Obviously she felt those more important considerations than love.'

'I wonder if she ever felt any true affection for Lord Trevellyn at all,' Madelaine said, feeling a swift surge of anger towards Lady Constance, and one of compassion for Trevellyn. 'If she could switch her affections so easily, I venture to say all she was ever after *was* a title.'

'Well, she would certainly not be the first lady to be motivated by such things, Maddie. After all, everyone knows that marriages are made for the betterment of social or financial standing, rather than in the hopes of finding true love. If one is fortunate enough to feel some affection for their chosen spouse, it is something to be thankful for, but not, I think, to be expected.'

Madelaine sat quietly for a moment, recalled to the rather cynical remark Lord Trevellyn had made last night regarding the tendency of the female sex to pursue a man for his wealth or social standing. No wonder he had made such a comment. Here was a perfect example of it. A woman had claimed to love him, and yet, in the end, had found his wealth and title insufficient.

What a foolish girl, Madelaine thought disparagingly. She would have taken Trevellyn over a hundred Winchelseas.

'Well, 'tis no wonder Lady Bourne aspires to a match between Lord Trevellyn and Phoebe,' Chloe was saying. 'I should not mind having a son-in-law like that in the family myself!'

Madelaine glanced at her aunt and laughed softly. 'Chloe, you truly say the most outrageous things.'

'I only say what other people think, my dear. Fortunately, given my age and the fact that I am a widow, I usually manage to get away with it. Still, you must own that Lord Trevellyn cuts quite a dash—even as a steward. Now I can understand why you looked so bemused every time you were with him.'

Madelaine's cheeks burned. 'I was not...bemused.'

'Of course you were—which is why I was so worried about you at the time. I did not think that you would seriously consider such a *mésalliance*, Maddie, but I could see that you were attracted to the man. And, indeed, what lady would not be? But you have not yet told me if you found his explanation with regard to his deception credible? He must have given you a rather lengthy one,' Chloe said, her eyes sparkling wickedly. 'The two of you were out on the balcony for some time viewing the breathtaking sight of the lake in the moonlight.'

The colour in Madelaine's cheeks deepened. 'Lord Trevellyn was merely anxious that I be acquainted with *all* of the circumstances surrounding his conduct.'

Chloe lifted her cup and regarded her niece over the rim. 'Then you found his explanation satisfactory?'

Madelaine reached for a piece of toast. 'It was presented in a manner that was…quite acceptable to me, yes.'

There was no mistaking the laughter in Chloe's eyes now. 'Mmm, given the colour in your cheeks when you returned, my dear, I rather imagined it was.'

At Carew, Gabriel stood by the window in the library and gazed out towards Pengarron. He could just see the grey stone chimneys poking above the distant trees, and the green hills which surrounded the house. Not surprisingly, his thoughts turned to its lovely owner, and to what she might be doing this morning.

Gabriel smiled as he recalled the rather embarrassed comment Madelaine had made the previous evening with regard to his knowledge of her breakfast habits. Would that he did know such things about her, he thought ruefully. Perhaps, if he did, he would know better how to go about resolving this other situation in which she figured so prominently.

Gabriel turned and walked back towards the large mahogany desk. His smile faded as his glance fell on the two letters which had arrived just that morning, and which had put him in his present mood of consternation. The one was from Madelaine; the other from his lawyer in London. Both letters disturbed him, though for entirely different reasons.

He picked up his lawyer's first.

My Lord:

Further to the matter concerning the purchase of Pengarron, please be advised that I have been in contact with Lady Trent's solicitors, and wish to advise you that your offer will soon be presented to the lady

for her review. They expressed their regrets for the
delay in reaching their client, but they were not aware
that the lady had removed to the country. I will contact
you again, as soon as I have had a reply from them…

Gabriel read the letter again before tossing it back on to
the desk. Then, he picked up the second letter which had
been delivered by hand no more than twenty minutes ago.

Dear Lord Trevellyn:
    My aunt and I would both like to thank you for your
gracious reception of us last evening. We enjoyed ourselves immensely, and I am relieved that the confusion
with regard to a number of things has, at last, been
cleared up. Having said that, I wonder if I might trouble you for the address of the lady who is tending the
little doe. A Mrs Abbey, I believe you said? I should
very much like to see how the animal is recovering.
If you would be kind enough to send back a note,
giving me some idea as to where she lives, I shall have
my groom accompany me. I trust you will understand
that I would not presume upon your time in any other
way, having now been made aware of the truth of your
identity.
    Thanking you again for your most generous hospi-
tality, I remain,
                           Yours most sincerely, Madelaine Trent

Gabriel sighed, and dropped Madelaine's letter on to the
desk next to the lawyer's. Unbidden, the memory of a pair
of soft grey eyes above dusky rose lips came to his mind,
and he knew a moment of grave indecision. This is what
he had wanted, wasn't it? To purchase Pengarron so that
he could give it to John and Cassandra?

Gabriel plunged his hands into the pockets of his robe and returned to his study of the scenery beyond the window. Of course it was what he wanted. And based on the discussions they had had over dinner last night, he knew that Madelaine was not ignorant of the fact that it made sense for her to sell it. Certainly Mrs Merrill and Lord Keswick had been happy enough to share their opinions on the subject.

The question was, why the hell wasn't *he* more pleased that it was all about to come to pass?

'You know damn well why,' Gabriel muttered aloud. And he did. Keswick had expressed the sentiments perfectly. He was having second thoughts about the whole thing—and he no longer wished to see Madelaine return to London.

It was a stunning revelation—especially given that it was only days away from his offer being presented to her. But Gabriel knew it to be the truth. He didn't want her to go. What's more, he wasn't even convinced that Madelaine *wished* to sell the house. Yes, she had looked to him for his advice, but that was probably because *he* had been the one to bring it up in the first place.

But if she did not wish to sell it, what would she say when she received an anonymous offer to purchase it? Would she be surprised that the buyer had wished to remain anonymous? Or angry because he had chosen not to make himself known?

More importantly, what would Madelaine think if she was to discover that *he* was the party behind it? How would she react when faced with the knowledge that, secretly, he had *wanted* her to sell the house so that he could buy it for another member of his family?

Gabriel knew the answer to that one all too well. She would believe that he had lied to her again. It was as simple as that. The fact that he had not offered an opinion as to the wisdom of selling the house would not spare him her censure. Indeed, the realisation that she would see it as a second deceit, and therefore be even less likely to forgive him, made the situation even worse.

The question was now, how did he go about fulfilling his promise to John and Cassandra, and not lose the respect and possibly the affection of Madelaine Trent—both of which were starting to mean far more to him than he cared to admit?

There was no simple answer to that question. And, with a decidedly heavy heart, Gabriel put the letters into the desk drawer and left the room.

Chapter Nine

Much to Madelaine's surprise, it was not a written reply which Lord Trevellyn presented her with little more than an hour after she had sent her own letter requesting his assistance, but a personal one. In the midst of finishing off some correspondence to friends in London, she was informed by Berkeley that his lordship had called and was waiting to see her.

Madelaine quickly set aside her letters and bid Berkeley show the Earl up.

'Lady Trent,' Gabriel said moments later as he presented himself at the door.

Madelaine rose and curtsied gracefully. 'Lord Trevellyn.'

'I hope I am not calling upon you too early.'

'Not at all. But I hope that your arrival here was not motivated solely by my letter.'

'It was indeed. I have come to offer my services as escort to Mrs Abbey's cottage.'

Flattered, but at the same time dismayed that he would go to such lengths to accommodate her, Madelaine said, 'My lord, it is exceedingly generous of you to offer your time, but surely you have more important things to attend to.'

Gabriel's eyes took on a devilish sparkle. 'It did not trouble you to bother my steward for such things, Lady Trent. Am I such an unworthy replacement?'

A hot wave of colour suffused Madelaine's cheeks. 'Certainly not. Nor did I mean to imply that you were.'

'Then why do you take exception to my offer?'

'I do not take exception to it, precisely,' Madelaine equivocated, even as a smile tugged unwillingly at her lips. 'It is simply that I did not wish to…disturb you.'

'If I am not disturbed, why should you be? Besides, I am not as heartless as you might think. I, too, should like to see how the little creature goes on.'

Madelaine sent him a bemused glance. It seemed that no matter what she said, Trevellyn had an answer for it. And given that she truly was pleased by the fact that he wished to accompany her, why *was* she arguing with him in the first place?

Little more than fifteen minutes later, Madelaine appeared at the front steps of the house. She was elegantly attired in a dark grey habit, the froth of white lace at the cuffs and throat serving to soften the military styling of the short jacket, while the cinched waistband of the full skirt drew attention to her slender waist and gently curving hips.

Gabriel did not even trouble to conceal his admiration at her appearance. 'I must say, it is a pity that we shall only be travelling to Mrs Abbey's cottage, Lady Trent. I dare say you would garner quite a few stares were you to ride through Hyde Park looking like that.'

Madelaine blushed with pleasure, but strove for a breezy tone. 'I would have thought such elegance *de rigueur* when riding out with the Earl of Trevellyn, no matter what the destination. Indeed, you would scarce discredit Mr Brummell himself, were the two of you ever to be seen keeping company.'

Gabriel chuckled deep in his throat. 'Thank you, Lady Trent, but as the gentleman was far more partial to the company of Alvaney and Pierrepointe than he was to mine, even before he fled to the Continent, I fear there is little chance of that ever happening. Shall we go?'

They set out for Mrs Abbey's cottage in a mood of complete charity. The sun shone down from the heights of a cloudless blue sky while the air was filled with the scent of the nearby sea. Madelaine smiled in contentment as she gazed at the breathtaking scenery all around her.

'You look remarkably pleased this morning, Lady Trent,' Gabriel observed as they walked their horses side by side. Her groom followed at a discreet distance behind.

'I am, Lord Trevellyn. I cannot recall having seen such a lovely day this many months. Is the weather here always so pleasant?'

'Of course,' Gabriel told her with a grin. 'We Cornish men would not have it any other way. But I am glad to hear you speak of it so well. Tell me, is Mrs Merrill enjoying her stay at Pengarron as much as you seem to be?'

'I think she is enjoying it a great deal more than she expected to,' Madelaine replied with a twinkle in her eye. 'My aunt pursues a rather active social life in London and had only just returned from a sojourn in Scotland before we left to come here. I think she was expecting to find Cornwall rather lacking in social activities.'

'Well, I admit there are not the elaborate garden parties and soirées to be had here as there are in London,' Gabriel acknowledged, 'but I, for one, am glad. I grow weary of the platitudes and posturing one is expected to do at such functions.' He paused for a moment before saying, 'Mrs

Merrill is a charming woman. I am surprised that she has not remarried.'

'My aunt was very much in love with her husband, Lord Trevellyn,' Madelaine told him sadly, 'and I think that, after he died, she lost interest in such things. But I do hold out hopes that she will marry again.'

'Is there, perhaps, a gentleman whom Mrs Merrill holds in esteem?'

'I believe she harbours a tendre for the Duke of Kenfield,' Madelaine admitted, 'though she prefers that few know of it.'

'Kenfield is a good man,' Gabriel commented with approval. 'He has been a friend of mine these many years. And it would be an excellent match for her. Does he return her regard?'

Madelaine sighed. 'I had begun to believe so, my lord, though I am not so sure any more. His Grace has always appeared to enjoy my aunt's company, and has sought her out on more than one occasion. But he has yet to say anything that would give her reason to believe that his affection was of a serious manner. It is highly provoking.' Suddenly aware that Chloe might not appreciate her discussing such a personal matter with a total stranger, Madelaine abruptly changed the subject. 'But tell me, my lord, this Mrs Abbey we are going to visit…is she trained in the area of animal care?'

'Not by any recognised sources, no,' Gabriel replied with a smile. 'Her methods are rather curious. Many of the villagers believe her to be a witch.'

Madelaine started. 'A *witch*!'

'There is no cause for alarm, Lady Trent, I can assure you that she is not. She is merely an eccentric old woman who possesses a remarkable knowledge of plants and their healing properties. I believe she learned a great deal about such things from her grandmother. But there is no denying that she has an uncanny way with animals. It is quite remarkable to see the way they behave around her.'

'Perhaps she has a touch of gypsy blood,' Madelaine suggested. 'My late husband used to say that the gypsies were remarkably close to their animals, and that they could train them to do things in a way that we could not.'

Gabriel kept his eyes fixed on the distant sea. 'You speak of Lord Trent with affection and respect, Lady Trent. You were happy, then, in your first marriage?'

Madelaine hesitated. Apart from Chloe, she had never spoken to any one of her relationship with Edward, and she found it strange to be discussing it now with Lord Trevellyn. 'Yes, I was happy. Edward was very kind to me.'

'I assume by the difference in your ages that it was an arranged marriage?'

'My father believed it to be an advantageous match and, as I was very fond of Edward, I saw no reason to object to it taking place.' Madelaine stroked her horse's neck absently. 'Did you know my late husband, Lord Trevellyn?'

'Sadly, I did not. As you probably already know, Lord Trent spent very little time at Pengarron, and I spent very little time in London. I believe that on the one occasion he was here, I was away fighting in France.'

'In France!' Madelaine's head came up quickly. 'Oh, but I had no idea. Were you there long?'

Gabriel's mouth twisted ruefully. 'Long enough to sustain injuries which forced my early return to England.'

Madelaine's brow furrowed at the note of self-recrimination in his voice. 'You sound bitter, my lord. Surely you should be grateful that there was anything left of you to be sent back.'

Gabriel guided the stallion around a deep pothole. 'I would have been more grateful had it had been my younger brother who was sent home, Lady Trent, rather than myself.'

'You have a younger brother? Forgive me, my lord, for some reason I had begun to think you an only child. Does he live in the area?'

'No. John and Cassandra were only married a few days before they went to France. There was no time for them to set up an establishment of their own.'

'Your brother's wife went with him to France?' Madelaine asked, clearly surprised. 'How unusual.'

'My sister-in-law has nursing experience and bravely volunteered to go,' Gabriel explained. 'But John was wounded in the fighting and has been waiting to be sent home. And, as Cassie is expecting their first child, it cannot be soon enough for me.'

'Oh, but how wonderful, my lord. Your brother coming home and you to be an uncle. You must be well pleased.'

'I confess, I am, but more than that, I am relieved,' Gabriel admitted. 'John and I have always been close, and I will be glad to have him back on English soil again after all this.'

'Were his injuries serious?'

Gabriel's eyes went back to a place she could not see. 'Not serious enough to warrant his being sent home, as mine were, but enough to keep him out of the front lines.' He uttered a short, harsh laugh. 'I suppose I should be grateful for that. I never forgave myself for being the one to go, while he was the one who had to stay behind.'

Madelaine heard the guilt and the anger in his voice, and tried to understand its source. 'My lord, surely you are not blaming yourself for the fact that your injuries were more grievous than your brother's? If the situations were reversed, would you think your brother justified in blaming himself for your misfortune?'

'Of course not, but he was my responsibility!'

'Not unless you were his commanding officer.'

Gabriel sighed heavily. 'I was, until the day of that wretched assault. After I was wounded, they sent in a replacement for me, a Colonel Philip Argyle. Argyle's a good man, but he and I differ on matters of military strategy. I would never have given the order to attack the way he did. He wasn't prepared for the enemy's numbers, and his stratagem resulted in half the regiment being injured, my brother included.'

'But that is not your fault, surely you can see that, my lord?' Madelaine repeated quietly. 'You cannot accept blame for something over which you had no control. That accountability must lie with Colonel Argyle. I am sure that your brother—and the rest of the men in his regiment— know that.'

Madelaine waited expectantly for his answer, but when none came, decided it might be better to change the subject. 'You said that your brother and his wife did not have a chance to establish themselves before they left for France. Are they intending to live in London when they return?'

'I think they would both prefer to live in Cornwall. John grew up here, and he loves the land as I do. Unfortunately, they haven't the wherewithal to buy anything of their own. After he was shot, John wrote and asked if he and Cassandra could stay at Carew until he got on his feet again. Naturally, I said yes.'

'Of course you would, and I am sure that you will be as glad of their company as they are of yours. And I have no doubts but that you will help them in any way you can, once they do return.'

There was nothing in her words that should have made him feel guilty, Gabriel reflected dimly. After all, he was only trying to buy the lady's house so that his brother and his wife could have a home to live in, and in which to raise a family. Surely there was nothing underhanded in that?

Why, then, did he feel as guilty as sin when he looked into Lady Trent's eyes and saw nothing but honesty and compassion in them?

'Mrs Abbey's cottage is located just over the next hill,' Gabriel said huskily. 'It will not be much longer now.'

It was as blatant a change in the conversation as Madelaine's had been earlier; for that reason, she did not attempt to engage Lord Trevellyn in conversation again. He suddenly seemed to have withdrawn into himself, sitting rigidly in the saddle in a posture which did not invite comment. Madelaine lapsed into silence herself, not sure how to break through the sudden wall of reserve the man beside her had erected. It was quite clear to her that Lord Trevellyn suffered a great deal over the entire matter. And she found herself wondering if even time could erase the guilt that he so obviously harboured over his brother's injuries.

They arrived at the quaint woodland cottage belonging to Mrs Abbey soon after. To Madelaine's delight—and astonishment—the little doe was already showing signs of improvement. Her back leg was securely fastened in a home-made splint, and she was actually managing to hobble about, albeit not for any length of time. But her eyes were bright and she accepted the food Mrs Abbey gave to her without hesitation.

With Mrs Abbey herself, Madelaine was thoroughly charmed. She was a woman of indeterminable age—though she looked to be somewhere in her mid-sixties—and had the whitest hair, the blackest eyebrows, and the most piercing blue eyes Madelaine had ever seen. There was a gentle, almost mystical quality about her, and as she moved amongst the animals in her care, Madelaine could indeed see that none of them were afraid of her. They did not run and hide when she approached, or pull away when she was tending to their injuries. It was almost as though they knew that she was trying to help them. Which was fortunate, given that, judging by the number of rudely constructed cages sprinkled around the garden, everyone who found a lost or injured creature brought it to Mrs Abbey for her help.

'Of course, they have no reason to fear me,' Mrs Abbey confided to Madelaine as they wandered through the large garden together. 'They recognise an animal spirit when they see one.'

Madelaine frowned. 'An…animal spirit?'

'Oh, yes, my dear. This is not our first time upon this earth, nor will it be our last,' the old woman said, her bright blue eyes sparkling. 'We travel many times through this life, sometimes as humans, sometimes as creatures of the forest. In my past lives, I have been a woodland creature, just as that little deer is now. And perhaps, in her next life, she will return as a beautiful young woman—like you.'

It was a little too far-fetched for Madelaine to believe, but she smiled politely and tried to steer the conversation back to more normal channels.

'You don't believe me,' Mrs Abbey said with a gentle, knowing smile.

'It is not that I do not believe you, Mrs Abbey,' Madelaine said, not wishing to hurt the old woman's feelings, but not wishing to lie to her either, 'but I confess, I do find the concept a little…difficult to grasp. I have never entertained the idea of…life existing in any other form than that which we live in right now.'

Mrs Abbey's smile grew. 'Sometimes it is good to question the things that you take for granted, Lady Trent. As humans, we tend to become very complacent. We see the same things every day, we believe what we are told, and we seldom question the world all around us. But things are not always what they seem—or people who they pretend to be. And in the end, we have only ourselves to blame when we are caught out.'

The old woman wandered off to tend to a small white rabbit, and Madelaine watched her go, wondering if, perhaps, there was some hidden message in her words. She could not help but feel that Mrs Abbey possessed a wisdom that went far beyond her years and life experience. It had been a very strange conversation indeed.

'So, are you pleased with the progress of your little doe, Lady Trent?' Lord Trevellyn enquired, suddenly appearing at her side.

Madelaine turned and smiled her relief at seeing him. He seemed to have regained his earlier good spirits and, once again, she felt the telltale quickening of her pulse when he smiled down at her. 'Indeed, my lord, I am well pleased. I do not think you could have given her to anyone kinder or more skilled to look after.' Madelaine risked a quick glance up at him, and then just as quickly looked away. 'Mrs Abbey is a remarkable woman.'

Gabriel nodded. 'She is, indeed. More than once I have seen her work miracles with her animals. The only ones she has failed to save are the ones who reach her too late.'

Madelaine walked towards the extensive herb garden, aware that the famous Culpepper himself was hardly likely to have had one more extensive. 'She has some... interesting ideas.'

'I take it you are referring to her belief that we have all travelled through this life before?' Gabriel replied mildly, 'and that she has lived some of those lives in...other forms?'

Madelaine glanced at him in astonishment. 'Do you not find the idea…bizarre?'

Gabriel inhaled a long, deep breath and slowly let it out again. 'I prefer to call it…intriguing. There are many things we do not understand, Lady Trent. Certainly, it is not the kind of belief advocated by the Church of England, but I like to keep an open mind to all possibilities.'

The fact that the mighty Lord Trevellyn would even entertain the idea caused Madelaine to laugh out loud. 'Well, you surprise me again, Lord Trevellyn. I would not have believed that a salt-of-the-earth Cornish man would hold with such curious ideas.'

'Ah, but we Cornish men are very much in tune with nature,' Gabriel reminded her. 'We live our lives in close proximity with its most powerful forces—the wind and the sea. Who am I to say that such things are not possible? After all, at one time, man thought that the world was flat too.'

Completely at a loss for a suitable reply, Madelaine just shook her head and walked on. The man seemed to have an uncanny knack for rendering her speechless—in whatever guise he chose to assume!

'What a remarkable woman Mrs Abbey is,' Madelaine commented to her aunt as they strolled past the shops in the village later that same day. 'I wish you could have seen her. The animals seemed to have no fear of her at all.'

'Remarkable, indeed,' Chloe replied. 'But I am delighted to hear that your little deer is doing so well. I know how upset you were the day you came back from the woods.'

Madelaine smiled and pretended to study a bolt of fabric in the shop window they were passing. She could hardly tell her aunt that a great deal of her distress had originated with the man she had believed to be a steward—and her reaction to him.

'Lady Trent! Mrs Merrill!'

Madelaine looked up, roused from her thoughts by the high-pitched voice of Lady Bourne, and sighed. Beside her, Chloe groaned. 'Oh, Lord, not the Bourne trio again.'

'Now, Chloe, you mustn't be like that,' Madelaine whispered. 'At least, not about all of them. I quite like Prunella.'

'Yes, I grant you, the elder Miss Bourne has more redeeming qualities than the younger, but…upon my word, Maddie, whatever has her mother dressed her up in this time? She looks like a beanpole over which someone has draped a sack and then tied it around the middle with a string.'

It was hardly a flattering description, but it was certainly accurate. The drab, shapeless gown Prunella was wearing did absolutely nothing for her complexion or for her figure. If anything, it seemed to detract from what tolerable good looks the girl did have.

'Do you know, it really is a shame, Chloe,' Madelaine said quietly, 'In the right clothes, and with a more suitable hair style, I think Prunella Bourne could be quite attractive.'

'Yes, I suppose she does have some potential. Her complexion is lovely, and she certainly has very fine cheekbones.' Chloe eyed the girl thoughtfully. 'I wonder…'

'My dear Lady Trent, Mrs Merrill, how are you this fine afternoon?' Lady Bourne greeted them effusively.

'Very well, thank you, Lady Bourne. And you?'

'Splendid. Come, girls, say your hellos to Lady Trent and Mrs Merrill.'

Both girls dutifully did as they were instructed, after which Lady Bourne turned back to Madelaine. 'And how are you finding the shops, Lady Trent? I dare say you miss the selection of materials and finery to be had in London?'

Madelaine smiled. 'As I brought all the clothes I intended to wear with me, Lady Bourne, I have not really noticed a shortfall.'

'No, of course not. Naturally, I also have a modiste in London who makes all of my own gowns, as well as Phoebe's,' Lady Bourne said quickly, not wanting Lady Trent to think that she made do with the talents of a local seamstress.

'And what of your eldest daughter's clothes, Lady Bourne?' Chloe enquired mildly. 'Where do you have those made?'

The slight note of sarcasm in Chloe's voice did not go undetected, and Lady Bourne flushed. 'You must understand, Mrs Merrill, Prunella has never cared overly much for clothes. Certainly not in the way my Phoebe does.' Lady Bourne drew the older woman to one side. 'Poor girl, bit of a Long Meg, you see, and it does not seem to matter what I dress her in. She just isn't able to carry it off as well as her sister. And it seems a shame to waste on one what could be used to such better advantage on the other, if you take my meaning, Mrs Merrill.'

Chloe nodded sagely. 'Oh, yes, I take your meaning quite well, Lady Bourne.'

The quiet of the afternoon was suddenly shattered by the clatter of a coach and four travelling briskly through the centre of town. There was no crest upon the door, but there was no mistaking the quality of the horses which drew it. It was piled high with luggage and it did not stop, but passed swiftly on and continued along the road in the direction of Carew. Madelaine was given little more than a fleeting glimpse of a young man and a lovely young woman inside the carriage before it passed them by and rounded the corner, disappearing out of sight.

'My word, I wonder who that was?' Madelaine turned,

surprised to see Lady Bourne staring after the coach with her mouth open. 'Do you know them, Lady Bourne?'

Phoebe tugged at her mother's sleeve. 'Yes, did you recognise them, Mama? For I declare, the gentleman inside was ever so handsome.'

Lady Bourne's mouth snapped shut. 'You needn't be casting your eyes on that one, my dear. That was his wife in the carriage with him.'

'Whose wife, Mama?' Prunella enquired softly.

'John Carew.' Lady Bourne turned back to Madelaine with the expression of one in possession of a tasty bit of news. 'No doubt there shall be some celebrating up at the lord's house tonight. The Earl of Trevellyn's younger brother and wife have come home at last!'

Gabriel had just returned from a lengthy ride along the cliffs when word reached him that John and Cassandra had arrived home. Tossing the reins to the waiting groom, he ran up to the house to find his younger brother already in the front hall and supervising the unloading of their luggage. 'John!'

Pandemonium momentarily ceased as the younger Carew turned and caught sight of his brother. 'Gabriel!' His face broke into a glorious smile, and covering the distance in a few long strides, the brothers embraced heartily. 'Gabriel! By God, it's good to see you again.'

'And you, John,' Gabriel said huskily, clapping his brother affectionately on the back. 'But what are you doing home so early? I hadn't expected you for another three weeks yet.'

'Colonel Argyle pulled some strings and had me switched with another chap,' John told him. 'There was no time to write and let you know about the change in plans. I hope it is not inconvenient.'

'Inconvenient! You young cub, of course it's not inconvenient. I have been waiting for this day for months. But where is Cassandra?'

'Here I am, Gabriel,' said a soft voice from the doorway behind them.

Turning around, Gabriel caught sight of Cassandra Carew coming out of the morning room. Her lovely face bore little evidence of the rigours of the long, tiring trip she and John had just completed, nor of the gruelling months which must have gone before. She was as she had ever been; smiling, serene, a woman of admirable courage and indomitable spirit.

Gabriel stepped forward and embraced his sister-in-law carefully, but with great affection. 'Cassie, my dear, welcome home.'

Cassandra kissed his cheek, and then laughed at his delicate handling of her. 'It is quite all right, Gabriel, I shan't break,' she assured him. 'I have been through a good deal worse than this.'

'She is right about that,' John said, grinning. 'I am beginning to think that nothing short of an explosion is going to unsettle that child.'

Gabriel turned back to regard his sister-in-law with a somewhat sheepish expression. 'You will have to forgive me, Cassie, I've not had much experience with this type of thing.'

'Nor have I,' John said ruefully, 'but I am learning very quickly.'

Suddenly perceiving the strain on his brother's face, Gabriel immediately took over. 'Right, lad, that's all the work you're going to do. Go into the drawing room, both of you. I shall be there in a moment.'

True to his word, in less than five minutes, Gabriel had seen to the removal of the baggage, dispatched a flurry of maids to have rooms prepared, and sent orders to Cook to prepare a late lunch. That done, he hurried to the drawing room to join his brother and sister-in-law.

'Your rooms will be ready shortly, and I have ordered refreshments,' Gabriel said. 'In the interim, I have asked Parker to bring tea. I hope that is all right? Tea, I mean.'

'A cup of tea would be wonderful, Gabriel, thank you,' Cassie said gratefully. 'You have no idea how much I have been longing for a good cup of English tea again. John, will you have some?'

John had his eyes closed and was leaning his head back against the settee. 'No, thank you, my dear, not just at the moment.'

Gabriel observed the younger man carefully. In the excitement of their arrival, he had not noticed the sling around his brother's neck, nor the pinched look around his mouth, evidence of a man in pain. 'Perhaps a brandy, eh, stripling?' he offered quietly.

John opened his eyes and fixed his brother with a grateful look. 'Yes, I think a brandy would be rather welcome right now, Gabriel, thank you.'

Gabriel got up to pour the drink himself. 'Well, you do not appear to have lost too much weight, lad. Cassie obviously took good care of you.'

John nodded and managed a weak laugh. 'I have no idea what I would have done without her. Ah, thank you, brother,' John said, taking the glass from Gabriel's fingers and swallowing a generous mouthful. He gasped slightly as the fiery liquid burned its way down his throat, and then eased himself back against the cushions, flinching slightly at the effort. 'By God, those Frenchies know how to make damn fine brandy, if they know nothing else. As I was about to say, now that we are home, Cassandra is not going to do another thing. I intend to start taking…very good care of…my wife.'

The strain was evident on John's face, and Gabriel quickly glanced at Cassandra, catching the look of concern on her face. 'It seems to me that you *both* need some taking care of,' he said gruffly. 'I shall send word to Dr Granger and ask him to call at his earliest convenience.'

'Have him here see to Cassie, by all means,' John said, 'but there is no need to fuss on my account.'

'There is every need,' Gabriel replied tersely. 'You are not well.'

'I think it would be a good idea that you see him, John,' Cassandra put in quietly. 'Colonel Argyle said that you were to have a thorough examination upon your return to England, you know he did.'

'Indeed. I can hardly have people coming to call and you not well enough to receive them,' Gabriel said, his teasing voice hiding the depth of his concern. He was anxious to talk to Cassandra alone and find out exactly how serious John's condition really was, but for the moment it would have to wait. 'In fact, I want both of you in prime form for the ball I intend to give in honour of your return.'

'A ball!' Cassandra's lovely green eyes deepened with pleasure. 'Oh, Gabriel, how exciting. I have not had a chance to dance in—'

'Dance!' John protested. 'Surely you do not intend to dance in your condition, madam!'

'Oh, fiddlesticks, John, I am perfectly well, and perfectly able to dance,' Cassandra retorted cheerfully. 'Having a baby is a normal part of a woman's life, and I certainly do not intend to hide myself away for the next five months simply because I am increasing. Besides, I am not showing all that much yet, and I am confident that I could have a gown made to conceal what little swelling there is.'

'Good Lord,' John said weakly.

Gabriel listened to the exchange with amusement. He was relieved to see that Cassandra had not changed in the time she had been away. She was as forthright and as sensible as she had been before she left. 'Well, I take it that's settled. Ah, good, here is your tea, Cassie, my dear. How long before lunch is served, Parker?'

'No more than twenty minutes, my lord. Cook asked me to tell you that she is preparing one of Master John's favourite pies. I have taken the liberty of setting lunch in the small dining room.'

'Thank you, Parker, that will do very nicely.'

'And thank Mrs Dawson for her trouble, Parker,' John spoke up. 'Tell her I shall be down to see her later.'

'Very good, sir.'

The butler bowed and withdrew. When the door closed behind him, Gabriel cleared his throat. 'Before we go in to lunch, there is something that I would like to tell you. Both of you.'

'Is something wrong, Gabriel?' John asked quickly.

Gabriel saw the look of concern on their faces, and smiled. 'Nothing at all. Quite the opposite, in fact. I know that you are concerned, John, about staying here at Carew. Some nonsense about crowding your older brother, or some such thing.'

'Well, you are a highly eligible bachelor after all,' John replied good-naturedly. 'And I should not like to think that our presence here would put a damper on that high-flying style of yours.'

'High-flying style? 'Pon my word, brother, I fear you are in for something of a shock. I have become quite the recluse of late. At any rate, what I wanted to tell you is that there is no need for you to concern yourselves with rushing out to look for a home of your own.'

Cassandra frowned. 'There isn't?'

'No. Because it is my intention to find a house for the two of you myself—in this area—as soon as possible. Call it a belated wedding present, if you like.'

John gazed at him in astonishment. 'You are buying us...a *house*?'

'Oh, Gabriel, we could never accept such a generous gift,' Cassandra said, glancing at her husband in dismay. 'You have already done so much for us.'

Gabriel shook his head. 'I have done little enough. But we need not talk about it any more right now. I just wanted you to know what I had in mind so that you would not feel obliged to leave, or to try to find something for yourselves in the next few weeks. I am well aware of the state of your finances and, until I do find something that will suit both of you, I want you to think of Carew as your home. There is more than enough room here for all of us. Now, I am sure you are ready for that cup of tea, Cassie. And after lunch, I expect both of you to rest for the remainder of the day.' He smiled at them in satisfaction. 'Now that you are safely home, we have all the time in the world to talk about your futures.'

Madelaine was arranging flowers in the drawing room when Berkeley approached her with an express just arrived from London. Wondering who could be sending her something of such import, Madelaine took the heavy cream parchment from the silver salver, and waited until the butler had left the room before breaking the seal.

The letter was from her husband's lawyers in London; in particular, a Mr Obadiah Jessop, the firm's senior partner. The letter was brief, but it could not have surprised her more, had it been three times as long. 'Good Lord,' Madelaine breathed.

Quickly crossing to the bell pull, she gave it a sharp tug. Moments later, the door opened again. 'Yes, my lady?'

'Berkeley, would you ask Mrs Merrill to come and see me at once,' Madelaine said quietly.

'Yes, Lady Trent.'

Madelaine moved towards the pale green brocade divan and sat down, her eyes still on the letter in her hand. Her aunt arrived almost immediately. 'You wished to see me, Maddie?'

'Yes. I have just received the most curious letter, Chloe. It seems that we are to receive a visit from Mr Obadiah Jessop within a few days.'

'Mr Jessop?' Chloe regarded her niece in astonishment. 'But...was he not Edward's lawyer?'

'He was, indeed.'

'But what business could he have with you that would necessitate his coming all the way down here?'

'Rather important business, by the looks of this.' Madelaine handed her aunt the letter to read. 'It would seem, Aunt, that someone wishes to buy Pengarron.'

Chapter Ten

Unaware of the events taking place at Pengarron, Gabriel began planning the ball that would officially welcome his brother and sister-in-law home. He knew that his own skills in the area were sketchy at best, so instructed his secretary, Mr Finch, to handle the bulk of the arrangements. He was confident that the young man would be able to deal with the issuing of invitations and the arrangement of food and decorations as efficiently as he dealt with everything else.

Thankfully, John's health was already showing signs of improvement. The doctor had expressed satisfaction with his condition, saying that, while his injuries would probably continue to bother him for some months yet, there was virtually no risk of infection setting in. All he needed was rest and good food, and his recovery would be swift. And with Cassandra, Dr. Granger expressed no cause for concern whatsoever. She had quickly resumed her rosy complexion and, with Mrs Dawson's excellent cooking, had even proceeded to gain weight. The long and arduous trip home seemed to have had no adverse affects on her at all.

That being the case, Gabriel felt free to turn his attention to the last matter which was of such importance to him: namely, the hiring of a new steward for Pengarron. He was anxious to put Lady Trent's mind at rest about the subject, and so, with Taylor's help, set about interviewing a number of applicants for the position. In the end, he narrowed the field down to three men, all of whom were extremely competent, highly trustworthy, and possessed of glowing references from their previous employers—all of whom Gabriel was acquainted with. He was confident that any one of them would make an excellent steward for Pengarron; with that in mind, he rode over to Pengarron the very next day and asked to see Lady Trent.

The two ladies were in the garden when Gabriel arrived. Madelaine, wearing a gown of pale lavender cambric, was seated in the very bower in which he had seen her that first day. She was idly flipping through a magazine while, across from her, Mrs Merrill sat on a shady bench, pleasantly lost in the pages of one of the romance novels she had brought with her from London. Both ladies looked up as Berkeley announced him.

'Good afternoon, Lady Trent, Mrs Merrill.'

Chloe was the first to speak. 'Good afternoon, Lord Trevellyn. This is an unexpected pleasure. We have seen so little of you recently.'

'I fear it was unavoidable. As you are no doubt aware, my brother and sister-in-law are home from France and, given their health, we have been enjoying a quiet reunion. But I hope you will forgive my delay in getting back to you regarding the matter of the steward.'

'Rest assured, the matter of the steward should be the least of your concerns right now,' Chloe said with a smile. 'Are your brother and sister-in-law well?'

Gabriel noticed that Madelaine had glanced at him upon his arrival and smiled in a rather preoccupied way, as though her thoughts were elsewhere. Strange, he thought. It was not like her to be so withdrawn.

'They are both very well, thank you, Mrs Merrill. My brother is still suffering some pain from his injuries, but overall the doctor is pleased and we believe that John is, on the whole, mending very quickly. And Cassandra is in the best of health. It is partially because of them that I am here.' He glanced at Madelaine again, finding it difficult to keep his eyes away from her. 'I am giving a ball at Carew in honour of their return to England, and I would like to extend a personal invitation to both of you to attend.'

For the first time since he had arrived, Madelaine's face brightened. 'A ball? Oh, but how lovely, Lord Trevellyn. When is it to be?'

'In two weeks' time. Cassandra told me it would take her that long to have a suitable gown made. Unfortunately, she is a little out of touch with what is *au courant*, and is somewhat concerned about going to town alone and finding a suitable modiste.'

'There is no reason for her to be concerned about anything,' Chloe spoke up. 'Why do you not suggest to your sister-in-law that she join us for tea tomorrow afternoon so that the three of us may become acquainted?'

'Yes, that is a splendid idea, Chloe,' Madelaine agreed. 'That way we will all have a chance to get to know each other before the ball. And I am quite sure my aunt and I would be delighted to take Cassandra shopping for a new gown.'

'That would, of course, be splendid,' Gabriel said. 'No doubt after following the drum all this time, Cassandra will welcome the opportunity of spending time in the company of ladies again.'

'As for matters pertaining to style,' Madelaine said, 'my aunt is something of an expert on women's fashion, Lord Trevellyn. I feel quite sure she will be able to guide Mrs Carew in the choice of something suitable to wear.'

'Yes, especially now that she is breeding,' Chloe said bluntly. 'I imagine she would like to disguise the fact somewhat.'

Gabriel nodded, appreciating the lady's candour. Like Cassandra, he did not particularly hold with the idea of a woman having to shut herself away simply because she was in a delicate condition, but he knew that others might frown upon her dancing in public. 'I know she would be most grateful for your assistance, Mrs Merrill, and I would consider it a personal favour if you would agree to lend her your aid in this matter.'

'You may consider it done, Lord Trevellyn,' Chloe said.

'Good. And now that the social aspect of the call has been taken care of,' he said, turning to Madelaine again, 'I wonder if I might speak with you on the matter of the steward, Lady Trent.'

'Yes, of course.'

'Well, you certainly do not need me for that,' Chloe said. She rose and cast a doubtful glance towards the sky. 'If you will excuse me, I think I shall fetch my shawl. I find it a bit chilly when the sun goes in.'

'But the sun hasn't gone in, Chloe,' Madelaine felt inclined to point out.

'Not yet, but it is going to directly. Just look at those clouds.'

Madelaine bit her lip as her aunt returned to the house. At times, Chloe could be so dreadfully obvious. There was hardly a cloud in the sky.

She turned back to smile at her visitor. 'I take it you have found someone suitable for the position, Lord Trevellyn?'

Gabriel sat down on the bench Chloe had just vacated, and nodded. 'I believe I have, Lady Trent. After interviewing a number of applicants for the position, I have narrowed it down to three gentlemen, all of whom are well qualified to do the job. I thought it only fair, however, that you be allowed to have a say in the final choice, rather than be handed a *fait accompli*.'

Madelaine bent her head in acknowledgement of his consideration, after which Gabriel proceeded to enumerate the qualities of each of the gentlemen. There seemed to be a great many of them, indeed, and Madelaine listened in growing confusion. Unfortunately, other thoughts kept intruding, and when at the end of the dissertation, Trevellyn looked to her for an opinion, Madelaine had to shake her head in apology.

'I am sorry, Lord Trevellyn. I did not catch the last bit about…Mr Owens, was it?'

Gabriel raised an eyebrow. 'Mr Owens was the first gentleman I spoke to you about, Lady Trent. Mr Heversaw was the last.'

'Ah, yes, of course. And tell me, which gentleman would you recommend?'

'Personally, I would choose Owens. He has experience on an estate of this size, and has been with the same family for the past twenty years. His reasons for leaving his previous situation are valid, and as it happens, I know his former employer quite well.'

Madelaine smiled. 'Then, by all means, offer him the position, Lord Trevellyn. Your experience in matters such as these is far more extensive than mine.'

'Very well. Shall he commence at what Diggs was being paid?'

'I believe Diggs was making a good wage?'

'A very good wage, my lady.'

'Not more than Taylor, I hope.'

Gabriel smiled. 'Not that good. Taylor has been at Carew all of his life.'

'Fine. Then Owens may start at what Diggs was making.'

Gabriel inclined his head. 'I shall advise him of your choice. Shall I set up a meeting between the two of you?'

Madelaine was about to reply, when Berkeley appeared again. 'Excuse me, Lady Trent, but Mr Jessop has arrived from London.'

Madelaine started, her dismay unconcealed. 'So soon? But I had not expected him for another day yet.' She bit her lip, and then nodded. 'Very well, I suppose I shall have to see him. Ask him to wait in the library, Berkeley, I shall be there directly.'

When the butler had gone, Gabriel glanced at Madelaine curiously. 'A gentleman caller all the way from London?' he enquired.

'Yes.' Madelaine rose graciously and held out her hand. 'I fear we will have to continue this at another time. Although, depending on the outcome of my meeting with Mr Jessop, it may not be all that important for me to meet with Mr Owens at all.'

Gabriel could hear the concern in her voice, and suddenly wondered who this unknown Mr Jessop might be. His arrival had clearly discomfited Madelaine, though not, he perceived, in a strictly personal way. 'I await your direction, Lady Trent.'

About to turn away, Gabriel suddenly took Madelaine's hand and raised it to his lips, pressing a soft kiss against her skin. Then, with another bow, he turned and walked away.

The unexpected gallantry startled Madelaine, and caused her pulse to quicken alarmingly. It seemed to her that Lord Trevellyn had intended the kiss to comfort her, rather than simply to say goodbye. And, oddly enough, it had.

But not nearly as much as it had disturbed her.

* * *

Obadiah Jessop was standing in front of the tall windows in the library, admiring, or at least viewing, the hills beyond when Madelaine walked in. As upon the occasion of their first meeting in London, just after Edward's death, the man did not make a strong impression upon her. He was a corpulent man, and his clothes proclaimed him for what he was. His features were not in any way remarkable, though his nose was, perhaps, larger than most. Still, at least his was not an intimidating personage, and as he turned to face her, his smile was as bland as his personality. 'Good afternoon, Lady Trent. I trust I find you well.'

'Well indeed, Mr Jessop, though I admit somewhat surprised.'

'Oh?'

'I had not expected to see you at Pengarron so soon. I hope you had a pleasant journey?'

'A passable one, Lady Trent. 'Tis many a year since I have ventured out this far, and I am pleased to note that the roads are in a much better condition than they were upon the occasion of my last trip.'

'Yes, no doubt your work keeps you close to London,' Madelaine murmured. She took her place behind the desk and indicated that Mr Jessop should sit across from her. Opening the top left-hand drawer, she removed the letter the lawyer had sent her, and placed it on the desk between them. 'So, Mr Jessop, would you care to explain what this is all about?'

Mr Jessop pulled a pair of spectacles from his breast pocket and dusted them off. 'It is really quite simple, Lady Trent. An offer has been made to purchase Pengarron. A rather unusual offer, perhaps, but a very good one, nevertheless.'

'And from whom has this offer come?'

'From the firm of Whitley, Henderson and Blake.'

'I was referring to the name of the buyer, Mr Jessop. Who is the party behind the offer?'

'That, I am afraid, is something I cannot tell you, Lady Trent.'

Madelaine glanced at him in surprise. 'Cannot? Or will not?'

'Cannot,' Mr Jessop replied, 'because I have not been made aware of the identity of the buyer myself. The offer has been made…anonymously.'

Madelaine sat back. 'Is that legal?'

'Oh, yes, quite legal. A firm can act on behalf of a client who wishes to remain, er, unidentified.'

'But why would anyone wish to do so?' Madelaine enquired. 'What would be the point?'

Mr Jessop shrugged. He opened his satchel and, from the depths of it, pulled out a bundle of papers, placing them on the desk beside the offer. 'The gentleman—since I assume it is a gentleman—purchasing the property may be intending to use it for purposes other than as a family home.'

'Other than… Oh, I see!'

Madelaine was dismayed to feel her cheeks grow warm. Whoever wanted Pengarron must be wealthy. Most gentlemen kept their bits of muslin close at hand, usually in a town house in a less fashionable part of London. This gentleman must be of the first consequence indeed to need to bury his mistress in the wilds of Cornwall.

'I do not like the idea of Pengarron being used for…such purposes, Mr Jessop.'

Mr Jessop was nothing if not astute. He noticed the frown between the lady's brows and correctly interpreted its source—as well as the note of censure in her voice. 'My dear Lady Trent, there are any number of reasons why a purchaser might wish to keep his identity concealed,' he

hastened to reassure her. 'Many of a more worthy nature
than the…er, one which seems to have come to your mind.
Do not forget that Pengarron was originally purchased by
Lord Trent's father as a hunting lodge. As such, it is very
possible that the purchaser has something like that in mind
for it again. I understand that the shooting here is quite
exceptional. Now, if you will address yourself to the
amount listed at the bottom of this page,' he said, conven-
iently pointing to it for her, 'you will see that the offer is
a most generous one.'

Madelaine gasped at the amount. 'Generous! Is the man
a nabob?'

'He may well be, Lady Trent.' Mr Jessop allowed himself a brief smile. 'I admit to being curious as to his identity
myself.'

Taking another look at the figure on the page, Madelaine
suddenly got up and walked across the room, coming to a
halt in front of the window. She remained that way for a
long time. 'Do you feel it in my best interests to consider
this offer, Mr Jessop?'

'Well, in all honesty, I cannot see that it would bring
you any grief, Lady Trent,' the lawyer replied truthfully.
'Pengarron is certainly the most remote of your late husband's properties, and as it was the one he spent the least
amount of time in, I cannot think that there is any senti-
mental attachment to it. The present Lord Trent has made
it clear that *he* is not interested in the house by the fact that
he has given it to you free and clear of any legal or family
entitlement. On the practical side, you stand to lose nothing
by selling the house. The money generated by the sale of
Pengarron would provide you with a healthy income.'

'I was not aware that I was lacking for funds, Mr Jessop.'

'Not in the least, Lady Trent, not in the least,' he replied,
detecting the faint note of criticism in Madelaine's voice.

'And I am pleased to say that, in my capable hands, the money Lord Trent left you has continued to grow. But there is no denying that an amount such as has been offered for the purchase of Pengarron would reconfirm your position as one of the wealthiest young women in London.'

Madelaine sighed, and shook her head. 'It is not a reputation I wish to perpetuate, Mr Jessop. My needs are few, and I am content that there is enough money for my aunt and I to live comfortably for the rest of our lives.'

'There is certainly that, Lady Trent, if we did nothing but leave what money you currently possess in the bank.' Mr Jessop hesitated, sensing that there was more to the widow's reluctance to part with the house than the issue of money. 'Lady Trent, let me assure you that there is no need for you to sell Pengarron. If you wish me to reject the offer, you have only to say so and it will be done, with no need for explanation whatsoever. I merely thought it was an offer which should be brought to your attention. As you know, I have always advocated the selling of Pengarron, simply because of its remote location. If you wish to purchase another residence closer to London, I would be more than happy to see to the necessary details.'

Madelaine smiled weakly. 'Forgive me, Mr Jessop, I did not mean to sound contentious. It is simply that I find this whole matter extremely confusing. Why would anyone want to buy Pengarron in the first place? It has not even been offered.'

Again, Mr Jessop shrugged. 'It may simply be that someone likes the house and felt that you might be of a mind to sell it, given that you are a widow and unlikely to want to live in a house this far from London. I am sure there has been speculation in town as to what you were intending to do with the property.'

That, Madelaine decided, was probably one of the truest

statements Mr Jessop had made thus far. Curiosity ran rampant amongst the members of the *haut ton*; no one knew that better than she.

'I will, of course, wish to give the matter some thought,' Madelaine said as she returned to the desk. 'Are you staying long in the area, Mr Jessop?'

'I had not thought to, Lady Trent. I have booked overnight accommodation at the local inn, but it was my intention to head back to London tomorrow.' Mr Jessop closed his satchel and rose. 'However, I think it a good idea that you take some time to consider the offer. I cannot but bring to your attention that it is an extremely generous one. However, the decision is ultimately yours. Please feel free to advise me of your decision at your convenience. Thank you for your time, Lady Trent, and I apologise if my visit has caused you any grief.'

Madelaine walked with him to the door. 'It has surprised me more than caused me grief, Mr Jessop. I confess, I had discussed the possibility of my selling Pengarron with my neighbour only the other evening.'

'Would that be Lord Trevellyn?'

'Yes. Do you know him?'

'I cannot claim an acquaintance with the gentleman, no. Lord Trevellyn is a man of considerable consequence but, unfortunately, one who does not do business with our firm. On the few occasions I have spoken with him, however, I have found him to be a most amiable gentleman. Have you seen Carew?'

Madelaine nodded. 'The Earl was kind enough to invite my aunt and I to dinner shortly after our arrival here. It is a beautiful house.'

'So I understand. It has been in the possession of the Trevellyn family for hundreds of years. It is, of course, entailed to the title, but even were it not, I doubt the Trev-

ellyns would ever consider selling it. A stubborn breed, the
Cornish. Like to hold on to what is theirs. Well, again, good
day, Lady Trent.'

'Goodbye, Mr Jessop.'

Madelaine watched the lawyer depart, and then slowly
wandered back towards the library, the memory of the
man's last words playing on her mind. A stubborn breed,
he had called the Cornish. People who held on to what was
theirs.

Madelaine sighed as she regarded the offer on her desk.
Strangely enough, she found herself unwittingly reminded
of Gabriel Carew, riding his fine horse, and pretending to
be a steward. Even in the guise of a servant, he had sur-
veyed his lands with the eye of a Cornish man, born and
bred. He had spoken to her of its rugged coastline, and the
bleakness of its moors. And he had held fast to his belief
that it was the finest place in all of England.

Was that being stubborn? she wondered. Or just inordi-
nately proud?

Cassandra Carew was as charming a young woman as
Madelaine could have wished to meet. Possessed of both a
sound mind and a gentle, caring nature, she quickly en-
deared herself both to Madelaine and her aunt. And while
it was easy to see the strength of character which had en-
abled her to follow her husband through the war-torn bat-
tlefields of France, there was no mistaking the degree of
happiness which her return to England—and the thought of
settling down to a happy family life in it—had brought her.

'It must have been frightening for you, though,' Madelaine said now, as she gazed at the composed young woman
with admiration. 'I do not know that I would have had the
courage to follow my husband into battle. I have heard the
most dreadful stories.'

Cassandra smiled in a manner that conveyed neither superiority nor condescension. 'I think you would have been able to find the strength, Lady Trent, if you truly loved your husband. Being there with John seemed far less worrisome to me than remaining behind in England and waiting for the weekly dispatches.'

'I am sure you were of great comfort to your husband when he was injured,' Chloe said sympathetically as the ladies lingered over a glass of sherry in the comfort of the green salon at Pengarron the following afternoon.

'Yes. Many times over I was grateful for my nursing skills. I only wish I had been able to offer similar comfort to Gabriel when he was wounded,' Cassandra remarked sadly. 'His injuries were far more grievous than John's, though you would not think so to listen to him.'

'No, indeed,' Madelaine said, surprised to hear that the wounds Gabriel had sustained were, in fact, quite serious. 'He told me that he was far more concerned with his brother's welfare than he was with his own.'

Cassandra's brows rose. 'Gabriel has spoken to you of this?'

'A little.' Madelaine smiled. 'Does that surprise you?'

'I confess it does. Gabriel shares very little of his life with others. He is, by nature, an extremely private man.'

'Yes, I gathered that much in conversation with him. And he did speak only briefly to me about it when the subject did arise,' Madelaine admitted, 'but he seems to harbour a great deal of guilt over the situation, as a result of being John's commanding officer.'

Cassandra sighed. 'Yes, though both John and I have argued endlessly with him not to. I think that is largely what has motivated him to go to the great lengths that he has in order to buy us a house.'

'A house!' Chloe put down her glass in astonishment. 'But, my dear, what a generous thing to do!'

'Yes. He is calling it a belated wedding present.'

'And what a wonderful present it is,' Madelaine said enthusiastically. 'Where is it to be? In Cornwall? Or would you prefer to live in London?'

Cassandra shook her head. 'I should much rather stay here, and I know that John feels the same. He grew up here, you see, and his ties to the land are almost as strong as his brother's. For that reason, it is my belief that Gabriel will try to find a house for us in the area.'

'But are there many suitable houses hereabouts?' Chloe enquired.

'I really do not know, Mrs Merrill,' Cassandra admitted. 'Having been away so long, I have no idea what houses are even available. But I am quite sure Gabriel does. And when he finds the right one, he will no doubt go to great lengths to secure it for us. When my brother-in-law sets his mind to do something, he seldom fails to achieve his goal.'

Madelaine managed a smile as she set her glass of sherry on the table, hoping that neither Chloe nor Cassandra noticed the way her hand suddenly began to tremble. How strange. Lord Trevellyn was looking for a house in the area—and she had just received an offer for the purchase of Pengarron. An *anonymous* offer. Surely it wasn't possible…?

'So Lord Trevellyn has not given you any indication as to which house he might be considering?' Madelaine heard Chloe ask their visitor.

'No. But then Gabriel has always been terribly closed mouth about his business dealings. He won't even tell John what he has in mind. For my own part, I am just delighted that we are to *have* a place,' Cassandra admitted. 'Given the limited state of our finances, there was certainly no chance of our being able to manage it on our own. And with the baby coming, it will be wonderful to have our own home.'

Madelaine smiled again, and decided that she must have been mistaken. After all, Lord Trevellyn had spoken about the possibility of her selling Pengarron over dinner the other evening, and surely if he had been any way interested in buying Pengarron for John and Cassandra, he would have broached the subject with her then.

No, the more Madelaine thought about it, the more she realised that her being presented with an offer for Pengarron at precisely the same time that Lord Trevellyn was looking for a house for his brother and sister-in-law had to be nothing more than a coincidence.

Suddenly aware that her extended silence had drawn the notice of the other two ladies, Madelaine said in embarrassment, 'I am sorry, Chloe, what were you saying?'

'I was asking your opinion as to the wisdom of green velvet for Cassandra's ballgown,' Chloe said. 'I thought perhaps the dark colour would be better than a pastel shade for concealing her condition. And the weight of the velvet will be far less likely to cling than a lightweight silk or muslin.'

Madelaine nodded her agreement. 'Yes, I think that would be...most flattering.'

'Splendid. Then green velvet it shall be. Now, Cassandra, when do you think you would be free to accompany Madelaine and me to town?'

As it turned out, Chloe's suggestion for Cassandra Carew's ballgown was a most judicious one. The luxurious silk velvet fell in soft folds from the high waist to the floor, drawing very little attention to the lady's burgeoning figure beneath, while the rich jewelled shade was extremely becoming to her pale complexion and fair, almost white-blonde hair. Mrs Harder in the village did a masterful job in the fitting of the gown, and even Chloe declared herself pleased with the results.

'It hides her condition admirably,' she announced with satisfaction. 'Excellent work, Mrs Harder, quite excellent.'

The ruddy-faced woman beamed with pleasure. 'Thank you, madam. Now, if I may suggest—oh, good afternoon, Miss Bourne.'

Madelaine glanced up in dismay, fearing that it might be the younger Bourne sister, and then smiled with genuine pleasure when she saw that it was Miss Prunella Bourne and her abigail.

'Miss Bourne, how delightful to see you again.'

'Good afternoon, Lady Trent, Mrs Merrill.'

'Good afternoon, Miss Bourne. Your mother and sister are not with you this afternoon?'

'No. Phoebe is having her dancing lesson, and Mama is resting.' Prunella suddenly caught sight of Cassandra, who was still standing in front of the glass in the velvet gown, and said, 'Oh, how beautiful!'

'Cassandra, allow me to introduce Miss Prunella Bourne,' Madelaine said with a fond smile. 'Prunella, Mrs John Carew.'

The two ladies exchanged greetings, before Cassandra slipped into the back with the modiste. Prunella glanced after her in admiration. 'Mrs Carew is so very pretty. And how splendid she looks in her gown. Is it for Lord Trevellyn's ball?' she enquired.

'It is indeed, Miss Bourne. Are you going to the ball?'

Prunella nodded, and then sighed. 'I believe so. Mama did receive an invitation.'

'You do not seem very happy about the prospect, child,'

Chloe observed. 'Are you not favourably disposed towards balls?'

'On the contrary, I enjoy them immensely, Mrs Merrill. I love looking at all the ladies in their finery.'

'No doubt in an effort to forget her own,' Chloe whispered in Madelaine's ear. Then, to Prunella, said, 'And what will you be wearing to Lord Trevellyn's ball, Miss Bourne?'

It was quite obvious from the blush which spread across poor Prunella's cheeks that Chloe's supposition had not been wrong. 'I believe Mama has ordered something from Mrs Harder, though I am not sure of the colour or the style. I seldom see the gowns until just before I am to wear them.'

Chloe's eyes sparkled with mischief. 'Mrs Harder, I wonder if I might prevail upon you to show us the gown Miss Bourne is to wear to the ball.'

Mrs Harder looked slightly embarrassed. 'I can bring you the material, madam, and a picture of the design, but I'm afraid I can't show you much more than that. Lady Bourne was most insistent that I finish the younger daughter's gown first.'

Madelaine stared. 'But I thought Lady Bourne said that Phoebe's gowns were made in London?'

'Yes, and no doubt the Prince of Wales dines regularly at her table,' Chloe said, lowering her voice so that Prunella could not hear. 'Mrs Harder, if you would be so good as to show us the fabric and the design, that will suffice.'

The modiste disappeared into the back room and returned a few minutes later carrying a bolt of fabric in a nondescript shade of mauve. Madelaine had no need to see the gown made up to know that it would be dreadful. The colour would look ghastly against the girl's dark hair and warm colouring.

Sadly, Prunella knew it too. The glimmer of hopeful anticipation, which had briefly illuminated the girl's eyes, died as soon as she saw the dreary swatch of fabric, to be replaced by a look of resigned acceptance. She smiled bravely, avoiding Mrs Merrill's eyes, and after picking up the embroidery silks she had come for, bid the ladies a pleasant afternoon and then quietly slipped away.

Madelaine truly wished there was something she could have done to make the girl feel better. 'It is not fair, Chloe. In a gown like that, Prunella Bourne is going to look a very plain little wren indeed.'

'Yes. Especially given that her sister is like to resemble a bird of paradise,' Chloe replied tartly. She was silent for a minute, and then narrowed her eyes thoughtfully. 'Mrs Harder, I wonder, have you the latest copy of *La Belle Assemblée*? The one showing the newest fashions from Paris?'

'Yes, madam, I have it in the back.'

'Good. In it, you will find a most attractive gown on page fifteen.'

'I know the very one, madam. And a lovely gown it is, too.'

'Good. Do you think you would be able to make it up for Miss Prunella Bourne in time for Lord Trevellyn's ball?'

Mrs Harder's face brightened. 'Aye, madam, I'm sure I could. The one I'm making for Miss Phoebe is similar, though not as fashionably styled.'

'Really?' Chloe winked at Madelaine in a conspiratorial fashion. 'How interesting. Now, Mrs Harder, would you be good enough to show me what you have in the way of apricot sarcenet?'

In the days leading up to the ball, Gabriel made a startling discovery. Startling, because it was in complete contrast to everything he had claimed to be true, both to himself and to Lord Keswick, only a few weeks ago. It had taken place at some time during the last month, and had crept up on him in a manner which was both subtle and immutable. Even now, he could not believe that it had happened.

He had fallen completely and quite hopelessly in love with Madelaine Trent.

It was an astonishing admission for Gabriel, and one which he had never contemplated making. But it was true none the less. Madelaine had worked her way into his heart and now occupied his thoughts constantly. He had only to close his eyes to see the image of her beautiful face, and to hear the sweet sound of her voice.

He began to wonder precisely when he had fallen in love with her, and then realised that there had been no one particular moment. It might have sprung from the compassion she had evidenced towards a tiny deer, or from her consideration for a lowly steward. All Gabriel knew was that his feelings towards her had been growing stronger by the day. From the very first moment of having met her, he had known that she was…special. She was everything that was good and loving in a woman and, in truth, Gabriel began to realise that he had never really stood a chance.

It was also his newly discovered love for Madelaine which caused him to make another startling discovery: that he no longer wished to buy Pengarron. He could not bear the thought of being the one who had caused her to leave her home, and he didn't give a damn what Keswick or anybody else thought about his change of heart. Madelaine's love for the land was unmistakable. He heard it in her voice every time she spoke of Pengarron, and the last thing he wanted to be was the cause of her losing it.

As such, Gabriel sent a letter to his lawyer and instructed

him to contact Lady Trent's solicitors at once and to withdraw his offer to purchase. He could only be grateful for
whatever impulse had compelled him to make it anonymously. He knew that Madelaine would surely have misunderstood his intentions had he not. After all, she could
hardly be expected to know that when he had first decided
to buy Pengarron, he had thought to find himself dealing
with a stranger rather than…well, with Madelaine.

Yes, it would mean that he would have to find another
house for John and Cassandra, and over the next few weeks
he would turn his mind to doing just that. But right now
he had more important matters to clear up. He would not
be the cause of Madelaine's returning to London.

Not now, when all he wanted to do was to be close to
her every hour of the day—and night!

To Madelaine's delight, Cassandra called in at Pengarron
a few days later on her way home from Mrs Harder's shop,
where she had been for a final fitting of her gown.

'It is wonderful!' Cassandra told Madelaine as she followed her into one of the smaller, cosier salons. 'And it
certainly gives no hint that I am breeding. I think it was an
excellent idea of your aunt's to employ velvet rather than
one of the more flimsy fabrics which are so popular.'

'My aunt has always been very good in that regard,'
Madelaine commented. 'But I am so pleased that you are
happy with it, and that you are feeling well enough to attend the ball. I know that it is in your honour, of course,
but I have heard that…the early days of your condition can
sometimes be very…difficult,' Madelaine said tactfully.

'You need not be politic with me, Lady Trent,' Cassandra said with a rueful smile. 'I suffered a great deal in the
early days of my confinement but, thankfully, that seems
to have eased now, and I am able to get through almost the

entire day without any bother at all. The only problem I have now is that I seem to be ravenous most of the time. Gabriel is quite astonished at the amount I am eating.'

Madelaine laughed softly, suddenly envying Cassandra her situation. How desperately she longed for a child of her own. Since the early days of her marriage to Edward, she had tried to forget about such things, but now, sitting here and listening to Cassandra talk about her condition, and realising what it portended, Madelaine felt the maternal longings rise anew.

'You must be very excited about the prospect of this child,' she said softly.

Cassandra's face glowed. 'I am happier than you can imagine, Lady Trent—'

'Maddie, please,' Madelaine interrupted. 'I think it is time we moved beyond such formalities.'

'I should like that very much. But, yes, I am very happy about having this child. I have always wanted children. Being an only child, I missed having brothers and sisters to play with and to take care of. Now I will have that opportunity. And I know that John will be the most splendid father. He has so much patience.' Cassandra hesitated for a moment, and then smiled. 'It is strange, is it not, how different two brothers can be?'

'Oh?' Madelaine was careful to instil a note of objectivity into her voice, as though the subject was only of passing interest. 'In what ways are they different?'

'Well, for example, John is so very easygoing. He is quite content to let life take its own course, whereas Gabriel is more inclined to take control of things, and guide them in the direction he wishes them to go. He hides his emotions under that gruff exterior, but I know for a fact that he feels things as deeply as anyone.'

'Perhaps that is what comes of being the eldest son,'

Madelaine suggested. 'He feels it is his duty to behave in a more stoic fashion.'

'Perhaps. Gabriel does take his responsibilities very seriously though,' Cassandra agreed. 'For example, I overheard him telling John yesterday that he had found a house that he wanted to buy for us—'

'Oh, my dear, that is wonderful news!'

'Well, I thought it was, until he went on to say that he had changed his mind about it. John told him that there was no need for him to put himself out on our account any further, and not to give the matter any more thought. Of course, Gabriel would not hear of it. He said that he had made a promise to us, and that he intended to keep it, but that it might take a little longer than he anticipated. For myself, I do not mind in the least. I am perfectly happy living at Carew,' Cassandra admitted contentedly. 'It is a beautiful house, and I confess, I am rather enjoying being spoiled by *two* Carew men. Gabriel is all attentiveness. Indeed, John declares that he has never seen his brother so…accommodating.'

Madelaine smiled. 'Sometimes a person's qualities are hidden until such time as circumstances warrant their revealing.'

'I suppose. But he is a good man, Maddie,' Cassandra said fervently. 'Indeed, I wish people knew better just how good and kind he is. I was not aware of it myself until John and I were courting. I always thought Gabriel a rather dour and cynical man when, in fact, he is anything but. It is…a façade he puts on for others, I think. But there, I did not come here to wax eloquent about my brother-in-law, for if you know him at all, I am sure that you have seen his admirable side on more than one occasion. Indeed, you must have, for he speaks very well of you.'

The remark brought the colour rushing to Madelaine's

cheeks. 'I am sure it was only politeness on his part which makes him speak so.'

Cassandra got to her feet and made ready to leave. 'Gabriel does very little for the sake of politeness, Maddie. He is a man of integrity. If he does not feel an emotion genuinely, he will not pretend that he does, merely for the appearance of good manners. Hence, his reputation for direct speaking. But now, I have taken up enough of your time. John will no doubt be wondering at my absence. He does tend to worry unduly about my condition.'

'And so he should,' Madelaine said fondly as she walked her visitor to the front door. 'But I am so pleased that you stopped by, Cassandra, and I do look forward to seeing you at Carew—and to meeting John.'

'And I know that he is just as anxious to meet you. Goodbye, Maddie. And pray do give my regards to your aunt.'

The ladies waved each other a fond farewell; after watching the carriage disappear down the long drive, Madelaine slowly walked back into the house.

So, Lord Trevellyn *had* been negotiating for the purchase of a house in the area. But he had changed his mind. Why? If he had believed his first choice of a house to be the right one, what could have happened to make him alter his opinion?

Whatever it was, the timely remark only served to convince Madelaine that she had been wrong to think that Lord Trevellyn had been interested in Pengarron in the first place. She had had no word from Mr Jessop advising her that the offer had been withdrawn, so, as far as she knew, the anonymous buyer still wished to purchase it.

Unfortunately for him, however, it was going to be necessary for him to look for another house, Madelaine reflected with satisfaction. For, while she had not yet had opportunity to contact Mr Jessop with her answer, she had made up her mind.

She was *not* going to sell Pengarron. Not now, when the man she had fallen in love with just happened to live right next door to it!

Chapter Eleven

Three days later, Gabriel changed into the proper attire for a gentleman intending to propose marriage to the woman he loved, and rode over to Pengarron.

His frustration at not being able to see Madelaine every day had grown in leaps and bounds since he had admitted to himself that he loved her. So much so that, in the end, he was capable of doing little other than think of her. That, more than anything, convinced him that it was time to remedy the situation.

With Pengarron, he was not in the least interested. If Madelaine agreed to marry him, she could do what she wished with the estate. Gabriel knew that any property she held rightfully became his upon their marriage, but Pengarron had been given to her by her stepson, and he had no wish to intrude upon that relationship. The dispensation of her assets would be left entirely up to her. He only wanted her to be happy, because her happiness was the only thing that mattered to him any more.

Madelaine was sitting at her embroidery frame when Gabriel arrived. She blushed prettily upon seeing him, and quickly rose to her feet. 'Lord Trevellyn, this is a pleasure.'

Gabriel bowed. 'Lady Trent, I apologise for calling upon you so early in the day, but with the ball this evening, I thought I might be prevented from visiting you later.' He glanced around the room and was surprised to see that she was alone. 'Your aunt is not indisposed, I hope?'

'Not at all. She has merely gone into the village to try to procure a pair of evening gloves. She was quite sure that she had brought at least one pair with her from London, but when her maid went to look for them this morning, she found there were none at all. I imagine she will be back soon.'

'In truth, I cannot say I am sorry for her absence,' Gabriel said quietly, 'since I came here today to speak to you on a matter of some importance.'

'Oh. A matter pertaining to Pengarron?'

He smiled. 'Indirectly.'

'The new steward, perhaps?'

Gabriel laughed, a deep throaty sound. 'Not the steward, no, though it certainly concerns the mistress of Pengarron.'

For the first time, Madelaine's smile faltered. Since Cassandra's visit, she had convinced herself that her suspicions regarding Lord Trevellyn's interest in Pengarron were unfounded, and she had relegated the anonymous offer—and the person behind it—to a position of non-importance. But now, hearing that he wished to speak with her on a matter of importance pertaining to both Pengarron *and* herself, her uncertainties came back tenfold.

Perhaps she was mistaken about his not wishing to purchase the estate. Perhaps he had withdrawn his anonymous offer so that he could come to her directly with it now. After all, he knew her well enough to do that. Was that what this was about? Or had he come to discuss something of an entirely different nature?

'Pray be seated, Lord Trevellyn.'

Gabriel could not fail to notice the look of concern which had suddenly appeared on Madelaine's face. 'You look troubled, Lady Trent. Is everything all right?'

'Yes, of course.' Madelaine strove for a more tranquil countenance, even as she felt her heart begin to beat. 'I am simply…curious as to what this important matter could be.'

Gabriel sat down beside her on the settee and looked into her eyes. 'It is something which has been on my mind for some time now.'

'I see. And has it something to do with the…future of Pengarron?'

Gabriel thought about that for a moment. 'It could be, depending upon how you answer my question.'

Fearful lest he see the way her hands suddenly began to tremble, Madelaine rose and crossed to the window, abruptly aware of a need to put some distance between them. 'Very well, Lord Trevellyn, you had best…ask your question.'

The note of foreboding in Madelaine's voice was evident, and it caused Gabriel to frown. Had he misjudged the situation between them? Was Madelaine not as enamoured of him as he had come to hope?

He slowly rose and walked across to where she stood by the window. Her back was turned towards him, and he could almost feel the stiffness in her shoulders. 'I hope I am not wrong in my assumptions, Lady Trent,' Gabriel began tentatively, 'but I had begun to hope that there were…feelings developing between us.'

Surprised, Madelaine said, 'I fail to see what personal feelings have to do with this, my lord, if this is to be a discussion of a…a business arrangement.'

Gabriel put his hands on her shoulders and gently turned her around to face him. 'Your first marriage might have been business, Madelaine, but I should hate to think that you would look upon your second one that way as well.'

Madelaine caught her breath. 'I...beg your pardon. Did you say...*my second marriage*?'

'Well, yes, of course,' Gabriel said gently. 'What do you think I have been standing here trying to tell you? I came here today to ask you to marry me.'

'Marry you?'

'Yes.' Gabriel glanced at her in amusement. 'Or did I neglect to tell you that I have fallen utterly in love with you, and that you have changed my life so completely that I can barely remember what it was like before you came into it.'

Madelaine stared at him in disbelief. 'You...*love* me?'

'Forgive me. It seems that I have indeed been remiss in making you aware of my feelings.' His eyes softened to a look of infinite gentleness. 'Yes, I love you, Madelaine. So much so that I cannot imagine my life without you in it any more.'

'But...I thought—' Madelaine broke off as Gabriel slipped his arms around her waist and drew her closer. 'I thought—'

'Yes, my darling. What was it you thought?'

Madelaine gazed up at him in bewilderment, not at all sure *what* she thought any more. The last thing she had been expecting from him was a proposal of marriage. But when Gabriel suddenly bent his head and brushed his mouth gently across her lips, then the dimple at the corner of her mouth, and the soft skin at the base of her throat, Madelaine found that she was quite unable to think of...anything. 'My lord...this is most...improper,' she gasped.

'Only if you do not return my feelings, sweet lady.' Gabriel felt her quiver in his arms, and pulled her closer. 'Tell me that you love me, Madelaine,' he whispered against her cheek, 'for I swear I cannot pass another day without hearing it. I love you more than I ever dreamed it possible to love a woman.'

And then, because he could not deny himself any longer, Gabriel lowered his mouth to hers and kissed her with a passion that left Madelaine breathless.

'My lord, I beg you…stop!'

'Can you blame me for wanting to show you how I feel?' Gabriel murmured huskily, as his lips left hers to find the sensuous curve of her neck.

Madelaine closed her eyes, feeling her knees go weak as he nuzzled the skin at the lacy edge of her gown. 'If you continue to show me…how you feel, I dare say you are going to have to beg forgiveness for a great deal more than that.'

Gabriel's eyes sparkled wickedly. 'And would you grant me that forgiveness, my darling?'

Madelaine bit her lip, unable to ignore the slow burning fire his touch aroused. 'Odious creature, of course I would.'

'Does that mean that you will marry me? Does it?'

Madelaine was unable to breathe…or to think. She could do nothing but stare up into the dark eyes that were gazing at her so intently. And suddenly, she started to laugh. 'Yes, I will marry you. But…are you quite sure?'

His smile was as intimate as a kiss. 'More sure than I have ever been of anything in my life. I love you, Madelaine Trent. Every independent inch of you.'

'I shall have you know—'

The rest of that sentence was never finished. Nor were any others, as Gabriel told the woman he loved exactly how much he loved her—without saying a word.

'Proposed!' Chloe stared at her niece in the semi-darkness of the carriage as it made its way along the road to Carew for Cassandra and John's ball, and shook her head in utter dismay. 'And you did not think to tell me?'

'It only happened this morning, Chloe,' Madelaine replied, laughing. 'While you were out seeing Mrs Harder. And with everything that has been going on—'

'Never mind everything that has been going on, I will not accept that as an excuse. Lord Trevellyn proposed to you more than eight hours ago, and you have kept it to yourself all this time? La, Madelaine, you are a most ungrateful child!' Chloe tried to appear stern, and then abruptly burst out laughing. 'But, oh, my dear, I am so very pleased for you!' She clapped her gloved hands together in delight. 'Only wait until Lady Bourne hears about this!'

'Oh, but you mustn't say anything,' Madelaine warned her quickly. 'Not right away, that is. Gabriel is intending to announce it at the ball tonight. He informed me that the only other people he planned on telling before the event were John and Cassandra.'

Chloe reached across the coach and grasped her niece's hands. 'Are you happy, Madelaine? Truly happy?'

Madelaine sighed. 'I love him so much, Chloe. He is truly the best of men. And I believe that he loves me—for all the right reasons.'

'Of course he does, how could he not? You certainly have no reason to worry about Lord Trevellyn marrying you for your money, my dear. He has more than both of us put together. And there is no deceit with him. His word is his bond.'

Madelaine smiled. 'Yes, it is. Do you know, I feel like such a ninnyhammer. I actually thought that...'

Chloe waited expectantly. 'Yes, dear? What did you think?'

Madelaine paused, and then quickly shook her head. 'It does not matter. It was only foolishness on my part.'

Yes, of course it was foolish, Madelaine chided herself. She knew that for a certainty now. Gabriel hadn't wanted to buy Pengarron. He would have told her if he had been. Because the man she loved was an honest man; a man of integrity. He would not have lied to her. Not when he knew how very important truthfulness was to her.

Madelaine smiled happily as the carriage drew closer to Carew. Yes, the man she was in love with was, in all ways, a most admirable man. And she knew, without question, that she, in turn, was the luckiest young woman in all England to have secured his love and affection.

Carew was ablaze with lights by the time Madelaine and her aunt stepped out of the carriage and made their way up the front steps to the magnificent hall. As they handed their cloaks to the butler and approached the reception line, Chloe could barely contain her excitement.

'Just think, Madelaine, before long you will be mistress of this splendid house and everything in it. You will stand in this very line, receiving your guests as the new Countess of Trevellyn!'

'Hush, Chloe,' Madelaine said, glancing around anxiously. 'No one is supposed to know.'

'Fiddlesticks! I am not sure that I can keep it a secret much longer. Oh, Madelaine. Only look at this room! How beautiful it is.' And, indeed, it was. The grand hall had been decorated with garlands of flowers, hundreds of them, all gathered from the Carew gardens in preparation for this night.

But it was not the decorations which caused the sudden softness in Madelaine's eyes, nor the thought of what lay ahead that brought the flutters to her stomach. It was the smile on Gabriel's face as he watched her approach from his position in the receiving line. A smile that she knew was meant only for her.

John was standing in the line beside Gabriel and, next to John, Cassandra, looking breathtakingly lovely in the gown of dark green velvet.

'Cassandra's gown is perfection,' Madelaine whispered in her aunt's ear as they slowly made their way towards their hosts. 'You would never know that she was breeding.'

Chloe nodded her satisfaction. 'I own, I am very impressed. Mrs Harder did an exceptional job. I might even allow her to make a gown for your betrothal party.'

Madelaine blushed, especially given that Gabriel chose that very moment to turn and smile at her. Dear Lord, had any man ever looked so handsome as her fiancé? she wondered. Surely none of the dandies of London Society could hold a candle to the elegance of Gabriel's black jacket over a shirt and cravat so white they were dazzling to the eye.

Madelaine saw the look of admiration in his own eyes as she and Chloe finally drew to a halt in front of him and smiled. Because in the gown of shimmering silver net over an underskirt of grey satin, Madelaine knew that she was looking her very best. The gown had cost a fortune, but seeing the pleasure in Gabriel's eyes now made it worth every outrageous penny.

'Lady Trent, words…escape me,' Gabriel said, taking one of Madelaine's gloved hands in his and raising it to his lips.

Madelaine looked up into his face and hoped that the others could not see the love in her eyes as she smiled back at him. 'Lord Trevellyn.'

'And Mrs Merrill,' Gabriel said without releasing Madelaine's hand. 'I am delighted.'

Resplendent in a gown of rich garnet-coloured satin,

Chloe was beaming almost as much as her niece. 'I would not have missed tonight for anything in the world, Lord Trevellyn.'

Gabriel then turned to introduce the two women to the young man standing beside him. 'Ladies, may I introduce my brother, John Carew, and his wife, Cassandra, whom you already know. John, our neighbours at Pengarron. Madelaine, Lady Trent and her aunt, Mrs Chloe Merrill.'

John extended his hand and smiled at Madelaine with undisguised warmth. 'Lady Trent, I am so very delighted to finally be meeting you. My brother speaks of you often, and with great affection. And having met you, I can understand why.'

Madelaine felt the gentle pressure of his hand, and blushed. 'Thank you, my lord.'

He held her hand a moment longer before releasing it, and then turned to greet Chloe. 'And, Mrs Merrill, I am all gratitude for your assistance to Cassandra since our return to England. She has been singing your praises for days.'

Chloe waved aside his compliments. 'It was a pleasure, I can assure you. But how are you feeling, my lord? Lord Trevellyn tells us that you are still recovering from your injuries.'

'I am feeling one hundred per cent better than I did when I arrived in England,' John said truthfully. 'And given the news that I received early today, I am feeling even better than that.' He glanced at Madelaine in a meaningful fashion. 'I cannot think of anything which would have given me more delight.'

Madelaine laughed, and moving down the line, found herself gazing into Cassandra's soft green eyes. 'You look lovely, Cassandra.'

'As do you. Oh, my dear Madelaine, I am so very—'

'Mrs Merrill,' Gabriel said, swiftly cutting across what

Cassandra had been about to say, 'I think there is another young lady here this evening who is particularly anxious to have a word with you.'

'There is?'

'Indeed. Miss Prunella Bourne is waiting to speak with both of you, actually,' he said significantly.

Madelaine squeezed Cassandra's hand and made to move on. 'I shall look forward to having a word with you later.'

So saying, Madelaine and her aunt moved towards the ballroom, marvelling at the sheer magnificence of the room. It was truly a most appropriate setting for the elegant night. Ladies wearing gowns every colour of the rainbow paraded about on the arms of gentlemen almost as resplendent. Madelaine saw a number of regimental uniforms, and assumed them to be friends of John's.

'I understand that the Earl extended invitations to some of his friends in London too,' Chloe informed her niece as they drifted through the crowd. 'And, judging by the number of people here tonight, I would venture to say that most of them chose to accept.'

'Yes. Lord Trevellyn may profess a dislike of London and its inhabitants, but it is obvious that they do not share his antipathy.'

Madelaine nodded and glanced around the room, looking for any faces that she might recognise. She was surprised to see a goodly few that she did, many of whom had, indeed, travelled down from London. But she was surprised by none more than Prunella Bourne, who came hurrying towards them in a highly excited state.

'La, Aunt,' Madelaine said as soon as the girl was within their hearing, 'can this lovely young woman approaching be the same Miss Bourne that we met only a few days ago?'

'To be sure, Madelaine, I cannot tell. Surely *that* Miss Bourne never looked as lovely as this one does?'

Prunella blushed, as radiant as a summer peach in her gown of apricot silk. 'Lady Trent, Mrs Merrill, I cannot find the words to express my gratitude for what you have done.'

Madelaine nodded in satisfaction. The dress had turned out better than she had dared hope, bringing out in the elder Miss Bourne a loveliness even she had not been expecting. The rich colour lent a warmth to her complexion that was extremely flattering. Even her hair was dressed in a new and most becoming style.

'That was my maid,' Prunella said when Madelaine made comment upon it. 'Sarah was so taken with my appearance in the gown that she felt it only fitting that she try to do something special with my hair.' Prunella blushed, and lowered her voice. 'She even applied a touch of kohl to my eyes. It does not look too…well, too much, does it, Lady Trent?'

It was not in the least too much, and Madelaine hastened to reassure her of the fact. The skilful use of cosmetics did, in fact, only serve to draw attention to the girl's dark, lustrous eyes and thick lashes, neither of which she had really noticed before. 'Prunella, I think you look absolutely beautiful. But tell me, what did your mother say?'

Prunella's face fell. 'I fear she was not at all pleased, Lady Trent. She did not see my dress when it came, you see, being more concerned with Phoebe's and with her own. When I opened the box in my room, I thought there must have been some dreadful mistake—until I found the note from Mrs Harder, telling me that you had switched the material and the style. Mama did not even see the dress until just before it was time to leave, and by then it was too late for me to go back upstairs and change. But I could tell that she was most displeased.' Prunella's wonderful dark eyes dropped guiltily. 'I dare say poor Mrs Harder shall have a peal rung over her head for this.'

'I shall endeavour to make sure that she does not,' Chloe promised. 'But, tell me, Miss Bourne, who is that handsome young man over there, the one in the Guard's uniform who keeps staring this way?'

Prunella blushed even deeper. 'I do not know his name, Mrs Merrill, but...I have noticed him looking at me... several times this evening.'

Madelaine turned in the direction of the young man, and then started to laugh. 'Oh, but how splendid, Chloe. That is Lady Fleming's eldest son, Simon.'

'Is it?' Chloe raised her quizzing glass and peered through it. 'Well, bless my soul, so it is. I hardly recognised him in that dashing uniform. Dear me, he seems to have grown considerably since the last time I saw him.'

Prunella stared at Madelaine in astonishment. 'Do you know the young man, Lady Trent?'

'I certainly do. His mother and I are good friends.' Madelaine waved gracefully in the gentleman's direction. 'Ah, good, he has noticed me. Now, Prunella, you shall have your introduction.'

By the time the young man eagerly made his way across the crowded floor, Prunella had made every excuse for leaving that she could think of, but to no avail. Madelaine simply would not hear of it.

'Lady Trent, this is truly a pleasure,' Simon said, trying very hard not to look at Prunella as he bowed towards Madelaine. 'I was not aware that you were in Cornwall.'

'My aunt and I are spending the summer at Pengarron, Mr Fleming. You remember my aunt, Mrs Merrill.'

'Indeed. A pleasure, Mrs Merrill,' Simon said with a gracious bow in her direction.

'And this is Miss Prunella Bourne, eldest daughter of

Lord Bourne, and a good friend of mine,' Madelaine said, knowing that the connection would stand Prunella in good stead, if and when news of the introduction were to reach Lady Fleming's ears. 'Prunella, may I present Mr Simon Fleming.'

Prunella blushed deeply as the young man made his bows, and then smiled, causing two enchanting dimples to appear in her cheeks. 'Good evening, Mr Fleming.'

Mr Fleming was quite clearly entranced. 'Miss Bourne. I…hope you will forgive me for staring at you earlier this evening.'

'Really?' Prunella fanned her cheeks prettily. 'I had not noticed.'

Madelaine nodded her approval. The girl would be just fine.

'Madelaine, if you will excuse me for a moment,' Chloe said, suddenly catching sight of Lady Bourne's foreboding countenance across the room, 'I think I had best go and settle the troubled waters before they blow up into a raging storm.'

Madelaine followed her aunt's gaze, and nodded. 'Yes, I think you are probably right.'

'Mama is still looking most put out,' Prunella said softly as she watched Chloe go. 'She really was very upset about my gown.'

Madelaine smiled at the handsome young man standing faithfully at Prunella's side, and chuckled softly. 'I would venture to say that is not the only thing your mother is put out about, my dear, but never mind. Mrs Merrill will put things right.'

Eventually, Madelaine drifted away from the young pair and, turning, found herself face to face with Gabriel.

'Lady Trent,' Gabriel said for the benefit of those in the immediate area, 'are you enjoying the ball?'

'Immensely, my lord,' Madelaine replied a touch breath-lessly. 'You are to be commended for the…masterful job you have done in preparation for it. Carew looks simply beautiful tonight.'

Gabriel shook his head, and gently drew her aside. 'On the contrary, my darling, it is you who look beautiful. All else pales beside you.'

'My lord, you flatter me too much.'

'I do not think so. You haven't changed your mind about marrying me, have you, Madelaine?'

'Surely you do not think me so fickle!' And then, turning suddenly serious, Madelaine said, 'I shall never change my mind about that, Gabriel.'

'Good. Because I plan to make the announcement of our engagement right before the dancing begins. John and Cas-sandra will lead off, and then you and I will follow.'

Madelaine knew that she should have been thrilled at the honour. All she felt, however, was a deep and abiding peace that she was beside the man she loved. Nothing else really seemed to matter any more.

'Does your aunt know yet?' Gabriel enquired as they fell into step together.

'I confess, I did tell her in the carriage on the way over,' Madelaine said. 'I could not keep it from her any longer.'

'I hope she was pleased.'

The note of anxiety in his voice touched her, and it was as much as Madelaine could do not to reach up and stroke his cheek with her gloved hand. 'She was as delighted as anyone could have been. Indeed, she scolded me quite mer-cilessly for not having told her the minute you left Pen-garron this morning. Were John and Cassandra pleased?'

'They are positively delighted that you are to become their sister-in-law—especially Cassandra,' Gabriel told her with a smile. Then, glancing towards the door, he sighed in exasperation. 'Forgive me, my dear, but it looks as though I must leave you for the moment. But before I go, I should warn you that I have invited a very special guest this evening. He should be arriving at any time.'

'Are you planning on telling me who this mystery guest is?' Madelaine asked, smiling up at him.

'Not at the moment.' Gabriel kissed her with his eyes. 'But you might like to keep watch on your aunt, and let me know what her reaction is.'

Madelaine glanced at him quizzically. 'Has this something to do with Chloe?'

Gabriel laughed softly. 'Indeed, but I shall not say another word, lest I spoil the surprise.' And with that cryptic remark, he moved away, leaving Madelaine to stare after him in puzzlement.

She was not left on her own for long, however. Cassandra hurried to her side and drew her away to a quiet corner. 'My dear Madelaine, I just had to talk to you alone. John and I are so very pleased about your news!' Cassandra whispered in excitement. 'I know that you will make Gabriel a splendid wife. Indeed, I was so excited I almost blurted it out when I saw you in line.'

'Yes, I think that is why Gabriel intervened. I fancy it would have taken the wind out of his sails had the news leaked out in the receiving line,' Madelaine offered with a smile.

'He would never have forgiven me,' said Cassandra. 'He is so looking forward to making the announcement later on. I hope Mrs Merrill was pleased.'

'Highly. In fact, this has been something of a triumph for her tonight. Have you seen Prunella Bourne?'

'I have indeed, and I scarce connected her with the plain little wren I met in the shop that day. Who would have thought that she might turn out so lovely? The apricot gown becomes her very well. Has she you to thank for it?'

'No, that was all Chloe's handiwork,' Madelaine informed Cassandra proudly. 'Lady Bourne has an unfortunate habit of playing down her eldest daughter in an attempt to build up her younger one. Chloe decided to step in and reverse the roles for a change.'

Cassandra's eyes widened in understanding. 'Ah, no wonder Lady Bourne was looking so furious this evening. I was sure I heard her mutter something about "that wretched Mrs Harder" when she moved past me in the receiving line. At the time, I could only wonder at her being so put out with the lady, when it seemed that she had done such a lovely job with the girls' gowns.'

'Oh, yes, she was definitely put out,' Madelaine acknowledged, laughing softly. 'Which is why my aunt is over there now, pouring oil upon the troubled waters.'

Cassandra and Madelaine glanced across the room to where Lady Bourne was looking considerably more pleased than she had been earlier in the evening, Mrs Merrill having just taken her leave of her. They waited expectantly as Chloe made her way regally back across the floor. 'Well, that little matter is nicely taken care of,' Chloe said triumphantly.

'Was she terribly annoyed?' Madelaine enquired.

'She was as mad as hops. Threatened to close down poor Mrs Harder's shop,' Chloe said, her shoulders shaking with mirth.

'How ever did you manage to calm her, Mrs Merrill?' asked Cassandra in admiration.

'Quite simple, my dear. I merely pointed out that the sooner Prunella established herself in a profitable alliance, the sooner Lady Bourne could devote her entire attention to Phoebe. And when I pointed out that Simon Fleming was of an acceptable family, she seemed to settle down very nicely.'

'Acceptable?' Madelaine gazed at her aunt in surprise. 'Lord Fleming is an extremely wealthy man. I should have thought that would have made his son and heir far more than merely acceptable.'

'Of course it does, Madelaine, but I did not wish to make too much of it,' Chloe replied complacently. 'Lady Bourne suffered enough of a shock when she saw her ugly duckling turned into a radiant swan. With her hopes pinned so high on Phoebe achieving the illustrious match, I thought it prudent to wait to tell her the rest of the news. Besides, it is early days yet. There is nothing to say that Prunella and Simon will make a go of it.'

But a quick glance in the direction of Prunella and her doting young man was enough to put paid to that assumption immediately. If ever there was a lovelorn gentleman, it was Simon Fleming.

'Speaking of admirable alliances,' Cassandra said beaming, 'I understand that we are to become indirectly related, Mrs Merrill.'

Chloe turned loving eyes towards her niece. 'Yes, so I was informed by this wretched girl on the way here this evening. Can you credit, Mrs Carew, that she purposely kept from me the most momentous piece of news I have had this many years, and for nearly an entire day!'

'If it is of any consolation, Mrs Merrill, Gabriel did not tell John and I of the news until barely an hour ago, and you can be sure I took him to task over it too!'

'Yes, he is a sly one, your brother-in—' Chloe suddenly broke off, her eyes going to the door and widening in astonishment and disbelief. 'Oh! *My word!*'

Madelaine looked at her in concern. 'Chloe, whatever is the matter, you have gone quite pink?'

Turning, Cassandra glanced in the direction of the door, and then smiled. 'Oh, how splendid. Gabriel was hoping that he would be able to come this evening.'

Madelaine turned in the direction of the door too, but her vision was momentarily blocked by the passing of a large crowd of people. 'That who would be able to come?'

'The Duke of Kenfield,' Cassandra said, indicating the tall, distinguished-looking man who was hesitating on the threshold. 'Gabriel told me that he had invited him, but he was not sure whether his Grace would be able to attend. Ah, there goes Gabriel to greet him now. My goodness, what a handsome man the Duke is. I have not seen him this three years. Is he still unmarried?'

It was as much as Madelaine could do not to burst out laughing. 'Yes, he is. Actually, my aunt has the better acquaintance of the gentleman than I. Are you going to greet him, Chloe?'

Chloe was more flustered than Madelaine had ever seen her. She opened her fan, closed it, and then hastily opened it again. 'Greet him? No, of course not, silly girl. It is not for me to force my attentions upon the Duke.' Chloe plied her fan rapidly in front of her burning cheeks and looked in the opposite direction. 'No doubt we shall…meet during the course of the evening,' she said, unable to resist, however, casting one quick glance back towards the door.

Madelaine was smiling from ear to ear. 'It seems that you shall not have long to wait. If I am not mistaken Lord Trevellyn is escorting the Duke this way even now.'

The sudden look of confusion which appeared on Chloe's face was almost comical to behold, and induced Madelaine to place a reassuring hand on her arm. 'The field is clear tonight, Chloe. No empty-headed young chits around to give you competition. Although I dare say Lady

Bourne may try to further Miss McClusky's case with the Duke, given the young lady's absence.'

'Humph, I detect your hand in this, Madelaine,' Chloe whispered.

'I am surprised that you would think such a thing,' Madelaine said, only just managing to sound convincing. 'I had nothing to do with it—except to mention to Lord Trevellyn some time ago that you were acquainted with the Duke and held him in some regard. But I can assure you that I have nothing to do with his being here this evening. That is likely due to John and Cassandra's homecoming, as I believe the Duke and Lord Trevellyn are old friends.'

Chloe's mouth twisted ruefully. 'Not that old, I shouldn't imagine.'

There was no time for further comment. Gabriel and the Duke of Kenfield arrived at their sides, and Kenfield smiled on Chloe with unmistakable warmth. 'My dear Chloe, what a pleasure to see you again. I trust your trip back from Scotland was not too arduous?'

'Not in the least, your Grace.' Chloe executed a graceful curtsey. 'May I present my niece, Lady Trent. And, of course, you already know Lord Trevellyn's sister-in-law, Mrs Carew.'

The Duke acknowledged Madelaine with a gracious bow, before turning to address Cassandra. 'Welcome home, Mrs Carew. You must be relieved to be safely back on English soil once more.'

'I am most heartily relieved to be home, your Grace. May I say how honoured both John and I are that you have come all this way for our celebration.'

'Wouldn't have missed it for the world,' he assured her in a jovial voice. 'I know how much Gabriel has been looking forward to your return, and when he wrote to say that he was holding this celebration, the thought of not attending never occurred to me. Even less so,' the Duke added, turning to regard Chloe, 'when he told me that my dear friend, Mrs Merrill, would also be in attendance.'

Chloe lowered her eyes with a demureness that would have done a debutante proud. 'Your Grace is too kind.'

'Lady Trent,' Gabriel said casually, 'I wonder if I might have a word with you?'

'But of course, Lord Trevellyn.'

'If you will excuse us, ladies. Your Grace.'

Gabriel offered Madelaine his arm and the two walked off in the direction of the balcony. Madelaine felt rather than saw the curious eyes following them, aware that this was the second time they had been seen conversing together, and wondered what the reaction would be when Gabriel made the announcement of their betrothal later in the evening. As they stepped onto the balcony and into the shadows, however, thoughts of other people were the last thing on her mind.

'I thought I would never get you alone,' Gabriel whispered fervently as he pulled her into his arms.

'Have a care, my lord, we are far from being alone,' Madelaine said with a wry chuckle. 'There are hundreds of people standing just beyond those doors.'

'Mmm, and that is where they can stay as far as I am concerned,' Gabriel whispered against her lips, enjoying the softness of her body close to his. 'Why, Lady Trent, I do believe you are blushing,' he said wickedly. 'And I haven't even begun to show you how much I love you yet.'

Madelaine's silvery laughter bubbled up in her throat. 'Odious creature, I remember the manner in which you tried to show me your affection last time, and it left me quite breathless. However, you know very well that someone could walk through those doors and catch us, and what would you say then?'

'I would say that I am perfectly within my rights to be kissing my future wife.'

'Ah, but at the moment, no one knows that I am to be your future wife—'

Gabriel silenced her protest with a long, lingering kiss which left Madelaine out of breath and very definitely pink. 'They will before very much longer, Maddie. Because I want to do far more than just kiss those beautiful lips of yours.'

The smile in his eyes contained a sensuous flame, and Madelaine felt her cheeks grow warmer. 'Gabriel, for heaven's sake, how do you expect my colour to return to normal when you keep saying such outrageous things to me?'

'I am not sure that I care about your colour returning to normal,' he chuckled. 'I rather like seeing you blush. The colour suits you—as it does your aunt.'

Madelaine gasped and tried very hard not to laugh. 'She was positively at sixes and sevens when the Duke walked in. And I know that you are *directly* to blame for that.'

Gabriel affected a look of innocence. 'For what?'

'You specifically invited the Duke of Kenfield here this evening because you knew of my aunt's affection for him.'

'My dear Lady Trent, why on earth would you think that?'

'Oh no, I shan't believe you this time,' Madelaine said. 'You are quite scandalous, my lord, and I shall tell my aunt so. Right now, she believes that *I* had a hand in this.'

By now, Gabriel was laughing openly. 'All right, I confess, I did think it would be pleasant for your aunt if the Duke was here. But I also invited him for John and Cassandra's sakes. Notwithstanding the distance in miles, our families have always been close.'

Madelaine glanced at him suspiciously. 'Are you sure

that it was not solely as a result of the conversation we had on the way to Mrs Abbey's cottage some days ago?'

'I admit that did have some bearing on it,' Gabriel relented. 'But it was definitely not my sole purpose. Am I to be forgiven for interfering?'

Madelaine quickly reached up to place a kiss on his lips. 'I suppose I shall have to, but only because you have quite made my aunt's night.'

Gabriel went to pull her into his arms again—but stopped when he heard the sound of voices approaching from the direction of the French doors. He cared little for the slight his own reputation might suffer, but he was mindful of Madelaine's and, as such, contented himself with a brief kiss. Then, tucking her hand into the crook of his arm, Gabriel turned and led Madelaine back into the light.

By the time they re-entered the ballroom, it looked as though they had been doing nothing more than enjoying a most animated conversation.

Shortly before the dancing began, waiters began to move throughout the room with trays of champagne. An expectant buzz echoed around the ballroom as Gabriel walked to the centre of the floor, and drew John and Cassandra with him. He held up his hand for silence.

'Ladies and gentlemen, I would like to thank all of you for coming this evening to celebrate the return of my brother John and his lovely wife, Cassandra. Most of you who know me know how much I have missed them both, and I hope all of you will join me in drinking a toast to their safe return to England. To John and Cassandra,' he said, raising his glass.

The crowd echoed the sentiment, and there was a brief silence as their health was drunk. Gabriel waited until the round of applause died down before saying, 'I would also like to make an announcement before the dancing commences, concerning my own happiness.' He slowly walked to the edge of the crowd and held out his hand to Madelaine. 'My dear.'

Chloe kissed Madelaine quickly on the cheek, her eyes bright. 'Off you go, my love.'

Madelaine walked back to the centre of the room with Gabriel, well aware of the murmurs that were swirling around the room.

'Ladies and gentlemen,' Gabriel said, drawing Madelaine to his side. 'I would like all of you to know that Lady Trent has most graciously consented to be my wife. A toast, my friends, to the future Countess of Trevellyn.'

The response to his announcement was immediate. As soon as the toast was drunk, Madelaine was besieged by well wishers; surrounded by friends and strangers alike, all of whom were eager to express their congratulations along with their best wishes for her forthcoming marriage.

Anxious to save his fiancée from being overwhelmed, Gabriel gave the signal to the orchestra, and soon, the opening bars of a waltz drifted out across the floor. The crowd reluctantly drew back as Gabriel stepped forward to claim Madelaine's hand. He nodded to John and Cassandra, signifying that they should lead off.

John, however, shook his head. 'Not this time, old boy. You and Lady Trent go ahead. I would not dream of taking this moment away from you.'

And so, Gabriel and Madelaine led the first dance, circling the floor in the beautiful, sweeping steps of the waltz. It was not at all usual for an orchestra to open with a waltz, but everyone in the room recognised that this was a very special evening, and a very special first dance. The newly engaged couple spoke not a word but, to everyone watching, it was as though they spoke volumes. The depth of their love for each other shone through in their eyes, causing many a soft-hearted young lady to reach for her handkerchief. Even Lady Bourne could not bring herself to look displeased, though Phoebe was hard pressed to smile at seeing her beloved Lord Trevellyn lost to someone else.

After a suitable interval, John and Cassandra took to the floor too, their young faces reflecting their own special happiness at being there. And soon, others began to claim their partners as the dancing began in earnest.

'Mrs Merrill, I wonder if I might have this dance?'

Chloe looked up into the Duke of Kenfield's face, and for the first time that evening, managed to smile without blushing. 'I should be delighted, your Grace.'

From her place on the floor, Madelaine saw Chloe stand up with the Duke, and watched with pleasure as she accompanied him on to the dance floor. Prunella Bourne had not yet received permission to dance the waltz, but Madelaine was delighted to see her sitting comfortably with Simon Fleming, the two of them obviously enjoying an animated conversation. Phoebe Bourne was also in the company of a rather handsome young officer, bringing a look of such satisfaction to Lady Bourne's face as to assure Madelaine that there would be no further trouble in that direction.

The party went on into the small hours of the morning. Gabriel, watching Madelaine dancing a lively country dance with the Duke of Kenfield, suddenly turned to find Lord Keswick standing at his side. 'Thomas, there you are. I was beginning to wonder if you had slipped off without saying goodbye.'

'Wouldn't do that, old man,' Keswick replied. 'Not without coming to offer my congratulations on the splendid news. So, you found Trent's widow more appealing than you expected to, eh?'

Gabriel had the decency to blush, remembering all too well their earlier discussions on the matter. 'I am perfectly willing to admit that I was completely wrong, Thomas. Madelaine is the most beautiful woman I have ever met, and not only in appearance. My apologies for sounding somewhat cynical when first we discussed the matter.'

'Good Lord, no apologies called for,' Keswick responded gruffly. 'Never meant to imply there were. I am just happy that it has all worked out so well for the two of you. Dashed convenient, though,' Keswick couldn't resist adding. 'Now you shall have Pengarron without having to lay out all that blunt. Or had the offer been accepted?'

'The offer no longer stands. I withdrew it weeks ago.'

'Withdrew it? Oh, but of course you would, how stupid of me,' Keswick said. 'There would hardly be any need for you to *buy* Pengarron when you were planning to wed its owner.'

Gabriel's smile faded ever so slightly. 'You misunderstand, Thomas, I withdrew the offer *before* I decided to marry Lady Trent, not after she accepted me. Once I realised that I had fallen in love with Madelaine, *and* that she had the same feeling for the land as I, I knew that I could not be the one to cause her to give it up.'

'Does she know that the offer has been withdrawn?'

'We have never spoken of it, though I have every reason to believe that she is aware of it. I instructed my lawyer to withdraw the offer some time ago.'

'Well, I cannot say but that it has all worked out for the best, Gabriel. And I am truly delighted that you have found a lady with whom to spend the rest of your life. And now, let us enjoy a drink together before I head off to my lonely bachelor existence.' Keswick laughed ruefully. 'I shall raise my glass to yet another eligible gentleman who has succumbed to the wiles of love!'

'You should give a thought to trying it yourself, Thomas,' Gabriel chuckled. 'About time you gave up your lonely bachelor existence too.'

Keswick winked as he tipped back his glass. 'Were I fortunate enough to find such an admirable lady as Lady Trent, I might just do that!'

Chapter Twelve

It was decided that the marriage would take place in the chapel at Carew Manor, after which a wedding breakfast would be held for family and invited guests. A trip to an undisclosed destination would follow—undisclosed, because Gabriel wished to keep it as a secret from his new bride—and then the newly married couple would return to Carew to set up housekeeping. The possibility of acquiring a fashionable London residence was discussed, with the decision being made to postpone that decision until their return. Which left only one more question to be answered.

What was to be done with Pengarron?

Madelaine deliberated over that for some time. Gabriel had already assured her that she was free to do whatever she wished with the property, informing her that he had no desire to intrude on that part of her life. But it was not until they were riding out along the coast together one afternoon the following week, that the solution suddenly came to her. And when it did, Madelaine could only wonder that she had not thought of it sooner.

'Gabriel, I have been such a goosecap!' she said, drawing Nightingale to an abrupt halt.

Reining in beside her, Gabriel smiled at his fiancée indulgently. 'You are many things, my darling, but a goose-cap is certainly not one of them.'

'Dear man, thank you for saying so, but I must admit that, in this instance, I have been. I cannot image why I have not thought of it sooner.'

'Thought of what?'

'What to do with Pengarron, of course,' Madelaine replied. 'Well, it is quite obvious to me that the best and only thing to do with it is to give it to John and Cassandra. Do you not think so?'

Gabriel's smile abruptly faded. 'What I think is that it is far too generous a gift for you to consider giving *anyone*, and that you should come up with another solution.'

'But do you not see? It will solve all of our problems. John and Cassandra will have a lovely home close to Carew and we shall be able to see them on a regular basis. I think it is a truly splendid idea!'

'But what about you, Maddie? By giving it to them, you will lose any financial benefit which might have accrued by the selling of it.'

'Tosh, I have no need of more funds, nor do I wish to see Pengarron go to a stranger. I have already received one such offer and turned it down.'

Gabriel's stomach muscles clenched. 'You have?'

'Yes. Do you remember the day you came to see me regarding the hiring of a new steward for Pengarron?'

'Very well.'

'And do you recall a Mr Obadiah Jessop coming to see me?'

'I do. I feared upon hearing his name that he was an ardent suitor come all the way from London to court you.'

'Mr Jessop a suitor?' Madelaine chuckled. 'Dear me, what an alarming thought. Obadiah Jessop was my late husband's lawyer. He came to see me about an offer which had been presented to him for my consideration. It concerned the purchase of Pengarron.'

For a moment, Gabriel did not know what to say. There was a lump in his throat as big as Gibraltar, and it was all he could do to meet her eyes. 'Did he say who the offer was from?'

'No, and that is the interesting part. He informed me that it had been made anonymously.' Madelaine turned to look at him. 'Is that customary?'

'What, that a lawyer would bestir himself to come all the way here from London?'

'Gudgeon. That an offer to purchase would be made anonymously.'

Gabriel shrugged his broad shoulders. 'It can be, depending upon the circumstances.'

'Mr Jessop led me to believe that a gentleman who wished to own the house for purposes other than as a primary residence might wish to submit his offer anonymously. I, of course, immediately put a negative connotation on his words. At the time, I was most upset about it.'

'Upset about the fact that someone might wish to use Pengarron as a love nest?'

Madelaine blushed at her fiancé's putting into words what she had only speculated upon before, and shook her head. 'No—although I cannot say that I would be *happy* about the idea of Pengarron being put to such use. No, what I was upset about was the fact that someone would approach me with such an offer and not have the decency to put their name to it. How can one be expected to deal intelligently with a nameless entity? I think it is a great affront to a person's dignity.'

Gabriel pretended a sudden interest in his stallion's left hind leg. 'It is not uncommon in such instances, Madelaine, that the matter would be handled by lawyers.'

'Mmm, so Mr Jessop informed me. Still, I think it a rather shoddy way of conducting business. But I digress from our original topic. I think John and Cassandra would be delighted to have Pengarron. Especially Cassandra. She is desperately longing for a home of her own.'

Gabriel frowned. 'Has she expressed her unhappiness to you at living at Carew?'

'Oh, no, my dear, not at all. In fact, she has remarked to me, on more than one occasion, that she is exceedingly taken with the house, and that you have been a most attentive and gracious brother-in-law. But I know that she would rather have a house of her own now that she and John are starting a family. After all, my dear, it is only natural.'

Gabriel turned to look at his beautiful fiancée, and sighed. How ironic. Here was Madelaine all but pleading with him to give Pengarron to John and Cassandra—something which he had tried to effect all along—and now *he* was turning her down. What a strange hand Fate was playing in all this.

'Will you allow me to give the matter some further consideration before mentioning anything to John and Cassandra?' Gabriel asked quietly.

'Well, yes, of course,' Madelaine said, surprised that Gabriel did not perceive it to be as wonderful a solution to the problem as she did. 'After all, there is no need to rush into anything. John and Cassandra are comfortably settled at Carew for the moment, and we have the wedding to concern ourselves with. But I do think it serves as an excellent solution to the question of what we are to do with Pengarron—'

'What *you* are to do with it,' he reminded her.

Madelaine smiled. 'Very well, what *I* am to do with it, then. But it also allows you to keep the promise you made to them as well.'

'My...promise?'

'Yes. To give them a house as a belated wedding present. Oh, now you needn't look so surprised, Gabriel, Cassandra told me about it weeks ago. She also told me that you had changed your mind about the house you were planning to buy, and that you were looking for another one.'

This time, Gabriel did not even attempt to meet her eyes. He stared out over the rolling waves and felt a terrible sense of foreboding. 'I was not aware that my sister-in-law knew anything about it.'

'Well, she did confess to me that it was only as a result of having overheard a conversation between yourself and John,' Madelaine felt obliged to point out when she heard the reserve in Gabriel's voice. 'But now it does not matter, because you have the solution to that problem as well. Do you not agree?'

Gabriel sighed. 'I agree that it is an exceedingly gracious and unselfish solution, my love, and one which only a truly gracious and unselfish lady could have suggested. Thank you.' Then, because he knew he had to ask, Gabriel said, 'By the way, you did not tell me what answer you gave Mr Jessop? Did you...agree to sell Pengarron?'

An unwelcome blush crept into Madelaine's cheeks. 'No. I wrote and told him that...I had no wish to sell Pengarron at the present time because it was not my wish to leave Cornwall.'

'And was there any particular reason why you did not wish to leave?'

'Yes.' Madelaine reached out her hand and lightly caressed Gabriel's cheek with the tips of her fingers, as she had wanted to do so many times in the past. 'I knew that I was...falling in love with you and I could not bear the thought of going so far away.'

Moved more than he would have thought possible, Gabriel leaned over in the saddle and placed one hand behind Madelaine's neck. Gently drawing her closer, he kissed her with all of the love, all of the admiration, and all of the respect that he was able to communicate through a single kiss.

And may God prevent me ever having to lose any one of the three, he prayed silently.

In the days leading up to the wedding, Madelaine's happiness knew no bounds. She drifted through the halls of Pengarron with a singular lack of attention that no one could fail to notice. That she was happy, no one questioned; that she was in love, no one doubted. Perhaps that was why, when a second letter arrived from Mr Obadiah Jessop, Madelaine was far less concerned about its contents than she might otherwise have been.

My dear Lady Trent,

You will no doubt find the arrival of this letter somewhat surprising, coming, as it does, so quickly on the heels of your own recently received note advising us of your decision not to sell Pengarron. I thought it might interest you to know that, before I was able to convey your sentiments, I was advised by the other firm that their client had withdrawn his offer, and that no reason or explanation had been tendered. If you wish me to pursue the matter further, I shall see what enquiries can be made. Given your own decision not to sell Pengarron, however, I do not suppose you will be unduly troubled by this…

The letter went on, but not to any matters of great relevance. The most important issue was that the offer had been withdrawn and that no explanation had been proffered.

Not troubling herself to show the letter to anyone, Madelaine put it in the desk drawer with Mr Jessop's first letter, and promptly forgot all about it. She had no intention of asking Mr Jessop to make further enquires because, as far as she was concerned, the matter was already closed. Pengarron was to go to John and Cassandra. Gabriel had not yet advised her of his agreement to the plan, but Madelaine had no reason to doubt that such would be his decision. After all, it was the only sensible thing to do.

At Carew, Gabriel was also in possession of a letter, albeit one whose arrival he deemed long since overdue. The correspondence was from his own lawyer, confirming the fact that he had, as per his lordship's most recent request, withdrawn the offer to purchase, and assuring him that the confidentiality of the matter had been strictly maintained. The letter went on to reassure Gabriel that he need have no fear that Lady Trent would, at any time, learn of his involvement in the matter from their firm.

The news should have made Gabriel feel a great deal better than it did. And yet, as he stood looking down at the piece of parchment in his hands, he knew that it was still there; that damned feeling of uncertainty. He couldn't shake it. It was like a dark shadow following him, lurking in the background until at some time, and without warning, it would rise up to strike.

And when it did, Gabriel feared that it would take every resource at his disposal to survive the effects of the devastating blow.

Ironically, the subject of the offer on Pengarron, and its subsequent withdrawal, came up quite innocently a few nights later, as Madelaine and Gabriel were returning from an evening card party at Lord and Lady Bourne's home. Neither of them had particularly wished to attend the function but, knowing that their refusal to do so would cause a great slight to their host and hostess, they had endeavoured to make the best of it. And, as it turned out, the evening had not been a complete loss. Lady Bourne had been considerably more agreeable than usual, given the fact that, just that afternoon, Mr Simon Fleming had asked Lord Bourne for his permission to address his eldest daughter, Prunella, and that when the young man had proposed marriage, Prunella had most graciously accepted him.

The news had brought a smile of genuine pleasure to Madelaine's face, and as she and Gabriel were preparing to leave Ashcroft, she gave Lady Bourne her promise that she would call within a few days to wait upon the newly engaged Miss Bourne.

'By the by, did I ever tell you that Miss Phoebe Bourne called you quite the most handsome gentleman of her acquaintance?' Madelaine commented idly as she settled back against the comfortable cushions of her fiancé's carriage.

'No, you did not,' Gabriel replied. 'But then, perhaps you thought it better to wait until we were safely betrothed before doing so.'

'And why, pray tell, would I wish to do that?'

'Because I dare say the lovely Phoebe will cause quite a stir when she makes her come out next year.'

Madelaine glanced at him in surprise. 'Are you trying to tell me that *you* would have been one of the anxious gentlemen clamouring at her feet?'

'Well, we shall never know now, shall we, because I am honour bound to marry you.'

Her mouth twitched with amusement. 'Dear me, had I known that you were of such a mind, I would have declined your proposal and allowed you to take your chances with the young lady at the appropriate time.'

'There is no need of that, Maddie, I am quite prepared

to make the best of it,' Gabriel told her stoically. 'And, in truth, I do prefer my ladies to be a touch more experienced—'

'*Gabriel!*'

'When it comes to the running of a gentleman's household.' Gabriel turned to regard his fiancée with a perfectly straight face. 'Whatever is the matter, my dear? Surely you did not think that I was referring to anything else?'

Madelaine tried very hard not to laugh, but in the end, she could do naught else. 'Gabriel, you are an unmerciful tease. I know perfectly well what you were referring to—and you needn't try to make me think otherwise!'

Enjoying the sight of her blushes, Gabriel pulled her close and kissed her. 'My darling Maddie, you are the only woman that I see, and the only woman I ever wish to see. I have no more interest in Phoebe Bourne than I do in... Lady Bourne herself. Satisfied?'

'Completely.' Madelaine sighed and snuggled into the warmth of his shoulder. 'Speaking of other gentlemen, I thought you might be interested to know that I had another letter from Mr Jessop.'

Gabriel stiffened, instantly on his guard. 'Oh?'

'Yes, regarding the offer I received on Pengarron. It seems that the anonymous gentleman no longer wishes to buy it. Strange, do you not think? Someone changing their mind like that?'

Inwardly, Gabriel breathed a sigh of relief. He had been wondering how long it would take before news of the offer's withdrawal would reach her, and thereby bring to a close, once and for all, the matter of Pengarron's purchase. 'What I think strange, my lovely lady, is that you have not told me once in the past three hours how much you love me.'

Madelaine sat up in surprise, her eyes widening before

the slow burning fire in his. 'My lord, you are uncommon bold. How could I have told you anything of a personal nature when we have been engaged in company for the past *four* hours? Besides, are you that insecure that you need to hear it so often?'

'No, I am that much in love that I *like* to hear it that often,' Gabriel told her, before leaning over and kissing her full on the mouth.

Madelaine's lips were sweeter than any wine he had ever tasted, and as Gabriel drew her close, he knew that he held a treasure far more precious than diamonds or gold. The fullness of Madelaine's breasts pressed up against his jacket caused the muscles of his lower body to ache, but he had no desire to press his attentions on her now. The day would come when he would be able to show her in the privacy of their marriage bed just how much he loved her, but for now, his need for Madelaine went far beyond the physical. Indeed, it went beyond anything he had ever known. He wanted all of Madelaine; her heart, and her mind, and her soul. He wanted to teach her what it was to love, and how to love in return.

And now, at such a time, and with such thoughts running riot through his body, she brought up the irritating issue of Pengarron.

Gabriel sighed as he broke off the kiss, and then rested his chin against the softness of her hair. Thank goodness he had withdrawn the offer in time. What would Madelaine have said had she found out that he had lied to her about his interest in Pengarron? She had been willing to forgive him once for pretending to be a steward, and then, again, for firing her servant. But he was very much afraid that if she found out that he had lied to her for a third time— especially about this—she might not be able to find it in her heart to forgive him—or to trust him—ever again.

* * *

The Duke of Kenfield stayed in the area for a full two weeks longer. He had a great many friends and acquaintances in Cornwall and, as he had not been to the area in some years, he took considerable pleasure in visiting them all. He was also a constant visitor to Pengarron, which pleased Madelaine—and her aunt—no end.

In fact, as Chloe grew visibly happier and more relaxed in the Duke's company, Madelaine felt sure that a marriage proposal would soon be in the offing. She rejoiced in the warm glow of contentment which seemed to settle upon her aunt's features each time the Duke was there. Consequently, it came as no great surprise to her when, upon returning from a ride one fine morning, her maid advised her that Mrs Merrill and the Duke were waiting to see her in the drawing room as soon as possible.

Suspecting that news of some import awaited her, Madelaine did not bother going upstairs to change her clothes, but hurried directly to the drawing room. There she found the Duke and her aunt standing together by the fireplace. There was a look of such joy on Chloe's face that, even had Madelaine not noticed the magnificent sapphire ring gracing her aunt's finger, she would still have known what had happened.

'My dear, we have the most splendid news,' Chloe said, holding out both hands to her niece.

'Indeed,' the Duke agreed, smiling almost as broadly as the lady beside him. 'My dear Chloe has just agreed to become my wife.'

'Your wife! But that is the most wonderful news, your Grace,' Madelaine cried as she went forward to congratulate them. 'I am so very happy for you both.'

Chloe's eyes were shining. 'Thank you, my dear. I think I speak for both…Ian and myself when I say that your blessing makes our happiness complete.'

'I could be nothing *but* happy,' Madelaine assured her. She embraced her aunt, and then impulsively reached up to press a kiss to the Duke's cheek. 'Shall you be married soon?'

'Just as soon as Chloe wishes,' Kenfield said in his deep, rolling voice. 'I tried to convince her to marry me today, but she would have none of it.'

'Impossible man,' Chloe chided him affectionately. 'You wouldn't even have time to procure a special license.'

'In Scotland, we do not waste time with such things,' the Duke replied, his blue eyes twinkling. 'We have our own way of doing things.'

'Yes, as I recall you do,' Chloe responded in a dry tone. 'I hope you do not have the pipes played *every* morning at six o'clock?'

'Of course not.'

'Thank goodness!'

'In the summer, we play them at half past five, when the birds begin to sing.'

'Half past five! But...surely no one with any sense is up and about at such an hour!'

The Duke chuckled. 'Then I fear you must call me senseless too, my dear, for that is the hour at which I rise every morning. Unless you give me a better reason for staying abed, that is,' he added, winking at her quite boldly.

Madelaine turned away to hide a smile, while Chloe actually looked embarrassed. '*Well!* I think we shall say no more upon *that* subject, my lord, lest you put both my niece *and* myself to the blush.'

The words were sternly spoken, but it seemed to Madelaine that her aunt's eyes were sparkling almost as brightly as his. It was obvious that the two of them shared a special rapport, and Madelaine had no doubts that, over time, that bond would grow even stronger. And so, after enjoying a glass of champagne to celebrate the news with them, Madelaine took her leave. She bade the Duke a fond farewell—knowing that he would be leaving within the hour to return to Scotland—and assured her aunt that she would be back very soon. Then, feeling that there was someone else who simply had to hear news of the wonderful event which had taken place that morning, Madelaine left the house and headed for Carew.

To Madelaine's disappointment, it was not Gabriel she saw walking down the front steps of Carew as she brought her mare to a prancing halt on the gravel drive, but Lord Keswick. He was pulling on his leather gloves in preparation for climbing up into the seat of his stylish, high-perch phaeton.

'Ah, good morrow, Lady Trent,' Keswick greeted her affably. 'What a pleasure to see you looking so bright and cheery this morning. Almost makes getting up before noon worthwhile.'

Madelaine laughed as the young lad who was holding Keswick's team reached over to take her own mare's reins. 'It certainly did this morning, Lord Keswick. But what brings you out visiting so early?'

'Not visiting, precisely. Came to borrow one of Gabriel's whips. Thought it might help my driving. Unfortunately, he's not about.'

Madelaine's face fell. 'Oh, what a shame. I was hoping to give him some excellent news.'

'Oh? Something of a personal nature?'

'Well, I had thought to tell Gabriel first,' Madelaine said, hesitating, 'but I suppose he shall know soon enough. I have just learned that my aunt and the Duke of Kenfield are to be married.'

'Married! But that is splendid news,' Keswick said, gen-

uinely pleased by her announcement. 'By Jove! This does
seem to be a dangerous area to live in. Two engagements
within a matter of weeks.' He lifted his nose and sniffed
delicately. 'Must be something in the air.'

Madelaine laughed softly. 'It could well be, my lord.'

'Is your aunt looking forward to living in Scotland?'

'I really cannot say. I did not wish to intrude on their
time overly much, as the Duke was getting ready to return
to Scotland.'

'Well, I dare say that you are well pleased with the way
everything has turned out,' Keswick observed. 'Your aunt
and the Duke in a castle in Scotland, and you and Gabriel
comfortably ensconced at Carew. Gabriel also tells me that
it is your wish to give Pengarron to John and Cassandra.'

'Yes. I think it an excellent solution to the problem of
what to do with the house, and one which will make everyone very happy.'

'It is, indeed, a most generous offer, Lady Trent. I know
that Gabriel is delighted that his hopes for seeing John and
Cassandra at Pengarron are finally being realised, and in
such an excellent manner.'

The statement was uttered in complete innocence and,
had she been anyone else, the proffered remark might easily
have passed by unnoticed. But Madelaine was not anyone
else. And as the relevance of the remark took hold, and its
meaning became clear, she felt the walls of her perfect
world begin to crumble around her.

…*his hopes were* finally *being realised*…

'Well, I suppose I had best take myself off,' Lord Keswick said, climbing up into the seat of the phaeton and
gathering up the reins.

'Lord Keswick, a…moment if you please,' Madelaine
said, her voice sounding strained and unnatural, even to her
own ears. 'Am I to understand that…Lord Trevellyn

has…long since held out hopes of his…brother and sister-in-law…living at Pengarron?'

'Well, yes, of course he has. That was his plan all along. But…surely he has told you of that?'

Gazing at him in stunned disbelief, Madelaine numbly shook her head. She was unable to do more than that. The depth of her grief was so great as to render it an almost physical pain.

Lord Keswick, watching the life and the colour drain from Lady Trent's face, knew that he had done the unpardonable. Gabriel had obviously *not* told his fiancée of his plan to buy Pengarron; in believing that he had, Keswick had inadvertently betrayed a confidence for which the repercussions could be devastating. 'Lady Trent, I can assure you—' he began hastily.

'No. Pray, do not…attempt to placate me, Lord Keswick,' Madelaine interrupted in a hoarse, broken voice. 'It will only…compound the injury already done me by Lord Trevellyn.' She took a long, deep breath, a simple exercise, yet one made exceedingly difficult by the fact that a hand seemed to be closing around her throat. 'Was my—was… Lord Trevellyn responsible for the anonymous offer made to me on Pengarron?'

'No, of course not,' Keswick lied automatically, for what else could he do? He had to protect his friend until he had a chance to explain the whole wretched situation to him. 'How silly of you to think that—whoa, Jezebel! Dash it all, Vixen, be still!' he shouted as the high-spirited horses suddenly started to plunge and prance. In truth, Keswick was glad of the diversion. It gave him a moment to gather his chaotic thoughts. 'Whatever made you think such a thing, Lady Trent?'

The telltale colour in your cheeks for one, Madelaine felt like telling him, for Lord Keswick had indeed turned a shade of red that owed nothing to his handling of the spirited bits of blood. And his continued avoidance of her eyes only served to confirm Madelaine's worst suspicions.

Gabriel had lied to her. He wasn't in love with her, he had only *pretended* to love her so that he could gain possession of Pengarron. *That* was what he had wanted all along.

A wave of nausea rose up and lodged in Madelaine's throat. *She had to get away.* The thought of staying here a moment longer, and risking Gabriel's return, could not be borne. Her feelings were too raw, and her pain too deep, to bear further discussion right now. She needed to be alone.

And so, raising her chin, Madelaine summoned what little dignity she had left and nodded to the stable boy. The moment he released the reins, she whirled the mare's head around and galloped back towards Pengarron—vowing never to set foot on Trevellyn property again!

The letter to Gabriel was not easy.

Madelaine knew what she wanted to say. She had thought about the wording of the letter all the way home from Carew. And yet, as she sat in her bedchamber at Pengarron, with her hand resting motionless upon the page, the words she so desperately wanted to say would not come. All she could think about was that Gabriel had lied to her.

That was the hardest thing for her to come to terms with: the fact that the man to whom she had willingly given her heart had betrayed her, without thought or compunction. His *only* purpose in courting her had been to win Pengarron. Madelaine knew that now. He had taken her love and her trust, and he had used them for his own purposes.

How humiliating to discover that it had all been nothing but an act!

Swallowing the sob that rose in her throat, Madelaine dropped the quill on the desk and pressed both hands to her face. *Why?* Why hadn't Gabriel told her that he wanted Pengarron? Would it not have been better to tell her the truth than risk having her hear it from a stranger? Yes, it was true, Gabriel had been the first to speak to her about the possibility of her selling Pengarron, but Madelaine had believed that his suggestion had stemmed from the financial prudence of the move, rather than out of any selfish interests of his own. He had never even expressed an interest in the house for himself. But the *truth* was that, all along, he had been scheming to get it away from her. First by submitting an anonymous offer to her lawyer, and then by marrying her.

Certainly, the latter made more sense, Madelaine reflected bitterly. After all, why pay good money for something that he could get simply by marrying her?

Madelaine closed her eyes and fought back the tears that trembled on her lashes. Oh, what a simpleton she had been. Only a matter of days ago, Gabriel had assured her that she could do whatever she wished with Pengarron. And only yesterday, she had told *him* that she wished to give it to John and Cassandra. But instead of jumping at the opportunity, Gabriel had told her that he needed more time to think about it.

'More *time*!' Madelaine cried out loud, dashing her hand across her eyes. God, how he must have laughed at her. And how very easy she had made it for him. What would he have said, she wondered, had she expressed an interest in doing something with Pengarron *other* than giving it to John and Cassandra? Would he have tried to persuade her that, as their new sister-in-law, it was the *right* thing to do? Or would he have said that it only made sense to keep the house 'in the family' as it were? And if she had still refused, would Gabriel have exercised his rights and *ordered* her to dispose of it in the manner *he* wished?

Sadly, Madelaine began to fear that he would. Because it was now quite clear to her that, as much as she might hate to admit it, Gabriel Carew was simply that kind of man.

When the letter was at long last done, Madelaine carefully folded it over and pressed her seal into the soft wax. She would write a second letter to Cassandra when she was able, bidding her goodbye and wishing her well for the future…but not now. She was too emotionally drained by the effort of writing Gabriel's to do any more. She needed time to be alone before putting pen to paper again. Instead, she tucked the letter into the top drawer of her writing desk, and then rang for her maid.

'Betty, after dinner, you are to begin packing our things,' Madelaine told her in a voice that was noticeably lacking in emotion. 'We will be setting off for London first thing in the morning.'

'For *London*, my lady?' the maid repeated.

Madelaine saw the look of surprise on the young girl's face, and nodded. 'Yes. And you are not to breathe a word of this to anyone, do you understand?'

'Y-yes, my lady.' The girl hesitated for a moment, clearly not understanding at all. 'Does that include my not telling…Mrs Merrill?' she asked uncertainly.

'Most assuredly. I shall speak to Mrs Merrill about this myself at the appropriate time.'

Without waiting for the girl's reply, Madelaine picked up her gloves and swiftly made her way downstairs. She was hoping to make good her escape without the benefit of witnesses, but she had reckoned without the ubiquitous presence of Berkeley.

'Ah, Lady Trent,' the butler said upon seeing her at the foot of the stairs. 'Mrs Merrill was just looking for you. She is in the dining room and was wondering whether you would be joining her for luncheon.'

Madelaine's heart plummeted. She had no wish to cast a shadow on Chloe's happiness, but she knew that, in her present frame of mind, it would be impossible for her to do anything but. 'Regrettably, I have an...appointment which begs my immediate attention, Berkeley,' she told him. 'Pray convey my regrets to my—no, wait, perhaps it is better that you do not tell my aunt that you have seen me. It will be...easier than trying to explain why I was suddenly called away.'

There was only a very slight pause before Berkeley bowed and withdrew, leaving Madelaine to continue on her way. Her groom was waiting for her at the front door, as she had instructed him to, and, signalling to him to bring the mare forward, Madelaine allowed him to help her mount. But she did not allow him to escort her. She had no desire for any manner of company at the moment. Only solitude would help in the sorting out of her emotions right now.

Without being consciously aware of it, Madelaine set the mare in the direction of the linden glade. At the point where she had found the injured deer, she finally stopped and dismounted, then listlessly began to wander through the tall grass. Her thoughts were as distracted as her steps. Memories of everything Gabriel had ever said came back to haunt her. His sweetly whispered words dogged her every step as she wandered deeper into the forest. Finally, unable to hold them back any longer, Madelaine raised her face to the sky and let the tears run freely down her face, tasting the saltiness of them on her lips.

'Oh, Gabriel, why did you have to lie to me?' Madelaine whispered softly. 'Why did you have to destroy… everything that we had together? Why couldn't you just have been Taylor—the man I first fell in love with.'

The long unspoken thought, finally put into words, should have surprised Madelaine—except that she knew it to be the truth. She *had* started to fall in love with Gabriel Carew when she had believed him to be a servant; a proud, strong man who had professed himself content with the simple pleasures of life.

Why could he not have stayed that way? Madelaine pondered sadly. Why had it been necessary for him to turn out to be the mighty Earl of Trevellyn: a man of her own social standing—and one who had made her fall so deeply in love that she was quite unable to see or think of anyone else?

The sound of a twig snapping in the grass behind her roused Madelaine from the misery of her thoughts, and she slowly turned around. Her eyes scanned the shadowy spaces between the trees, looking for the source of the noise. But she could see nothing. The forest was still. She was quite alone.

Feeling sure that it must have been a bird or some other small woodland creature routing through the undergrowth, Madelaine turned and walked on. Nightingale followed, her hooves leaving deep imprints in the soft ground. They had not gone very far, however, before Nightingale suddenly threw up her head and whinnied nervously. Turning again, Madelaine stopped—and this time she went quite pale.

A man was sitting astride a bay gelding, watching her.

Madelaine stood very still, a shadow of alarm touching her face. She did not recognise the man. His clothing was dirty and his face was covered with a dark stubble of beard. There was a vicious twist to the set of his mouth, and his nose looked as though it might have been broken more than once. But it was his eyes that disturbed Madelaine the most. They were small and dark, almost hidden beneath a shaggy fringe of heavy, black eyebrows. They seemed to Madelaine to be filled with a kind of burning resentment—and they frightened her almost as much as did the pistol held loosely across the man's saddle.

She wiped the tears from her eyes and strove for composure. 'Who are you, and what is your business here? This is private property.'

'Aye, I know that, Lady Trent,' the man said quietly.

He made no moves towards her, but the fact that he knew who she was told Madelaine that this was not a chance encounter. 'How do you know who I am?'

'Doesn't matter how I know. Just that I do.'

'Then…perhaps you would be so good as to tell me who *you* are.'

'Can't you guess?'

Apprehension darted through Madelaine's body. 'No. Should I be able to?'

'I would have thought you might, being as how you're so friendly with the Lord of Carew.'

Madelaine frowned. What had *Gabriel* to do with this? 'Forgive me, but I am none the wiser for your saying that.'

'The name be Diggs, ma'am.'

Madelaine gasped. *Diggs!*

Her reaction caused the man's sinister smile to widen in satisfaction. 'I see you have heard of me, then.'

She tilted her head in a nod. 'You were my…late husband's gamekeeper.'

'I was. Until his great and mighty lordship sent me packing.'

Madelaine hesitated, trying to gauge the man's emotional state. He sounded rational enough, though she judged by his appearance that he had been living on his wits for some time. The question was, what did he want? He hadn't made any overly-threatening gestures towards her. Could it be that he simply wanted to talk?

'Lord Trevellyn told me that you were…stealing from my husband, Diggs,' Madelaine said quietly. 'And that it was…because of that, he dismissed you.'

Diggs laughed unpleasantly. 'I weren't stealing, Lady Trent. I was merely…living off the land.'

Madelaine's finely shaped eyebrows drew together in a frown. 'My husband paid you a good wage. Surely there was no need for you to…live off the land.'

'And what would the likes of you know about that?' Diggs snapped, his smile vanishing. 'Have you ever had to live by your wits, Lady Trent? Not sure where your next meal was coming from, or where you was going to sleep that night? Do you know what it's been like since he turned me off? *Do* you?'

Madelaine shook her head, aware that the man was beginning to sweat. 'No.'

'I haven't been able to find work because nobody will take me on. Lord Trevellyn and his bloody servant saw to that. He had no right to turn me off. It weren't his place.'

It was obvious that the man was working himself into a state of considerable agitation, and Madelaine knew that now, more than ever, she had to remain calm. If she provoked him, there was no telling what he might do. 'No, I agree, it was not Lord Trevellyn's place to dismiss you, Diggs, but—'

'I told him it was nobody's business but yours, but he wasn't having any of it,' Diggs muttered. He pressed his heels into the bay's side and urged it forward. 'And you wouldn't have turned me off, would you, Lady Trent?'

A cold knot formed in the pit of Madelaine's stomach at his approach, and unconsciously, she took a step backwards. 'Diggs, I don't know what you're planning, but... you must believe me when I say that no good can come of it. It would be...best for all concerned if you just...let me get on my horse and ride back to Pengarron.'

'Ride back to Pengarron? Oh, no, Lady Trent, I can't do that,' Diggs said quietly. 'Because I warned his lordship that he hadn't heard the last of me. I told him as much the day he turned me off.'

'But...what have I to do with your vendetta against Lord Trevellyn?' Madelaine asked in confusion.

'You've got a lot to do with it,' Diggs said, beginning to smile in a manner that made Madelaine's skin crawl. 'You see, I know about you and him. I still have a few friends up at the manor, and they tell me what's going on. They told me that you and him were getting married, and *that's* when I started thinking about getting me own back. I can't let you ride back to Pengarron now, Lady Trent,' Diggs said, suddenly lifting the pistol and aiming it straight at her. 'Because I need you to get even with him. That's why you are coming...with me.'

Chapter Thirteen

At half past six, Chloe sat in the drawing room at Pengarron and tried to keep her mind focused on the words of the page that she was reading. Unfortunately, with everything that had happened today, she was finding it an exceedingly difficult thing to do.

What a summer it was turning out to be! Her favourite niece happily betrothed to the dashing Earl of Trevellyn, and now, today, her own dear Duke proposing marriage to her. Truly, she was blessed to have been loved by two such admirable men in her lifetime.

But where could Maddie be? When she had left this afternoon, Chloe had assumed that she had gone to Carew to share her good news with Lord Trevellyn. But that was several hours ago. Surely she should have returned by now—especially since she had given no indication that she intended to be gone for long.

Setting aside her book, Chloe got up and crossed to the bell pull. When Berkeley opened the door moments later, she asked him whether or not he had seen Lady Trent within the last few hours.

'Er...not since she left to go riding this morning, madam,

no,' the butler said, suddenly remembering the promise he had made to his mistress.

'I see. Did she tell you if she was planning on returning for dinner?'

'No, madam, she did not.'

Chloe frowned. How strange. It was most unlike Madelaine not to say what her plans for the evening might be. 'And you are sure that no message has come for me from Carew?'

'Quite sure, Mrs Merrill.'

Chloe tapped her foot. No letter and no news. Strange indeed. 'Thank you, Berkeley, that will be all.'

The butler bowed and started towards the door. At the threshold, he faltered. 'Madam, if I may say one thing—'

'Of course.'

'Lady Trent…did come back to the house this morning. But she told me that…I was not to tell you that she had.'

'I beg your pardon?' Chloe glanced at him sharply. 'Why would Lady Trent not wish me to know that she was here?'

'She did not say, madam. She just left to go riding again.'

'I see. Did she take a groom with her?'

'Not to my knowledge.'

'And to your knowledge, she has not returned.'

'No, madam.'

Chloe glanced at the clock on the mantel again and saw that it was getting on for seven o'clock. 'Have Lady Trent's maid come to me at once.'

'Of course, Madam.'

The butler bowed and withdrew. As soon as he did, Chloe got up from the chair and walked across to the window. Madelaine had come back from Carew and then left again almost immediately. And she had instructed Berkeley

that he was not to say a word to anyone about her return.
Why?

'You wished to see me, Mrs Merrill?' a voice said tim-
idly from the doorway.

'Hmm? Oh yes, child, come in. I understand from Berkeley that Lady Trent was in the house for a short time after
coming back from her ride this morning. Did you see her,
by chance, before she left again?'

'Y-yes, ma'am, I did.'

'And did she say anything to you?'

The girl suddenly began to look nervous. 'Yes, ma'am,
but...she told me I...wasn't to say anything to you about
it.'

Chloe went very still. 'She said that?'

'Yes, ma'am.'

Skilfully concealing her dismay that her niece had instructed *two* servants to keep silent about her whereabouts,
Chloe raised her eyebrows imperiously. 'I do not approve
of servants keeping secrets, Betty. Now, I want to know
the truth. *What* did Lady Trent tell you that I was not to
be made aware of? Oh, come along, child, you need not
fear that I shall punish you, I am merely concerned about
Lady Trent and I wish to know where she is.'

At that, Betty began to look frightened. 'There's nothing
happened to her, is there, ma'am?'

'Of course not. But if you know where my niece is, I
should like to hear it.'

'I don't know where she is, ma'am,' Betty said anxiously. 'All she told me before she left, was that I was
to...start packing her things because we were...returning
to London first thing in the morning.'

Chloe stared at the girl. 'Returning to London! But what
on earth could have put such an idea in her head? She has
said nothing to me about it.'

'No, ma'am.'

'So she did not tell you where she was going?'

'No, ma'am. She just took up her gloves and left.'

'And you haven't seen her since?'

Betty's bottom lip started to quiver. 'No, ma'am.'

For the first time, Chloe started to feel the stirrings of real concern. 'Thank you, Betty, you may go.'

The maid tearfully bobbed a curtsy and left. Five minutes after she did, Chloe quit the drawing room and climbed the stairs to Madelaine's chamber. Why would Maddie wish to return to London now, when there was still so much to plan for the wedding? Chloe asked herself. Unless it had something to do with the wedding, of course. But if that had been the case, why hadn't Maddie told her about it? And surely a brief trip to London did not warrant her packing *all* of her things?

Opening the bedroom door, Chloe paused for a moment on the threshold and glanced around the room. She had no idea what she was hoping to find, but she was convinced that something was going on. Unfortunately, at first glance, nothing seemed to be amiss. Betty had not yet begun to pack her mistress's things, and everything was still in its place.

Not sure why, Chloe went first to Madelaine's writing table. Hoping that her niece would forgive the intrusion into her privacy, she reached for the top drawer and pulled it open.

She saw it at once. A letter, sitting atop Madelaine's other things. It was formally addressed to the Right Honourable Gabriel Carew, Fifth Earl of Trevellyn. And it was sealed.

Chloe picked up the creamy parchment and felt icy fingers wrap around her heart. Why would Madelaine be writ-

ing such a formal letter to her fiancé? And why had she
done it in secret?

Convinced now that matters were definitely not as they
should be, Chloe tucked the letter into the pocket of her
gown and hurried back downstairs. The sooner she found
out what was troubling Madelaine, the better. As such, she
ordered the carriage brought round at once and informed
the driver that he was to take her to Carew.

Gabriel was just sitting down to dinner when his butler
appeared in the doorway. He had spent the entire day on
the estate with Taylor, and was looking forward to a hot
meal, followed by a quiet evening filled with pleasurable
thoughts of his lovely Madelaine and the life that they
would soon be starting together. So when he was given the
news that Lord Keswick had arrived and wished to see him
at once, Gabriel could not find it in his heart to be particularly pleased.

'He did say that it was on a matter of extreme urgency,
my lord,' the butler added, when he saw his master hesitate.

Gabriel sighed, and reached for his glass of wine. 'Very
well, Parker, show him up. And set another place at the
table. No doubt Lord Keswick has not yet dined.'

'Very good, my lord.'

Moments later, Lord Keswick appeared at the doorway.
He was breathing heavily, as though he had run the entire
way to Carew, and it was evident from the look on his face
that he was extremely agitated.

'Good lord, Thomas, whatever is the matter?' Gabriel
enquired, cutting a slice of succulent roast beef from the
joint before him. 'You look as though the hounds of Hell
have been after you.'

'Gabriel, pray forgive my…intrusion on your dinner, but

the…matter upon which I needed to see you could not… wait another moment.'

The genuine note of apprehension in his voice caused Gabriel to glance across at him in surprise. 'What can be so serious that it warrants you speaking to me with such haste? Will you not join me for dinner?'

'Thank you, no. I find myself quite without appetite this evening.' Drawing his hand across his forehead in a gesture of abject frustration, Keswick suddenly began to pace back and forth in front of the table. 'My dear friend, it was neither my…wish nor my intention to cause a problem for you, but I fear that, by my very actions, that is precisely what I have done.'

Wiping his mouth on the snowy white napkin, Gabriel said, 'And what is it, precisely, that you have done?'

At that moment, the dining room door opened again and Parker appeared once more, looking decidedly embarrassed at having to disturb his master yet again. 'Excuse me, my lord, but…Mrs Merrill is asking to see you.'

'Mrs Merrill! At this time of the evening?'

'She bid me tell you that it was regarding a matter of the utmost importance, my lord.'

Across the room, Lord Keswick sighed. 'Yes, I have no doubt that it is.'

Sending a probing glance towards his friend, Gabriel pushed back from the table and rose. 'Very well. Show Mrs Merrill in, Parker.'

'Yes, my lord.'

'Am I to understand that you *know* what the lady is here about, Thomas?' Gabriel asked.

'I fear I do, Gabriel, but we may as well wait for her to confirm it.'

Moments later, Chloe walked into the room. Her normally tranquil expression was marred by tiny lines of worry. 'Lord Trevellyn, pray forgive my untimely interruption.'

'There is no need to apologise, Mrs Merrill. Is everything all right?'

'No, my lord, I have reason to believe that things are far from all right. I am most concerned about—oh, Lord Keswick,' Chloe added, suddenly catching sight of the other gentleman standing quietly to one side. 'Forgive me, I did not mean to interrupt your dinner with Lord Trevellyn.'

'I am not here to dine, Mrs Merrill. I dare say that you are employed on the same mission as I. Before we speak of that, however, please allow me to offer my most sincere congratulations on your recent betrothal.'

'My betrothal?' Chloe's attention was momentarily diverted. 'But...how did you know of that?'

'I chanced to meet Lady Trent this morning when she came to give Lord Trevellyn the good news.'

Gabriel started. 'Madelaine was *here*?'

Lord Keswick nodded. 'We both were. I came to see if I might borrow your new whip, and Lady Trent arrived just as I was leaving. We spoke...briefly.'

'When was this?' Gabriel enquired.

'Around half past eleven, I should think.'

Chloe took a deep breath. 'My lord, forgive me for interrupting but...have you seen my niece today?'

Gabriel frowned deeply. 'No, Mrs Merrill. I have been occupied with Taylor on the estate since early this morning.'

'So it is safe to assume that the two of you have not had...words?'

Gabriel's eyebrow rose in bewilderment. 'Words? Of course not. What would make you say such a thing?'

'*That* is what I came to talk to you about, Gabriel,' Lord Keswick interrupted in a melancholy tone.

Gabriel glanced at him sharply. 'Then I would encourage you to speak at once so that we may all know what is going on.'

'Mrs Merrill,' Lord Keswick began, 'am I to understand that…Lady Trent is very…upset?'

'I do not know, Lord Keswick,' Chloe answered him truthfully, 'because I have not seen my niece since she left Pengarron this morning. The Duke and I had, in fact, just told her of our betrothal, and after a brief celebration, Madelaine left. I assumed that she was coming here to tell Lord Trevellyn the news. But when she had still not returned by half past six, I started making enquiries with the servants.'

'And what did you learn?'

'That she *had* come back to Pengarron, but that she left messages with *two* of the servants that I was not to be told about it. More importantly, my niece instructed her maid to begin packing her things as she was returning to London first thing in the morning.'

'Returning to *London*?' Gabriel echoed in surprise.

'Damn and blast,' Lord Keswick swore, sinking heavily into the nearest chair. 'It is worse than I thought. I knew that Lady Trent was upset when we parted company this morning, but I had no idea it would come to this.'

'Thomas, I think you had better start telling me what you know of this, and quickly,' Gabriel ordered, beginning to feel a prescience of doom.

'Before you do,' Chloe said, extracting Madelaine's letter from her reticule and handing it to Gabriel, 'perhaps you should read this.'

Gabriel took the folded parchment. In silence, he read the formal writing of his name and, beginning to fear the worst, quickly broke the seal. He recognised Madelaine's flowing hand at once:

Lord Trevellyn:

It would seem that I have foolishly allowed myself to be taken in yet again. I give you your due; you were certainly more convincing than any of the gentlemen who went before you. At least I knew what they were after.

By the time you read this, I shall be on my way back to London. I find that I have no wish to reside in Cornwall, and take leave to tell you that I will not be returning. Thus, you may consider our engagement at an end. No doubt you will be relieved to learn that it will not be necessary for you to marry me in order to gain possession of Pengarron, as I now understand was your original intent. Though your offer to purchase has been withdrawn, and no doubt shortly after my accepting your proposal of marriage, I am sure you will wish to tender it again. I plan to offer the property for sale, as I no longer wish to have anything to do with it. My lawyer, Mr Obadiah Jessop, will handle the transaction.

As regards your engagement ring, I did not wish to enclose it for fear of arousing suspicion. It will be returned to you by my aunt, in whose possession I intend to leave it, after explaining the reasons for its return. I have also written a brief note to Cassandra, explaining simply that I changed my mind...

The letter went on, but Gabriel could read no more. He closed his eyes and swore softly under his breath. *He had lost her.* Through his own deceit, he had lost the most precious thing in his life. And he had no one to blame for it but himself.

'Did Lady Trent give this to you?' he asked Chloe tonelessly.

'No. I found it tucked away in a drawer in her room. But...whatever is the matter, Lord Trevellyn?' Chloe asked quickly, seeing the stricken look on his face. 'Has something happened?'

'Yes, I fear it has, Mrs Merrill.' Gabriel turned his gaze on Keswick. 'What took place between you and Lady Trent this morning?'

Keswick sighed like a man guilty of having committed a heinous crime. 'I told Lady Trent that you were...very pleased that your...wish to see John and Cassandra happily settled at Pengarron was finally coming to pass. And when she asked if...you had long since hoped to see them living there, I said that...yes, you had. That it was what you had...planned for all along. When I saw her looking... much as you do now, I realised that you...had not told her the truth.'

When Gabriel said nothing, Lord Keswick hung his head. 'Forgive me, Gabriel. I was so sure that you would have...told her. I remember you saying that you wanted honesty between the two of you, and I felt sure that...if Lady Trent had agreed to marry you, she must have known what you wished to do and...understood it. I swear, I never meant to offend—'

'Thomas, I understand,' Gabriel interrupted quietly. 'I do. And you are perfectly right. I *should* have told Madelaine the truth, right from the start.'

'Lord Trevellyn, I am not sure that I understand,' Chloe said, frowning. ' Are you saying that...you lied to my niece?'

'Yes, Mrs Merrill, I did,' Gabriel admitted. Wordlessly, he handed her the letter.

There was a long, brittle silence as Chloe read through her niece's correspondence.

'Then *you* were the gentleman behind the anonymous offer,' Chloe whispered in stunned disbelief.

'Yes. An offer I withdrew *before* I asked Madelaine to marry me,' Gabriel said dully. 'It had long been my wish to buy Pengarron for John and Cassandra, but that was before I met Lady Trent. Once I had and realised that I was…falling in love with her, I withdrew the offer at once. Unfortunately, she was not made aware of it until *after* she had accepted my proposal. And now, it is quite clear that she believes the *only* reason I asked her to marry me was so that I could gain ownership of Pengarron without having to pay for it.' He sighed heavily. When he spoke, his voice was filled with anguish. 'I have caused your niece grievous injury, Mrs Merrill, and I must speak with her as soon as possible.'

'Yes, I think you should, Lord Trevellyn,' Chloe said coldly. 'Unfortunately, I have no idea where she is. When her maid informed me that she had gone out riding, I came here hoping that this might have been her destination.'

Gabriel thought for a moment, trying to pick up on something he might have missed. 'Mrs Merrill, did you find a second letter in your niece's desk? The one she mentions having written to Cassandra?'

'No, there was only the one.'

'Which means that she was planning on returning to Pengarron to finish the other one, and no doubt to leave instructions that this one not be delivered to me until she had safely departed for London in the morning.'

'But…where can she be, Lord Trevellyn?' Chloe asked, her anger towards him being replaced by her concern.

'That is what we have to find out, Mrs Merrill.' Gabriel crossed to the bell pull and tugged on it hard. 'If Madelaine did not come home from her ride, and there is nowhere else she is likely to have gone, we must assume that she has met with an accident. For that reason, I intend to have the entire property searched. Ah, Parker, good. Send word to the stables. Have my horse saddled and brought round. Then tell Taylor to round up some of the lads and meet me on the drive.'

'I should like to go with you,' Lord Keswick offered, 'if you can spare another horse.'

'Yes, of course. See to a mount for Lord Keswick as well.'

'Very good, my lord.'

After the servant had gone, Gabriel ran the fingers of his left hand through his dark curls, hopelessly dishevelling them. 'I am relieved that John and Cassandra are dining out this evening. I would not wish either of them to be alarmed by this.'

'Is it *all* true?'

Gabriel swung round to find Chloe watching him, the letter still in her hands. He shook his head, sadly. 'No. Very little of it, in fact. I did not ask Madelaine to marry me for the sake of Pengarron, Mrs Merrill. And contrary to what your niece believes, the offer will not be made again. Because like her, I want nothing more to do with Pengarron, if she is not to be a part of it.'

He saw a flicker of relief in Chloe's eyes, but it did nothing to assuage the guilt that he was feeling. If anything had happened to Maddie, he would *never* forgive himself. 'Mrs Merrill, was anything gone from Madelaine's room?' he asked her now.

'Not that I could tell. Her maid told me that…Maddie had instructed her to begin packing, but as far as I know, she did not take anything with her when she left.'

'Then it is safe to assume that she planned on coming back.' Gabriel paused, and then glanced down at the letter. 'I venture to say she was too angry and upset after writing this letter to me to write another one to Cassandra, and thought to go out for a ride to calm herself.'

'But why hasn't she come back?' Chloe asked anxiously.

Gabriel made no reply. He couldn't, given the insidious fear that was beginning to eat away at his insides.

'Perhaps she rode out and became disoriented,' Lord Keswick suggested helpfully. 'I doubt Lady Trent is familiar enough with the woods to know her way through them yet. She may have ridden too far in and lost her bearings. The question is, where was she headed in the first place?'

'The linden glade,' Chloe said suddenly, glancing at Trevellyn.

Gabriel nodded, aware that the same thought had already crossed his mind. 'I think you may be right, Mrs Merrill. At any rate, we will head there first. Perhaps it will give us a clue as to her present whereabouts.' He cast an anxious glance towards the window. 'We won't have the benefit of daylight much longer, and finding Madelaine in the forest after dark is going to be extremely challenging.' *If she is still in the forest alone*, Gabriel added silently.

As it turned out, his fears were not without cause. The ransom note from Diggs arrived shortly thereafter.

The building Diggs took Madelaine to was little more than a hovel. It was hidden in woods that were far more dense than the linden glade had been, and at such a distance from Pengarron, that Madelaine feared she would never have been able to find her way back, even if she had been able to break free of Diggs.

Upon reaching their destination, Diggs dragged Madelaine down from her mare and quickly ushered her inside. 'Welcome to your new home, my lady,' he said with a sneer.

Madelaine glanced around the crudely furnished room, and shuddered. It contained only a narrow bed, a battered table with two rickety chairs, and a cupboard of some kind. Fragments of light filtered in through the two windows, while on the far wall was a fireplace where, judging by the few smoke-blackened pots thrown haphazardly on the hearth, Diggs did his cooking. That was all; little more than the bare necessities, and certainly nothing in the way of comfort.

'Quite a change from what you're used to, eh, my lady?' he whispered close by her ear.

Madelaine tried not to flinch, but failed. The odour rising from Diggs's body was nearly overpowering. She said nothing, however, as he pushed her towards one of the two chairs and roughly forced her to sit down. Pulling some lengths of rope out from under the bed, he quickly tied her wrists and ankles together, then, with a longer piece of rope, secured her upper body to the back of the chair. Finally satisfied that she wasn't going anywhere, Diggs went back outside to see to the horses.

Left on her own for the first time since the horrible ordeal had begun, Madelaine closed her eyes and dropped her head wearily on to her chest. *Dear Lord, however was she going to find her way home?* They were miles from anywhere, and in a cottage that was so far buried in the forest Madelaine was sure no one even knew of its existence.

More importantly, what was Diggs going to do with *her*? He might not have a grudge against her personally, but it was clear that he was intent on using her to get his revenge on Lord Trevellyn. What would he do if Gabriel refused to cooperate?

Madelaine glanced around the room, desperately searching for some method of escape. Unfortunately, even if she could have reached one of the two windows, they were far too small for her to have climbed through. Quite apart from which, the manner in which Diggs had bound her made it impossible for her to do anything. Even now, the rough cord was cutting into the softness of her flesh and bringing the blood to the surface. She was helpless. There was nothing she could do but hope that someone would find her—that Gabriel would find her.

At the thought of her fiancé—and the memory of his treachery—Madelaine choked back a sob. Why, why, *why*, had she allowed herself to be taken in by his lies? Just thinking about it now tore at her insides. She had recognised deceit before—why hadn't she been able to recognise it with Lord Trevellyn? Chloe had told her that she was intelligent enough to know the difference between empty words of flattery and true expressions of love, and Madelaine had agreed.

And yet, as it turned out, she was no better at recognising the difference than a lovesick young girl. She had believed everything that Gabriel had told her; every sweet word about how much he loved her, and how she was the only woman he ever wanted. She had not expected from him the perfidy she had found in her other suitors.

But then, why *should* she have expected lies from him? The Earl of Trevellyn was a wealthy man. She would have had no reason to suspect that he was after her fortune. The problem was, it wasn't her money he was after. It was Pengarron.

'Right, that's the horses taken care of,' Diggs said, suddenly reappearing in the doorway. He closed the door behind him and dropped a crudely constructed wooden bar across it. 'Now we should be set for a while.'

'What do you intend to do with me?' Madelaine asked in a low voice. 'If no one comes looking for me—'

'Oh, they'll come,' Diggs interrupted confidently. 'They

won't find you without my help, because nobody knows where this place is, but they will come. *He'll* come, for sure.' Diggs sat down at the table across from her and grinned. 'His lordship is going to pay for what he's done to me. Cost me a lot, did your bleeding Trevellyn.'

Madelaine shook her head. 'It was *you* who forfeited your living, Diggs, not Lord Trevellyn. My husband paid you a good wage. Certainly better than most. And yet, you still felt obliged to cheat him by poaching on his lands. No doubt you expected to continue doing so even after I came to live here.'

Diggs face darkened with anger. 'I weren't poaching.'

'Then how did a deer come to be caught in a trap in the linden glade?' Madelaine enquired coldly. 'My husband did not allow such things on the property.'

Diggs sneered unpleasantly. 'Well, that's really neither here nor there any more, is it, my lady? Because now that I have you, I'm going to get on me feet again. Trevellyn will pay handsomely to see you returned to him safely.'

Madelaine blanched. *'Pay?'*

'Aye. He should be getting the little note I left for him any time now. And if he cares to see his lady again, he'll meet the terms I've set out. I figure you're worth at least a thousand pounds to him.'

'A thousand pounds!' Madelaine gasped. 'You must be mad!'

Diggs shrugged his shoulders. 'The Earl's a rich man. I should think he'd be prepared to pay a lot more than that to get his future wife back.'

Madelaine glanced up sharply, her brow furrowing in consternation. His future *wife*?

But of course! Diggs still thought that they were to be married. That was why he had kidnapped her in the first place. He had no idea that the marriage was no longer to take place. And for the first time, Madelaine realised that she might have found a weakness in his plan.

'I am sorry to have to tell you this, Diggs,' she said quietly, 'but I fear that you may be in for a disappointment.'

'Eh? How's that, then?'

'I doubt Lord Trevellyn will be willing to pay *anything* for me since we are...no longer betrothed.'

Diggs guffawed. 'That's right, and I'm dining with Lord and Lady Muck tomorrow night. Of course you're betrothed. Gussy told me so.'

'Gussy?'

'Aye. Kitchen maid up at Carew. Tells me everything, does Gussy.'

Madelaine carefully tucked the name away for the future. 'I am telling you the truth, Diggs. Lord Trevellyn and I had an...argument this morning and I broke off our engagement. We are no longer going to be married.'

'Is that right?'

'Yes. I was...planning on returning to London tomorrow morning, in fact.'

Diggs regarded her suspiciously. 'So what's all that to me, then?'

'Well, surely you understand that...if I am not to become Lord Trevellyn's wife, he is unlikely to pay an inordinate amount of money to get me back. Why would he bother, if I no longer mean anything to him?'

Madelaine held her breath. She could see that Diggs was mulling over what she had just said, trying to figure out whether she was lying or not—and, if she wasn't, how it would affect him. His next words confirmed it. 'How do I know you're not having me on?'

'Why would I lie?' Madelaine replied. 'If I thought there was any chance of Lord Trevellyn coming to rescue me, do you really think that I would warn you about it?'

Diggs glanced out of the window. 'You'd better hope that he does come, my lady. Or that somebody does.' He turned back and stared at her menacingly. 'Because nobody gets away with making a fool out of Jake Diggs. *Nobody!*'

Chapter Fourteen

In all, eleven men set out from Carew. Gabriel divided them into five teams of two and gave them each a section of property to explore; a search that would take them through Pengarron, Carew, and all of the surrounding areas.

Gabriel set out on his own. He knew that no one would be able to keep up with him in his present mood. He was consumed by anger and fear; anger that Diggs would stoop to using Madelaine to get his revenge, and fear over the fact that she had been kidnapped as a result of something he himself had done.

'I swear by all that's holy, if you touch a hair on the woman's head, Diggs, I'll kill you myself,' Gabriel muttered as he urged the stallion on.

He rode to the linden glade first, knowing that it had a special meaning for Madelaine. Reaching the open ground, he kicked his feet free of the stirrups and jumped down from the saddle. With any luck he would be able to find some clue, no matter how small, that would prove that Madelaine had been here earlier in the day.

It did not take him long to find it. The ground was soft under Gabriel's feet, and when he saw the marks where a horse and rider had travelled through, he knew that Madelaine had come here. He dropped to one knee and traced with his hand the outline of a horse's hoof and, beside it, a small boot, obviously belonging to a woman.

He followed the prints a while longer. When he discovered a second set of hoof prints further along the path, Gabriel knew that he had found the point at which Diggs had joined her. Moments later, he spied a lacy white handkerchief, delicately embroidered in one corner with the letter 'M', snagged on a branch.

Gabriel straightened, the look on his face grim. The second set of prints, and the carelessly dropped handkerchief, left him in no doubt as to Madelaine's fate. Just as the deer had been trapped in the leafy green glade, so had his beloved.

The onset of darkness brought the men reluctantly back to Carew. They would need to equip themselves with torches and lanterns in order to continue the search into the night.

Telling the younger lads to gather what they needed, Gabriel assembled Taylor and Lord Keswick in the library. He was dismayed to see that John and Cassandra had returned and were waiting for him too, along with Mrs Merrill.

'Let me help, Gabriel,' John said, immediately coming up to him.

Gabriel shook his head. 'I can't. You're not strong enough.'

'I am strong enough to ride and I can still take a man down if I have to,' John told him. 'All that's weak is my pistol arm. But I have a feeling that if shots are required, you shall be the one firing them.'

A grudging smile lifted Gabriel's lips. 'Indeed. If Diggs has harmed her in any way, his death will be on my hands, no one else's.'

In the corner, Cassandra gasped, while Chloe's face went deathly white. 'Surely it will not come to that, Lord Trevellyn!'

'I hope it will not, Mrs Merrill,' Gabriel said quietly, 'but I have no idea what Diggs is capable of. All I know is that he made a mistake in thinking that he could use Madelaine to get to me. Might I suggest that you and Cassandra go back to Pengarron and wait there?'

Chloe shook her head stubbornly. 'No, my lord. I will stay here until you bring my niece safely home.'

'I shall not go either, Gabriel,' Cassandra said firmly. 'We will wait here together, as a family.'

Gabriel swore softly, but he knew there was nothing more he could say. 'Very well, if that is what you wish. All right, gentlemen, I found indications that Diggs and Madelaine were in the linden glade, so we shall set out from there. Taylor, equip the men with torches, and regroup them into parties of three. Make sure that each group is armed, whether it be with pitchfork or pistol, and warn them that Diggs will be too. And he will not be easy to find. He knows these woods like the back of his hand. One of your men could be within three feet of him and not even know it. We will set off again as soon as—' Gabriel suddenly broke off, his eye catching a slight movement at the door. He was astonished to see that it was Mrs Abbey.

'Mrs Abbey! But…whatever are you doing here?'

Everyone turned to stare at the white-haired old lady who was standing uncertainly in the doorway. 'Excuse me, my lord,' she said softly, 'and begging your pardon for coming in unannounced, but I did knock and no one answered—'

'That's quite all right,' Gabriel said quickly. Though he might have wished her anywhere else at the moment, he gently ushered the old woman into the room and introduced her to the others.

'So *you* are the lady taking care of Maddie's deer,' Chloe said abruptly.

'That's right.' Mrs Abbey nodded. 'And very nicely she's doing, too. I'll be setting her free again soon.'

'Mrs Abbey,' Gabriel said, trying to hide his impatience, 'what did you come to see me about?'

'Oh, yes, well, I thought I should tell you that I saw something rather peculiar in the woods this afternoon, my lord.'

Assuming that the something peculiar referred to yet another wounded creature, Gabriel sighed impatiently. 'Mrs Abbey, we really do not have time—'

'I remember what you said about your telling Lord Trent's man to leave, and not to come back,' Mrs Abbey continued, 'and I thought you might like to know that I saw him this afternoon on my way back from Dorkins Glen.'

'You *saw* Diggs?'

'Aye. He and Lady Trent were—'

Gabriel froze. 'Lady Trent was *with* him?'

Chloe was instantly on her feet. 'Mrs Abbey, was my niece all right?'

'As near as I could tell, my lady. She were riding ahead of Diggs, and it looked as though…her hands were bound, but I might have had that wrong. My eyesight isn't what it used to be.'

Gabriel's features hardened into a rigid mask. 'Where did you see them, Mrs Abbey? On Pengarron?'

'Oh, no, my lord. They were way out past Trathrevor Pond, on the road to Lower Tewes.'

'Trathrevor Pond?' Gabriel frowned. 'But that's nearly…ten miles away.' Then, abruptly, he glanced at Taylor as an almost forgotten childhood memory came to mind. 'Isn't there an old abandoned cottage out that way?'

The steward nodded slowly. 'There is, my lord, if you

can call it that. More like a shack, as I recall, hidden way back in the woods.'

Gabriel smiled, his suspicions confirmed. 'All right, Taylor, tell the lads you won't be needing them any more. I think you and I can handle this on our own.'

'Let me come too, Gabriel,' John said quickly. 'If Diggs knows his way in the woods as well as you say, you may need my help.'

Gabriel nodded, and grasped his brother's good hand. 'Thank you, John. Thomas,' he said to the older man, 'can I count on you to take care of the ladies?'

'Only if you are sure that I cannot be of service in some other way. My eyesight isn't the best in the dark, but I would be more than willing to give it a try.'

'Thank you, but now that we have located Diggs, I think the three of us should be able to take care of it. In fact, I would venture to say that the fewer of us who go now, the better. No doubt Diggs will be waiting.'

Taylor nodded briskly. 'I'll fetch the horses, my lord.'

Gabriel turned towards the elderly woman and placed a tender kiss upon her forehead. 'Thank you, Mrs Abbey. You have saved us a great deal of time and worry. Please stay and partake of some refreshments. Thomas, ring for Parker and ask him to have a meal prepared for Mrs Abbey and the ladies.'

But Mrs Abbey shook her head. 'Thank you, my lord, but I must be heading back. I have animals who need tending.'

'Then I shall see that you have a trap to take you there.'

The woman smiled at him, and then, in a gesture which surprised them all, pressed her hand against his heart and closed her eyes. After a moment, she said very softly, 'Your lady will come to no harm, my lord, if the love between you is strong enough.'

A shutter dropped down over Gabriel's eyes. He covered her small hand with his own, and held it tightly. 'I hope that it is, Mrs Abbey. For *everyone's* sake, I hope that it is!'

Madelaine sat up with a start, instantly alert. She was astonished that she had fallen asleep, and wondered what had woken her. She blinked her eyes a few times and tried to get her bearings. Unfortunately, she couldn't see a thing. The cottage was in utter darkness.

'Diggs?' she whispered tentatively into the gloom.

There was no answer. She was alone.

Realising that this might be her only chance, Madelaine began to struggle in earnest against her bonds. If she could loosen the ropes enough to slip her hands free, she might be able to undo the ones holding her ankles and get out of the cottage. Once outside, she could hide herself in the forest until help came. Surely, someone must be looking for her by now. Perhaps Gabriel...

No! She would *not* think about him, Madelaine told herself firmly. He meant nothing to her any more. He had lied to her all along. Surely that was reason enough to stop loving him. Wasn't it?

Unfortunately, it wasn't long before Madelaine realised that she was having no more success with her physical struggles than she was with her emotional ones. She couldn't stop loving Gabriel any more than she could free herself from the ropes Diggs had tied her up with. Indeed, they were no looser now than when she had started. She was trapped. There was no way out of the cottage—

Out of the cottage...

Madelaine gasped. Oh, dear heavens, why hadn't she thought of it before! *She* might not be able to get out of the cottage, but she could certainly try to stop Diggs from

getting back *in*! The fact that he had gone out meant that
the wooden bar on the inside of the door would be *up*. All
she had to do was get to it before he came back and drop
it into place.

Galvanised by the thought, Madelaine redirected all of
her energies to the task at hand. Diggs had tied her upper
body to the back of the chair, but he had *not* secured her
ankles to it, probably believing that it would be impossible
for her to lift the heavy wooden chair off the floor.

Fortunately, he had reckoned without his victim's single-
minded determination! Madelaine found that by pressing
her feet to the floor and leaning her body slightly forward,
she could edge the chair towards the door in a series of
hops. How she was going to drop the heavy wooden bar
across the door once she reached it, she had no idea. For
the moment, it was challenge enough just getting there. And
it was exceedingly painful too. Every time Madelaine
leaned her body forward, the ropes cut deeper into her
tender flesh. So much so that, by the time she had gone a
few inches, tears of pain were trickling down her cheeks.

But she steadfastly refused to give up. This might be her
only hope!

The minutes ticked by. As silently and as quickly as she
could, Madelaine inched her way towards the door, trying
to ignore the dreadful pain in her wrists and ankles. She
had to be close to the door now, she told herself. Only
another few hops and—

Suddenly, Madelaine froze. *Somebody was coming.*

And then, without warning, the door swung open.

Madelaine had no time to prepare herself. The heavy
wooden door hit her hard, catching her just below the knees
and sending her sprawling backwards into the darkened
room. She cried out once as she landed on the floor, and
then lay still, gasping in pain.

'What the—what the 'ell do you think you're doing?' Diggs demanded angrily.

Stars danced in front of Madelaine's eyes as he shouted at her, but she would not answer. It was all she could do not to pass out. Her right leg was throbbing unbearably. She wondered if it might be broken—

'Little bitch!' Diggs cursed vehemently in the darkness. 'Thought to get the better of me, did you?' The man seemed to be blessed with the vision of a nocturnal creature. Unerringly, he made his way across the floor and, ignoring Madelaine's cry of pain, grabbed her by the arm and dragged the chair upright. 'We won't be having any of that again.'

'You won't get...away with this, Diggs,' Madelaine spat at him, fighting back a wave of dizziness. 'One way or another, they'll find you.'

'They won't find me,' Diggs said confidently. Stopping only long enough to light a small candle, he placed it on the table in the centre of the room and then bent to pull another length of rope from under the bed. 'When I gets me money, I'll be off like bloody greased lightning, see if I'm not.'

About to reply, Madelaine suddenly caught sight of a movement just beyond the window.

Gabriel?

Her heart began to beat furiously. She glanced down at her captor and realised that he hadn't seen the movement. Thank God. She had to make sure that he didn't see it either.

'Look, why do you need to ransom me at all?' Madelaine said quickly. 'I'm a wealthy woman in my own right.'

'And what's that to me?'

'I can afford to pay you...far more than Lord Trevellyn is likely to, given that we are...no longer betrothed.' She risked a quick glance towards the window—then froze as she caught sight of another movement. Someone was definitely out there.

Diggs straightened and slowly walked towards the table. 'That's fine to say, my lady, but I don't think you'd pay up. I think you'd run straight back to Trevellyn, and tell him what I done,' he said harshly.

'But why would I? What would be the point?' Madelaine asked desperately. 'I have already told you that he and I mean nothing to each other any more. And that being the case—'

Suddenly, Diggs tensed, freezing like a rabbit who senses the stealthy approach of a fox. *'What was that?'*

Madelaine blanched. 'What?'

'I heard something.'

'I'm sure it was just—'

'Shut your mouth!' Diggs snapped. He jumped to extinguish the candle, then pulled the pistol out of his jacket. 'If you so much as breathe a word—'

A twig snapped in the blackness beyond the door.

The sound echoed eerily in the silence of the night, and made Madelaine jump. She held her breath as Diggs slowly made his way towards the door. She heard the sound of a pistol being cocked—and closed her eyes in silent prayer. *Please keep Gabriel safe. Please keep him...*

Suddenly, a gunshot ripped apart the night.

'Bloody 'ell!' Diggs spun around wildly. He aimed his pistol towards the window, and fired. The second he did, the front door burst open and two men rushed in. 'Maddie, *get down*!' Gabriel shouted harshly.

Without stopping to think, Madelaine threw all of her weight to the right. She felt the chair begin to sway, then held her breath as it tipped over, gasping in pain as her right knee and elbow hit the floor again. She felt her head swim and bit her lip to keep from passing out. But at least she was out of the way. She tucked her head tight against her chest, and listened in terror to the sounds of the scuffle going on all around her.

A faint shaft of moonlight lit the tiny room. The two men who had rushed in flung themselves on Diggs and struggled to take him down. Seconds later, a third man appeared in the doorway. 'Gabriel, where are—?'

'John! For God's sake, get—*agggghhhh*!'

The rest of the shout was lost in the explosive sound of a pistol discharging. Madelaine heard a harsh groan of pain, followed by another shot, and then a dull thud, as of a body hitting the floor. Seconds later, a heavy weight landed with crushing force on her legs. '*Gabriel!*' she screamed.

It was the last thing Madelaine remembered before the pain finally overtook her. Lying broken and bleeding on the floor, she closed her eyes and let herself succumb to the blessed darkness.

'Maddie? Can you hear me, dearest? Maddie?'

Madelaine's eyelids slowly fluttered open. She blinked a few times, and saw her aunt hovering anxiously above her. 'Chloe?' she said weakly.

'Thank the Lord, you're back with us,' Chloe whispered. 'How are you feeling, dearest?'

'I'm…not sure,' Madelaine replied unsteadily, and wearily closed her eyes again. In truth, she knew precisely how she felt. She was lying on a soft bed, and her body was aching as though it had been trampled by a team of runaway horses, not to mention the fact that her wrists were on fire. Madelaine glanced down the length of the bed and was astonished to see that they were both heavily bandaged. 'What—?'

'It's all right, Maddie,' Chloe assured her quickly. 'The

doctor just wanted to make sure that your wounds stayed clean and dry. The ropes cut you…quite badly. Lord Trevellyn did try to—'

'*Gabriel,*' Madelaine whispered frantically. 'Where is he? I heard a shot—'

'Lord Trevellyn is going to be fine, dearest. He has been waiting downstairs to see you.'

'But…I heard a shot, I remember that clearly.' Madelaine's eyes opened very wide as she glanced up at her aunt. 'Diggs. Is he—?'

'No, he isn't, though I wish to God he were,' Chloe informed her in a terse voice. 'And you needn't look at me like that, Madelaine, I was so worried about *you* I couldn't see straight, never mind sparing a thought for the horrible man who caused it all.'

Madelaine swallowed painfully. 'But you are sure that…Gabriel is all right. I distinctly remember hearing… two shots.'

'Lord Trevellyn was slightly injured,' Chloe admitted, 'I will not lie to you about that. But the doctor assured us that the wound was not deep and that he is going to be fine.' She hesitated for a moment, and then took a deep breath, knowing that something had to be said, and soon. 'I found the letter you wrote to Lord Trevellyn, Maddie. And I…gave it to him.'

Madelaine stared at her aunt in dismay. 'You went through my desk?'

'Forgive me for intruding on your privacy, my dear, but you cannot know how worried I was about you. I had to try to find out what was wrong. And when Betty told me that she had seen you…writing a letter, I thought it might give me some insight into your whereabouts. When I found the letter and saw that it was addressed to Lord Trevellyn, I decided it would be best to take it to him right away.'

Madelaine stared down at the white bedsheets in bewilderment. 'Then Gabriel *knew* that I had...broken off our betrothal *before* he came looking for me?'

'Yes.'

'And he came regardless.'

Chloe gently stroked her fingers over Madelaine's cheek. 'He loves you, Maddie. Truly *loves* you. I saw that by the way he reacted to your letter. And he blames himself for everything that has happened to you.'

Madelaine felt the sting of tears and quickly averted her eyes. 'He doesn't...love me at all. He lied to me. All he ever wanted was Pengarron,' she whispered in a choked, bitter voice. 'He lied to me about...everything.'

Chloe shook her head. 'I don't believe that for a moment. And neither would you, had you seen the expression on his face when Mrs Abbey arrived, and told him that she had spotted you and Diggs heading towards Trathrevor Pond.'

'*Mrs Abbey* saw us?'

'Yes. It was thanks to her that Lord Trevellyn knew where to search for you. She came and told us yesterday evening. If she hadn't, I think Lord Trevellyn would have torn down every inch of wood between here and Lower Tewes looking for you.'

'But he *lied* to me,' Madelaine repeated dully, closing her eyes in an effort to hold back the tears. 'He is no better than Lord Rakesley, or Lord Otley, or...or any of the others. He may not have wanted my money, but he still wanted me for something other than my love. He wanted what I could give him.'

'Nothing could be further from the truth, Madelaine. I only hope you can find it in your heart to believe that.'

The words were spoken in a voice choked with emotion, and glancing towards the door, Madelaine felt her heart turn over in her breast. '*Gabriel!*'

A heavy silence followed. After looking from one to the other, Chloe suddenly bent to kiss her niece's cheek, well aware that nothing would be accomplished by her remaining in the room. 'Listen to him, dearest,' she urged gently. 'Listen with your heart *and* your mind open.' Then, with an encouraging smile, she rose and headed for the door. 'As for you, Lord Trevellyn,' Chloe said, pausing for a moment beside Gabriel, 'I know that I shouldn't be leaving you alone with my niece like this but, all things considered, I think the two of you need some time to talk over what has happened. And to that end, I shall give you all the time that I can. But know that when I return, you must come back downstairs with me.'

'Thank you, Mrs Merrill,' Gabriel said gratefully. 'I shall not overstay my welcome.' He waited until the door closed behind her, before crossing the width of the room and stopping by the side of the big bed. Gazing down at the woman lying there—painfully aware that her face was as white as the bandages that were wrapped around her wrists—Gabriel knew that he had been very, very lucky. 'Dr Granger said that your...wrists and ankles should heal...quickly,' he began tentatively.

Madelaine swallowed. 'Yes. Thank you for...calling him in so promptly.'

'I could do...nothing else.' Gabriel tried to go on, but the words lodged helplessly in his throat. He sank to his knees at her bedside, and hung his head. 'Forgive me, Madelaine. I never intended that any of this should happen to you—'

'It...does not matter, Lord Trevellyn,' Madelaine said hastily, hoping to spare him further anguish.

'But it does. When I realised what Diggs had done...when I thought about you all alone in the woods with him, you must have been so frightened—'

'Gabriel, please, there is…no need to take on so,' Madelaine told him, her own voice husky with emotion. 'Thanks to you, everyone is safe. But…however did you manage to find us? I was sure that…no one would be able to, all the way out there.'

Gabriel stared into the distance, remembering how shaken he had been last night at seeing Madelaine tied to a chair, her wrists and ankles bleeding from the ropes that bound her. 'One of the benefits of being a boy here was that I had the entire countryside to explore, and I did explore it, every chance I got. So when Mrs Abbey told me that she had seen you and Diggs heading towards Trathrevor Pond, I knew exactly where she meant. I also remembered an old, broken-down cottage which I had stumbled upon quite by chance, many years ago. I recalled that it was close to the pond, and since it was hidden well back in the woods, I suspected it might be the type of place Diggs would use to hide out in. Unfortunately, it wasn't so heavily covered in vines then as it is now. When I first tried to peer in through the windows last night, I could see nothing inside.'

'I thought I caught a movement at one of the windows,' Madelaine told him, 'but I had no idea whether it was you or not. I just tried to keep Diggs occupied in case it *was* someone come to rescue me.'

Gabriel sighed heavily. 'It was fortunate for us that you were able to keep his attention diverted. We knew that the only chance we had of getting you out safely was to catch Diggs off guard. The only problem was, I had no idea where you where—until Diggs lit the candle. That was what saved us. Once I saw you sitting in the chair, I told John to fire.'

Madelaine blinked quickly. 'Was he trying to…kill Diggs?'

Gabriel shook his head. 'No. Aiming at Diggs with you in the room would have been far too dangerous. I only wanted to draw his attention away from the door so that we could have time to get inside. As soon as Diggs returned John's fire, Taylor and I rushed the door.'

'Then it was…John who came in afterwards.'

'Yes.' Gabriel closed his eyes for a moment, reliving that horrible moment when he had looked up to see his brother standing directly in the line of fire. 'Just before we subdued Diggs, he managed to break away from us. I saw John standing in the open doorway—and realised that Diggs had a clear shot at him, and shouted at him to get down. At the same time, Taylor grabbed Diggs around the waist and tried to wrestle him off balance. For all his size, Diggs fought like a mad man,' Gabriel murmured, recalling every painful second of that fight. 'He was thrashing wildly, kicking at anything that came close to him. He caught my bad leg with one of those kicks, and I went down like a pile of bricks. Fortunately, by doing so, I probably saved my own life,' he admitted ruefully. 'When Diggs's pistol discharged, the ball caught me on the shoulder, rather than full in the chest. Thankfully, Taylor was able to hold him after that, and the second shot you heard was mine. And no, I did not kill him,' he added, seeing the alarm in Madelaine's eyes. 'My only intention was to disable him, which I did.'

Madelaine closed her eyes and felt her throat tighten at the memory. 'I thought…you had been shot. I was…so afraid—'

'I know you were, but it's all over now. Diggs is on his way to prison, and you will never have to see him again. Ever!'

Madelaine smiled weakly. 'I am very relieved to hear it…Lord Trevellyn.'

Gabriel heard the note of reserve in her voice, and

sighed. It seemed that, while Madelaine might be willing to thank him for rescuing her from Diggs, he had a long way to go before she was willing to *forgive* him for the way he had behaved prior to that—*If* she forgave him at all.

'Madelaine, I think you should know that I…read the letter you wrote to me,' Gabriel told her quietly. 'Your aunt brought it to me last night after you were kidnapped.'

Madelaine bit her lip, and nodded. 'I know. She told me that she had…found it in my drawer and…taken it to you. And I am truly sorry, Lord Trevellyn. I had not thought to be here when you read it. I thought it would be…easier for everyone if I were…back in London before you saw it.'

'It would never be easy for me to read a letter like that, Madelaine, surely you must know that?' When she said nothing, Gabriel sighed. 'I take it that…your feelings have not changed since you wrote the letter, and that it is still your wish to…end our betrothal?'

'I fear I must, Lord Trevellyn,' Madelaine said unhappily. 'The circumstances which prompted me to write it have not changed. The lies that were told, the deceits that were perpetrated—'

'It was never my intention to deceive you, Madelaine,' Gabriel interrupted. 'Please believe that, if you believe nothing else. I did not propose to you because of Pengarron. I proposed to you because I *love* you.'

Madelaine bit her lips and sighed. 'I…wish I could believe that, my lord, but with everything that has happened—'

'Believe it, my love. When I originally began to think about buying Pengarron for John and Cassandra, I had no idea that I would be taking it away from you,' Gabriel told her, knowing that the time had come for him to tell her everything. 'I had expected to be dealing with the new Lord Trent and his lawyers.'

'And when you learned that Pengarron was mine, why did you not approach me then?'

'Because I feared that you might be aware of the long-standing feud between our families and resist my offer on principle.'

That caused Madelaine to frown. 'You believed that I would have used an old feud as an excuse for rejecting your offer? But surely no one has ever taken the feud that seriously?'

'Lord Trent's grandfather and mine took it seriously enough that they refused to speak to one another for over thirty years,' Gabriel informed her gently. 'And though you may not be aware of it, your husband had strong feelings about it too. It was one of the reasons he never came to Pengarron.'

Madelaine was surprised to learn that Edward had harboured such a silly grudge, but knowing that there was nothing to be gained by belabouring the point, she offered no further argument. 'Very well, Lord Trevellyn, I am willing to concede that your explanation for not approaching me directly with the offer is valid, as are your reasons for not wishing to identify yourself as the prospective buyer. But what I do not understand is why you went to so much trouble to show me the property, if you had every intention of buying it even without my knowledge. If you were convinced that I would not wish to live at Pengarron, and that I would return to London at the first opportunity, why were you so concerned about…what I thought of it when I first arrived?'

'Because when I learned that you were to come to Pengarron, I decided that it would be worth my while to *try* to find out what the likelihood of your selling it was,' Gabriel admitted. 'Please understand, Madelaine, when I rode up to the house that first morning, it was not with the intention of pretending to be someone else. I had every intention of introducing myself as the Earl of Trevellyn. But once I realised that you thought I was a steward, I began to see…an opportunity for myself. I realised that, in the guise of a servant, I could take you around Pengarron and see with my own eyes how you felt about it. The problem was,' Gabriel told her with a lopsided grin, 'I had no idea that I would find myself as attracted to you as I was, even then.'

Being far from immune to his charm, Madelaine felt a reluctant smile tug at the corner of her own lips. 'Yes, I recall your behaviour on that day as being somewhat… bold. But you have not yet convinced me of your innocence in this matter, my lord,' she added quickly, not wishing him to feel that she was softening towards him. 'Because when you *were* presented with the perfect opportunity to tell me of your interest in Pengarron, you still said nothing. That night at Carew, when we talked about the possibility of my selling Pengarron with Lord Keswick and my aunt, why did you not tell me of your interest in the house *then*?'

'Because it was that very night that I realised I was having…second thoughts about the whole thing. And very soon after that, I knew that I no longer wished to buy Pengarron at all. I feared that if I did, you would…leave Cornwall and never come back,' Gabriel told her in a husky voice. 'And that I could not allow to happen.'

Madelaine blinked rapidly, aware of a lump forming in her throat. 'Is that why you…withdrew your offer?'

'Yes. The day I received your letter asking for Mrs Abbey's address, I knew that it was too late. I had fallen quite hopelessly in love with you,' Gabriel told her softly. 'And it was within the week that I contacted my lawyer and instructed him to withdraw the offer. If you would care to check my correspondence, you will see that the dates do coincide.'

'I see. So, after you fell in love with me, withdrew your offer, and finally asked me to marry you, why did you still not tell me the truth?'

'Because by that time, I was afraid,' Gabriel said, knowing that this was the hardest admission he would have to make. 'I considered myself…extremely fortunate to have been able to withdraw the offer without your ever having known that I was behind it, because I knew how much the truth mattered to you. I was afraid that…if you found out that I had not been completely honest with you, I would lose you forever. And it was my hope that, with the offer withdrawn, and you and I engaged to be married, the subject of Pengarron need never come up again.'

Madelaine raised a questioning eyebrow. 'And what of your promise to John and Cassandra?'

Gabriel shrugged his shoulders. 'That has not changed. I promised them a house, and a house they shall have,' he told her simply. 'But it will not be Pengarron—not if your lawyer was *giving* it away. How could I visit a place, even if it belonged to a member of my own family, which was so filled with memories of you, and not have you beside me? How could I ride through the forest without remembering the times that you and I rode there together? I could never go to the linden glade without seeing the look of despair on your face when you saw the little deer. You must believe me, my darling. I never meant to lie to you.' Gabriel gently lifted one of her bandaged hands to his lips and carefully kissed the exposed fingertips. 'I love you, Madelaine, in a way that I have never loved any one else in my life. But I have not been completely truthful with you, and if you cannot forgive me for that, or if you ask me to leave now, please know that I will. I will *not* be the cause of any more sadness in your life. Tell me to go, and let that be an end of it, once and for all.'

In silence, Madelaine looked up into Gabriel's dark eyes, and saw first-hand the pain and anguish that he was suffering. It had been a difficult conversation for both of them; difficult for her to hear, and difficult for him to utter. Because in telling her the truth, he had risked losing... everything. And perhaps it was that, more than anything else, which finally convinced her of the depth of his love.

'Do you know, I think I shall miss living here,' Madelaine said. She gazed around the bedchamber which, like the rest of the house, had become so very dear to her, and sighed. 'I know that, no matter where I go, Pengarron will always hold...special memories for me.'

Gabriel nodded, but did not trust himself to speak. *I shall miss living here...* With those few brief words she had told him...everything he needed to know.

It was over. Madelaine had made her decision.

He went to rise and found that his legs were trembling badly. 'Pengarron,' he whispered sadly. 'How ironic that...the very house which brought you to Cornwall in the first place should be the cause of your leaving it forever.' He tried to smile, but found it more than he could manage. 'No, that is unfair. I think *I* must bear the blame for sending you away from Cornwall.'

Slowly and carefully, Madelaine raised the hand which he had so recently kissed and placed it gently upon his sleeve. 'I think you take too much upon yourself, my lord, for I did not say that I was going...anywhere.'

Like a man in a trance, Gabriel stared down at the slender fingers resting lightly on his arm. 'You said that...you shall miss living at Pengarron.'

'And so I shall. Once John and Cassandra are settled here, I hardly think they will expect me to be living with them.'

'But…if you are not to be…my wife, why would you still wish to give it to them?'

A smile trembled over Madelaine's lips. 'Who said that I was…not going to be your wife, my lord? Unless you have…changed your mind and decided not to marry *me*, that is.'

Gabriel faltered in the silence that engulfed them. Was it possible? After everything that had happened, was it possible that…she still wanted him?

Very slowly, he reached out his hand and grasped her chin, gently tilting it back so that she had to look into his eyes. 'I have not changed my mind, Madelaine. I love you more now than I did upon the day that we first met and, God willing, I will only love you more on the day that I die. But…is that enough for you? Is that truly enough in light of everything that has happened?'

The touch of his hand was almost unbearable in its tenderness, and Madelaine swallowed hard, blinking back tears. 'It is more than enough, my love. Because I cannot imagine living my life…anywhere without you in it.'

It seemed to her that he was silent for a very long time. Then, with a smile that Madelaine knew she would remember for the rest of her life, he dropped to one knee at the side of the bed, and said very quietly, 'Will you marry me, Madelaine? Will you live with me at Carew, and be my wife and lady?'

A tiny pulse beat at the base of Madelaine's throat, and her eyes were bright. 'I will marry you, my lord. I will live with you as your wife, and together we shall have children enough to make the empty halls of Carew ring with laughter. Because I do love you, Gabriel, so very, very much.'

'Then I shall make you a promise here and now, my darling Maddie,' Gabriel whispered huskily. 'A promise made by a Cornish man born and bred, to the fair London lady who would marry him. I promise to spend the rest of my days showing you how much I love you, so that you never have cause to regret the day you first came to Cornwall and met a man who called himself Taylor. And with your permission, I should like to begin keeping that promise, just as soon as you say that I may.'

Madelaine smiled up at him with eyes that were filled with love and a heart that was blissfully free of shadows. 'You have my permission to begin as soon as you wish, my lord. For I could no more regret the day that I came to Cornwall than I could meeting the man who made me fall in love with it. A bold, brash and thoroughly wonderful man who, by *any* name, gave me the best possible reason of all to stay!'

* * * * *

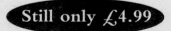

2 FREE
books and a surprise gift!

We would like to take this opportunity to thank you for reading this Mills & Boon® book by offering you the chance to take TWO more specially selected titles from the Historical Romance™ series absolutely FREE! We're also making this offer to introduce you to the benefits of the Reader Service™—

* ★ FREE home delivery
* ★ FREE gifts and competitions
* ★ FREE monthly Newsletter
* ★ Exclusive Reader Service discounts
* ★ Books available before they're in the shops

Accepting these FREE books and gift places you under no obligation to buy, you may cancel at any time, even after receiving your free shipment. Simply complete your details below and return the entire page to the address below. *You don't even need a stamp!*

✂ **YES!** Please send me 2 free Historical Romance books and a surprise gift. I understand that unless you hear from me, I will receive 4 superb new titles every month for just £2.99 each, postage and packing free. I am under no obligation to purchase any books and may cancel my subscription at any time. The free books and gift will be mine to keep in any case.

H9EA

Ms/Mrs/Miss/Mr ....Initials.................................
BLOCK CAPITALS PLEASE

Surname ....

Address ....

....

....Postcode..................................

Send this whole page to:
UK: FREEPOST CN81, Croydon, CR9 3WZ
EIRE: PO Box 4546, Kilcock, County Kildare (stamp required)

MILLS & BOON®

MEDICAL ROMANCE™

A FAMILIAR FEELING by Margaret Barker

Dr Caroline Bennett found working at the Chateau Clinique with Pierre, the boy she'd adored as a child, wasn't easy. It didn't help that his ex-wife was still around.

HEART IN HIDING by Jean Evans

Dr Holly Hunter needed respite, and the remote Scottish village was ideal. Until Callum McLoud turned up accusing her of treating his patients!

HIS MADE-TO-ORDER BRIDE by Jessica Matthews
Bachelor Doctors

Dr J.D. Berkely had a good job in ER, a delightful son Daniel, and a truly good friend in nurse Katie Alexander, so why would he need a wife?

A TIMELY AFFAIR by Helen Shelton

Dr Merrin Ryan sees that widowed Professor Neil McAlister needs nurturing and she falls in love! But Neil is aware that he could damage her career…

Available from 5th November 1999

Available at most branches of WH Smith, Tesco, Martins, Borders, Easons, Volume One/James Thin and most good paperback bookshops